THE RED PLANET

JOURNEY INTO SPACE

VOLUME TWO

THE RED PLANET

by
Charles Chilton

fantom
publishing

First published in 1956 by Herbert Jenkins Ltd, and
republished in 1960 by Pan Books Ltd

This edition published in 2012 by Fantom Films
fantomfilms.co.uk

Based on the BBC radio serial *Journey into Space* first broadcast in 1954

A catalogue record for this book is available from the British Library.

Paperback Edition ISBN: 978-1-78196-025-7

Typeset by Phil Reynolds Media Services, Leamington Spa
Printed by MPG Biddles Limited, King's Lynn

Jacket design by Stuart Manning

Foreword

'**R**ogers is asleep… He cannot be woken.'

What on earth is happening on Freighter Number Two? Why can't the strange Whitaker wake his crewmate Frank Rogers? In April 1971, aboard the flagship *Discovery*, Captain Jet Morgan and his colleagues – Doc, Mitch and Lemmy – can only guess at the strange behaviour of construction engineer James Edward Whitaker as he continues his unnerving, monotone radio conversation from another vessel in the Mars fleet. At home, listeners to the BBC Light Programme in September 1954 could only guess along with them as the latest instalment of the new *Journey into Space* serial hurtled to another tantalising cliffhanger.

Over the last twenty-five years of writing professionally about television and radio, I still get a particular thrill when the subject is *Journey into Space*. And *The Red Planet* – the second part of the series' 1950s trilogy – is my *favourite* piece of radio adventure because of Charles Chilton's mastery over the sound medium. Charles understands sound *so* well. Some of the most wonderful sequences in *Journey into Space* are those where the listener is in *exactly* the same position as Jet and his crew. In addition to the strange events in Freighter Number Two alluded to above, later on after the Martian landing, Jet's group are similarly dependent on the vocal commentary from one of their colleagues on the strange visitors who have arrived at a crashed freighter. The mystery for the listener and their anticipation of the next clue is every bit as vivid as it is for Jet.

Apart from being brilliant radio adventure, *Journey into Space* is also historically very significant. Alongside Frank Hampson's *Dan Dare – Pilot of the Future* blasting off in the pages of the *Eagle* comic and Nigel Kneale's Professor Bernard Quatermass confronting the unearthly in evocative thriller serials for BBC Television, Charles Chilton's *Journey into Space* forms the final part of the key triumvirate which brought science-fiction to the British public via popular media of the 1950s.

It's difficult to convey now how *big* Charles' radio serial was. The first series had debuted in September 1953 as an eighteen-part serial. *The Red Planet* was the title given to the second series, broadcast as a run of twenty half-hour instalments at 7.30pm on a Monday from 6 September 1954 on the BBC Light Programme (later reborn as Radio 2), with a repeat at 6pm the following Sunday. In January 1955, the tale's penultimate episode attracted a 17% share of the UK's adult audience to tune to the Light Programme... compared to a mere 16% who watched the BBC Television Service newsreel on their new-fangled television receivers. A radio show grabbing a bigger audience than television – that *does* seem like science-fiction these days.

In the days before the major exploitation of successful brandings, *Journey into Space* was hot property right from its debut in 1953. The BBC was swamped with enquiries from manufacturers wanting to licence space helmets and space suits, toy kits, 'picture stories' (i.e. comic strips), feature film projects, stage plays... and book deals. Following an approach by Allan Wingate in December 1953, other offers of novelisations or novels in the coming months originated from Routledge and Kegan Paul Ltd, Frederick Muller, Herbert Jenkins, Putnam, Birn Brothers and Michael Joseph. It was Herbert Jenkins – the first company to make a formal book offer – that clinched the deal to take Jet and his chums to the printed page, with Charles Chilton agreeing terms in March 1954. The novelisation of the first series under the title *Journey into Space* appeared in hardback from Herbert Jenkins in November 1954, concurrent with the transmission of the second radio series.

By the start of 1955, director David Lean – then known for his acclaimed versions of *Oliver Twist* and *Great Expectations* – had his team making enquiries about the availability of the movie rights to *Journey into Space* while Rembrandt Films proposed a filmed TV serial for the US market. However, Charles Chilton was very firm that *Journey into Space* was something uniquely crafted to exploit the sound rather than visual medium, even mischievously going to the extent of setting some episodes in total blackness with the characters having to explore and vocalise their surroundings. What Charles had crafted was true sound drama: captivating dialogue enhanced by strange new sounds and the rich, evocative music score of Van Phillips; indeed, *Theme from 'Journey into Space'* as recorded by Frank Weir and his Orchestra was released by Decca in March 1955.

Journey into Space returned for a third series – subtitled *The World in Peril* – in September 1955, picking up with events in April 1972 and concluding the epic Martian story arc started in *The Red Planet* in another twenty episodes. In the meantime, *The Red Planet* was published by Herbert Jenkins in January 1956. The closest to a visual version of the programme would come in April 1956 when *Express Super Colour Weekly* launched a *Journey into Space* strip within its pages, initially boasting stylish artwork from Italian artist Ferdinando Tacconi.

In 1957, one episode of the first series was remade under the title of *A Trip to the Moon* as part of a BBC Schools Radio science unit – an accolade possible because of Charles' determination to draw upon hard science as much as possible in his narratives. A condensed thirteen-part remake of the original *Journey into Space* serial – now entitled *Operation Luna* – was recorded for the BBC's Transcription Service in 1957 and broadcast domestically from March 1958. 1958 also saw the paperback appearance of *Journey into Space*, courtesy of Pan Books, followed by softbacks of *The Red Planet* in 1960 and *The World in Peril* in 1962 (following its 1960 Herbert Jenkins hardback). As Jet Morgan and his crew faded into the world of radio nostalgia, it was these novelisations which kept the story of *Journey into Space* alive for the next twenty years.

Being born in the 1960s, my own introduction to *Journey into Space* didn't come until 1981 when Jet and his team were revived for a one-off play in Radio 4's *Saturday Night Theatre* strand – part of a sporadic smattering of SF plays throughout the year including H. G. Wells' classic *The First Men in the Moon*, John Wyndham's *The Chrysalids*, Arthur C. Clarke's *A Fall of Moondust* and Harry Harrison's *The Technicolor Time Machine*. *The Return from Mars* was a very enjoyable ninety minutes for this sixth former, but – thirty years later – it is all too clear that this new offering for the *Discovery* crew was merely a shadow of the complex, epic narratives that 1950s audiences had been treated to.

In the wake of *The Return from Mars* came *Journey into Space*'s natural descendent: Charles Chilton's *Space Force* serials which offered engaging, higher calibre adventure when broadcast by Radio 2 in 1984 and 1985 (although commissioned originally in 1979). Now studying at university, I eagerly followed the missions undertaken by Captain Saxon Berry and his colleagues: engineer Lauderic Sincere, scientist Professor Magnus Carter and radio operator Chipper Barnet – the grandson of Lemmy Barnet himself! At the same time I was able to collect the Pan paperbacks of the three *Journey into*

Space novelisations, and so was finally able to get a taste of what all the fuss had been about at the time.

Thankfully, the radio serials – believed lost over the years – had in fact survived. In June 1987, BBC Sound Engineer Ted Kendall located 33rpm sixteen-inch coarse-groove discs of *Operation Luna, The Red Planet* and *The World in Peril* in the basement of Kensington House in Shepherd's Bush. Repeats were scheduled on BBC Radio 2 in due course, with *Operation Luna* taking to the air again on Friday nights from May 1989 and being released commercially on cassette by BBC Enterprises. In the coming years, *The Red Planet* and *The World in Peril* would receive similar re-runs, attracting positive comments in the media about how well the unearthly adventures of Jet and the *Discovery* crew had stood the test of time.

Now graduated and working in the technological world, this was when Charles Chilton's stories captivated me. During the 1980s, I had started to research British telefantasy series and was writing for a number of publications – both professional and amateur. But now I was developing a particular passion for this amazing *radio* serial which offered such tension and excitement on a Friday evening. It was a struggle but – after months of research – I was able to persuade the professional 'zine *Dreamwatch* to take an article and brief guide to the series in 1991. This appreciation was enriched by a phone conversation with the great man himself, Charles Chilton – a helpful, affable and enthusiastic voice at the end of the telephone line.

When it came to a reissue of the serials on cassette in 1998, my editors at the late, lamented magazine *TV Zone* offered me the opportunity to interview Charles Chilton in a piece of promotion set up by BBC Audiobooks. Eagerly, I booked a day off from building databases and travelled down to meet Charles at his London home, spending a joyous morning discussing his amazing career with us both enthusing over Tacconi's amazing comic artwork as I spread newly acquired back-numbers of *Express Weekly* across Charles' living-room floor. In the coming years, I was able to work with BBC Audiobooks on various science-fiction and comedy titles, compiling booklets of notes and advising on possible bonus material. When it was decided that a restored set of episodes for *Journey into Space* would be released on CD and download from 2004, I was overjoyed to be able to write at length and in detail about the making of my favourite radio adventure series of all. Most recently, AudioGO have re-released the CDs in a new uniform edition at an even more attractive price, and so the rich source material remains available to own.

In taking these amazing stories and turning them into prose, Charles chose to stick predominantly to the radio narration by Doc Matthews – mellifluously delivered by Guy Kingsley-Poynter in the original – and embellish it with more of the real science of the day; the descriptions of life on the lunar colony which open this volume are vivid and captivating. However, to fit ten hours' narrative into a couple of hundred pages, some sacrifices were made to achieve this abridgement. Mitch's almost lethal spacewalk from *Discovery*. The shocking fate of Freighter Number Seven. Peterson's final, tragic message. Lemmy's nightmarish regression to the London of his childhood...

I still work in the database arena during the day – and am even fortunate enough to have a line manager who is a Jet Morgan devotee, having been brought up in the 1980s by a father who generously passed on his passion for sound drama. A few months ago my wife Julie – who was sensible enough not to adopt my rather bizarre surname at the altar but retain her maiden name of Rogers – was taken ill and required extensive rest at home, with myself in attendance. Apologising for my absence from the office over the phone as Julie slept, I was delighted when my boss Robin adopted the uncanny tones of Whitaker to reply, *'Rogers is asleep... She cannot be woken.'*

It's a pleasure to be able to share my enthusiasms for *The Red Planet* in this foreword, so my thanks to Dexter O'Neill of

Fantom Films for his kind offer to let me supply this eulogy to the story, and of course to the amazing Charles Chilton for setting Jet's adventures in motion almost sixty years ago.

Ahead of you in this volume is a brilliantly gripping and solid piece of space adventure. Orders are that you enjoy it. And orders must be obeyed without question at all times.

Andrew Pixley
December 2011

Chapter 1

As everybody knows, there is no air on the Moon and temperature there varies between great extremes of heat and cold; in fact, the only comfortable time for men to be abroad on the Moon's surface, even in heated or cooled space suits, is during the hours of the lunar morning and evening.

Yet today, in the Bay of Rainbows, stands Luna Colony – a vast monument to man's engineering skill. There all air has to be manufactured and every article of food, clothing and equipment still has to be brought from Earth, for the Moon, being a barren globe, can supply us with nothing but a few raw materials which have to be ferried back to Earth before they can be put to any kind of use.

That men are on the Moon at all is due to the now historic trip of the first atomic-powered space ship *Luna,* captained by Jet Morgan and manned by his crew of three: Lemmy Barnet, radio engineer, Stephen Mitchell, the Australian astronautics engineer who designed the ship, and myself, Dr Matthews, known to the rest of the crew simply as 'Doc'.

But why bother to establish a Colony at all, you may ask? There are a number of reasons, but the most important is that from the time *Luna* first landed on the Moon it was realised that at last man had a jumping-off ground from which to reach the more distant planets – in particular, Mars. And it was to this end that the work of Luna Colony was principally directed, for there was a time limit on the project, as I will now explain.

Mars is the nearest planet to the sun outside the Earth. In other words, the orbit of the Earth lies inside the Martian one.

Neither orbit is circular, but elliptical. However, the Martian orbit is more elongated than the Earth's and the direction of the elongation is not the same. In consequence, the paths of the Earth and Mars lie closer together in some places than in others. Earth and Mars travel round the sun in the same direction, but do not, as it were, travel hand in hand. Not only does Mars travel more slowly than the Earth, it also, because it is farther from the sun than our own planet, has much farther to go. Consequently the Earth is constantly overtaking and passing Mars.

When the Earth lies in a direct line between the sun and Mars, it is said to be in 'opposition' to the Red Planet. Oppositions occur about every 780 days and it is then that the distance between the two planets is at its minimum; this minimum distance varying, of course, according to whether the opposition takes place at points along the orbits which are close or not so close to each other. The smallest possible distance during an opposition is around thirty-five million miles; the greatest, sixty-three million.

'Close' oppositions occur approximately every fifteen years and since 1900 there have been five. The opposition of 1924 was one of the closest of the century and, although nobody on Earth could have had the remotest idea of it at the time, not even the astronomers realised that it was one of the most important Martian oppositions in history. But just as important, perhaps, was the last which took place in 1971. In that year, using the Moon as a jumping-off ground, the attempt to reach Mars was made.

You may wonder why we should go to the trouble of assembling a fleet on the Moon when we could take off from the Earth direct. It is because the lower gravitational pull enables us to take off with larger ships and propel them with far less fuel expenditure.

The construction of *Luna* had been child's play compared with the present project. Now, instead of just one ship, we were to take a whole fleet. It was estimated that the quickest possible time in which a space ship could reach Mars was approximately six months. But, perhaps, before I go into any details of the type of ship necessary for this great journey to the Red Planet, I had better remind you of a few more facts about the planet itself.

Mars is, of course, with the exception of Venus, the nearest planet to our own and, as planets go, it is quite small. Its diameter is approximately 4,200 miles, nearly half that of our globe; its mass is little more than one-tenth that of the Earth and, in consequence, its gravitational pull is also far less. A man weighing fourteen stone on Earth would weigh nearer five on Mars.

But, in many other respects, Mars is very similar to Earth and has been called by some astronomers 'Earth's little brother'. Mars rotates on its axis in almost the same time as the Earth and its day is 24 hours 37 minutes in length. (The Moon's day, you will remember, is 14 Earth days in length.) The Martian axis tilts at an angle of 25 degrees to its orbit; the Earth's at 23½. Seasonal conditions, therefore, are very similar to those we know on Earth except that, because of its longer journey round the sun, the Martian year is nearly twice as long.

Like the Earth, the poles of the Red Planet are ice-covered and, as summer approaches, these ice caps are seen to melt, and then to expand again during winter. The existence of these changing climatic conditions and the fact that Mars has an atmosphere made it almost certain that some kind of plant life existed there.

The sharp contrasts of colour that characterise the Martian surface – greens, blues, purples and reds – have been closely studied from the observatory established at Luna Colony, and what is believed to be vegetation has been observed to change colour with the seasons, just as vegetation does down on Earth. But what this vegetation is, whether it is forest, grass, fern or just moss, could never be established until man set foot on his little neighbour in space.

And then there was the vexed question of the 'canals' (or 'canali', to give them their correct name). For years after they were first discovered by Schiaparelli in 1877 these elusive features were the subject of fierce controversy. Many astronomers declared the canals did not exist at all. The argument was not settled until the establishment of the lunar observatory where, with no atmosphere to blanket out or distort the physical features on the Red Planet, the canals were indisputably proved to exist and were photographed hundreds of times. But it no longer seemed that the canals could have been made by any intelligent beings and it was almost certain that they did not contain water (which was a popular belief of the nineteenth century).

The problem of the 'canals' was one of many mysteries which we hoped to solve by our journey to Mars. But first we had to get there. Although we planned to land on Mars when it was close to the Earth, it was necessary to travel 355 million miles through space to reach the planet, for our ships could not travel in a straight line as the Moon ships virtually did. The reason for this is not hard to see. As I have already explained, the Earth, revolving in its orbit inside the Martian one, is constantly overtaking the planet. We travel round the sun at an average speed of 18½ miles per second. Mars, on the other hand, travels at an average speed of only 15 miles a second.

If it were possible for the Earth to move over from its orbit into that of Mars, it would overtake it at a rate of 3½ miles a second and eventually the two globes would collide. The Earth cannot, of course, deviate from its orbit but a space ship, leaving the Earth-Moon system at a carefully calculated speed and on an equally carefully calculated course, can. It can 'drift' outwards from the sun on a *spiral* path until the orbit of the Red Planet is reached. Once in the Martian orbit the speed of the ship can be adjusted until it matches that of the planet and, provided, of course, that the planet has already reached the same point, a landing can be made.

Such a journey takes six months or more and in that time the Earth will have travelled halfway round the sun and reached a position directly between the sun and Mars.

You can see that the slightest miscalculation could mean disaster to such a project and almost certain death for every man connected with it. But this was the least consideration in the minds of those chosen to take part in the great adventure.

We would be away from Earth for two years in all; six months' travel each way and a year on the planet itself. Consequently, nearly all our ships were freighters, carrying equal amounts of fuel, food, water, oxygen and scientific equipment. Our supplies were estimated to be enough to last for three years – after our experience on the Moon we intended to leave a wide safety margin.

Of the ships we were taking – and we were taking eight in all – only three could actually make a landing on the Martian surface. In the interests of economy the others were constructed to travel only in airless space. Because of this, only ten men would be able actually to touch down on Mars. The remaining crews would have to stay within the freighters in free orbit about a thousand miles above the planet's surface.

We would land on the southern ice cap. We realised that the temperature would be extremely low in those regions and that it was almost certain we would be unable to venture out of the ships at night. But it was only at the ice caps that we could be sure to find a surface smooth enough to land on. Once we had established a Polar Base, we intended to unload tractors and make our way towards the Martian equator, exploring the planet as we went.

The flagship of the fleet, the *Discovery*, was to be manned by the same men who had made the first journey to the Moon. We were to take off on April 1st, 1971.

By March the Mars Fleet was ready to leave but, looking back over the project now, I realise that from the very start it was ill-fated for, even before takeoff, things were against us – ominous portents, had we then known it, of what was to come.

The floor of the Bay of Rainbows is as flat as any surface you can find on the Moon, and measured from cape to cape (Laplace to Heraclides) the bay is 143 miles in width. In the north-east are the Jura mountains; a magnificent sight when the low sun lights up their peaks, many of which rise to twenty thousand feet or more.

The bay was chosen as the site of Luna Colony for various reasons. Being situated at a high latitude (only 45° from the lunar pole) the day temperature does not rise to the heights it reaches at the equator. The bay also offers a flat and fairly solid surface (the depth of dust there being far less than in all other 'seas' so far explored) on which to construct the launching ground and, at the same time, a cliff face into which the Colony is built.

Why is it necessary to live underground? For protection; from the extreme heat, intense cold and meteor showers. On the moon, meteors take the place of weather as a subject of conversation. Sometimes days go by (Earth days, that is) without a meteor fall being recorded anywhere near the Colony. At other times, fortunately rare, they fall so thick and fast that it is not safe to go outside until the shower has passed.

Ninety-nine per cent of the meteors which travel Earthwards never reach its surface; they have burned themselves out long before. But every meteor that approaches the Moon is vaporised, not by an atmosphere, but by striking the lunar surface. And whenever a meteor strikes, an explosion, large or small according to the size of the missile, takes place and another scar is added to the Moon's face.

These small pits, or craters, looking rather like small shell holes, dot the lunar surface everywhere. However, the northern hemisphere of the Moon is less affected by meteor bombardment than the southern and, in particular, that part of the Sea of Rains in which the Bay of Rainbows lies.

The Colony extends into the mountains for a depth of two miles. The only outbuildings are the Colony entrance, the observatory domes and the 'rest rooms' where men off duty can sit and gaze through a thick, transparent roof at the stars or the Earth, a huge, brilliant globe which waxes and wanes just as the Moon does when seen from home.

And it was in one of the observation domes that the first disaster occurred.

The chances of a meteor hitting Luna Colony, protected as it is by the mountain range, are very remote. The chances of a meteor actually hitting the dome, the most vulnerable part of Luna City, are incalculable – and yet it happened. One moment the four men who were in there had been enjoying their view of the universe, the next the precious artificial atmosphere had rushed out of a gaping hole, leaving the men in a vacuum. It happened so suddenly that none of them could have realised it.

Fortunately the rest of the Colony suffered no harm. The airtight door leading into the observation room stood up to the pressure and did not give way. Soon the damaged section was permanently and hermetically sealed off from the rest of our underground city.

Two freightermen were killed in that accident. For two years they had been training as crew members of the Mars Fleet and then, only a few days before takeoff, their lives had suddenly come to an end. Of course, we were prepared for such an emergency and had replacements standing by for every man in the expedition. But it was a sad business and something we could well have done without.

However, the next few days were a fever of activity. Not far from the entrance to the Colony stands a shallow crater. It is about a mile in diameter and almost spherical in shape; in fact, it could hardly be called a crater at all, though it obviously had been once. But over the aeons of time its walls had been worn down and are now no more than a few feet high at their summit. It was in this crater that the Mars Fleet had been erected.

The ships were huge; nearly three hundred feet tall and ninety feet in diameter. Only one of them, the Flagship

Discovery, was of conventional rocket shape; the rest were quite out of line with the popular conception of what a space ship should look like. As they would never have to travel through any atmosphere they were not streamlined. They consisted of only the barest essentials: solar reflectors, radio antennae, fuel tanks and other equipment held together by what appeared to be a tangle of girders. The whole was topped by a large sphere which, besides carrying most of the cargo, also housed the tiny cabin which served as living quarters for the two men needed to man each vessel. The freight ships stood in a large circle about three quarters of a mile in diameter. And in the centre of that circle stood the *Discovery*, painted a bright blue for identification.

Twelve hours before takeoff, every man not on duty was looking towards the lunar horizon, waiting for the sun to rise. Behind us, hanging motionless in the void, itself like a great moon, was Earth.

Then suddenly there appeared behind the rugged skyline a spearpoint of its approach. Instantly, as though some giant hand had turned a switch, the whole area was bathed in the sun's hard glow, the mountains, rocks and crater rims throwing long, black, pointed shadows across the Moon's surface.

The lunar day had begun – the space fleet to Mars could now leave.

Chapter 2

Three hours before takeoff, all crew members assembled in the briefing room for last-minute instructions. Then we put on our space suits and gathered in the huge airlock that constituted the entrance to the Colony.

It was 'zero, minus two hours'.

Once we had passed into the airlock and the great, oval-shaped door had closed behind us I put on my helmet which until then I had carried under my arm. Its rim slid comfortably into position in the groove of the suit's collar. I fastened the catch and tested its security. Then I switched on the radio, listened for the faint 'mush' in my headphones that told me the receiver was alive and waited for further orders.

There were twenty of us in the lock, all similarly dressed in reinforced rubber-like, white, plastic suits. They were, except for the helmet, of one piece. The knees, elbows and shoulders were fuller than the rest of the suit and were ridged for flexibility. The soles of the feet were thick and hard and over them we had pulled our boots; tough, snugly fitting articles that were expected to last (even with almost continuous wear) for longer than our expedition was estimated to take.

Every man carried a back-pack containing his oxygen and battery power units. A small panel in the front of the suit just below chest height held a set of switches by which each man could control his radio, regulate the temperature of his suit, and increase or decrease the oxygen supply.

Standing in a tight little bunch, we all faced the door on the other side of which lay the Bay and the space ships. A white light gleamed above our heads. It was the signal that the air in the lock was about to be extracted.

A cold, flat voice sounded in my ear. *'Zero, minus one hour fifty minutes.'*

As the pressure went down and my suit inflated, I could feel the flexible joints tightening. Soon I was a stiff, rounded figure, like a knight of old in a shapely suit of armour.

Now a blue light glowed, indicating that air pressure was down to zero and that the door to the outer Moon was opening.

An intense glare greeted us from outside. It was so brilliant I instinctively closed my eyes against it. Quickly I felt for my control panel and dropped a neutral-tinted light filter into place. When I opened my eyes again it was to see the floor of the Bay, indented and rock strewn, stretching clear to the horizon.

The scene was a study in black and white; night and day at the same time. The sun lit up the rocks and mountains with a dazzling light. Where the sun could not reach all was black – blacker than the deepest Earth night – and it was impossible to see any detail where the shadows lay.

The sky, black as pitch, was studded with millions of multi-coloured stars in numbers far greater than can ever be seen from Earth. The Milky Way shone out as though a giant hand had dipped a huge whitewash brush into a bucket of shining stardust and swept it in a mighty arc across the heavens.

Owing to the sharp curvature of the Moon's surface, the horizon was no great distance away and we could just see the tops of the space ships rising above it. The sun, lighting up the spherical cabins of the freighters, gave them the appearance of huge beacons.

Parked outside the door of the Colony were two land trucks. Drivers were already seated in each of the hermetically sealed cabins and, as we left the airlock and walked towards them, they smiled and waved their hands at us.

Ten men climbed inside the passenger compartment of each vehicle and, once we were as comfortably seated as our suits would allow, we began to move swiftly along the red, concrete road. Nobody spoke for, as conversation could be held only via the radio, any unnecessary speech would have jammed the channel.

We rode, at twenty miles an hour, in complete silence. Not even the sound of our motors could be heard in that airless atmosphere; it was like living in an old, silent film.

Massive rocks slid by and were gone. Gradually the Jura mountains sank below the horizon behind us while the ships rose up slowly in front, as though mounted on a vast, rising platform.

We entered the great circle of rocketships half an hour later. Every ship was still enclosed within its elevator gantry; scaffolding on wheels into which was built the lift that would carry the men to the open doors of the crews' cabins. In the centre of the circle stood the *Discovery*, resting on a concrete platform of about one hundred yards' diameter. Radiating from the platform and built of the same red concrete as the road were eight tracks, each leading to a freight ship. Another road, like the rim of a great wheel, connected the ships on the outside.

When we reached the perimeter, the other truck turned off towards Freighter Number One while we continued our journey in towards the hub where *Discovery* towered above the launching ground. On reaching her, Jet, Mitch, Lemmy and I boarded the little elevator and soon the ground began to fall away beneath us. I could see the two trucks making their way from freighter to freighter. The ships cast great long shadows across the ground and when the trucks drove through them only their headlights were visible. Shadows on the Moon are so dense headlights are essential if you are to steer your way through them safely.

When we were all inside the cabin airlock, Jet closed the outer door and filled the vacuum with ship's air. As the chamber filled up, our suits lost their stiffness and the hum of the air-pump gradually grew in volume. Finally the pressure reached maximum and, even through our helmets, we could hear the low whirr of the cabin hatch as it opened above our heads.

Jet led the way and as soon as we were all in the cabin we closed the hatch and removed our helmets.

Lemmy spoke first. 'Well, Doc,' he said, still holding his helmet in his hand, 'this is it. All aboard the *Skylark*. A trip round the sun and back in time for dinner.'

The tone of Lemmy's voice told me he was keyed up. We all were, but Jet showed it least of all. 'All right, gentlemen,' he said coolly, 'take off your suits, stow them away and carry out pre-takeoff checks.'

As calmly as we could, we did as we had been ordered, carrying out a familiar routine in an unfamiliar mood of excitement and tension. By the time Lemmy had established radio contact both with Control and Freighters 1 to 8, Mitch and I had finished our inspections and had reported to Jet that everything was in order. 'Then get on your bunks,' he said, 'and strap yourselves in.'

We moved to our takeoff couches and as we did so we heard the voice of 'Tim'. *'Zero, minus thirty minutes.'*

We lay on our backs and tried to relax as we had been taught. One by one we heard the freighters check in to Control and ask for their gantries to be removed. The last ship to ask was Number Two. After that the radio was silent, and silence also reigned over our little cabin.

It was broken finally by Mitch. 'Well, there's one thing to be said for these new atomic motors,' he observed; 'with their slow acceleration we're not likely to go through the agony we did when we first took off from Earth on our way to the Moon – remember?'

'Will I ever forget?' said Lemmy. '*Luna* was no more than an old crate compared to this job.'

'Lemmy,' said Jet, ignoring both his engineer's and radio operator's remarks, 'televiewer.'

The little screen above my head glowed and in it I could see a small picture of the Moon's surface outside. Even in the short time we had been on the launching ground it was noticeable that the shadows thrown by the mountains, trucks and crater rims were already shorter.

Suddenly an arc of light rose up from the darkness, seemed to tower above the mountains for a second and then burst into a brilliant cascade of light.

'There goes the first flare,' I said. 'Takeoff imminent.'

'*Zero, minus twenty minutes*,' observed 'Tim' by way of confirmation.

'Well, gentlemen, it won't be long now,' said Jet. 'Remember, takeoff is fully automatic. Nothing should go wrong.'

'Let's hope not,' said Lemmy, with mock fear in his voice. 'Thirty-five million miles is a long way from home.'

'We'll be first off,' went on Jet. 'The others will follow at two-minute intervals. Thirty thousand miles above the Moon's surface the motors will be cut and we'll be coasting the rest of the way. Next stop – Mars.'

We lay back in silence. In spite of two years' preparation, Jet's last sentence came almost as a shock.

The time passed slowly, and every few minutes 'Tim' announced the fact. Five minutes before Zero we received a direct call. 'Hullo, *Discovery*. Control calling Flagship *Discovery*.'

'Hullo, Control – *Discovery* answering,' replied Jet.

'Takeoff time is less than five minutes away. Are you ready?'

'All set. Lemmy, televiewer – stern view.'

'Televiewer, stern view – contact.'

The picture above me changed. The view now was of the launching platform directly beneath us. At the top edge of the screen I could see the rim of our motor exhaust.

'*Zero, minus forty-five seconds.*'

'Stand by,' said Jet.

The voice of Control came through from the loudspeaker. 'Hullo, Freighter Number One. Control calling.'

We heard Number One reply.

'Your takeoff time is imminent. Are you ready?'

'All set,' confirmed Number One.

'Zero, minus fifteen seconds.' This was to us.

'*Minus ten seconds. Minus five – four – three – two – one –*'

'Here we go!' shouted Lemmy.

There was a pronounced vibration and a dull, muffled, distant explosion as the rocket motors came into play. For two or three seconds we did not rise, although the ship shook considerably. Suddenly the vibration ceased and there was the gentlest rocking sensation. The ship was leaving the ground. Perhaps poised no more than a foot above it. I tensed as I felt the ship move and then suddenly forced myself to relax.

We increased speed, slowly at first and then extremely rapidly. As speed increased, so did our weight. I felt myself growing heavier and heavier; being pushed down into the inflated bed which prevented my being pressed against its metal base. I had made many trips from Earth to the Moon since that first historic takeoff back in 1965 but I could never get used to the sensation of takeoff. It is the only thing I dislike about space travel. But, fortunately for us, the low gravitational pull of the Moon and the revolutionary type of rocket motor we were now using enabled our maximum acceleration to be reached gradually. Consequently, although my body felt like lead and it was impossible to move even a muscle, the experience was nothing like so unpleasant as that which we had all endured in *Luna*.

'*Zero, plus thirty seconds.*'

Control spoke now for the first time since takeoff. 'Hullo, *Discovery*. Height forty-five point one, velocity five thousand two hundred; maximum acceleration rate will be reached in thirty seconds.'

I looked again at the picture above my head. Below us was the Moon's surface. Now we were high enough to see not only the whole of the Bay of Rainbows but also a considerable part of the Mare Imbrium to the south and the Sinus Roris (which lay on the other side of the Jura Mountains) to the north. The Moon's terminator, the division between light and darkness on a 'non-full' Moon, lay directly below us. To the east all was black; to the west the Moon was bathed in brilliant light; and down the middle, where light met darkness, where the angle of the sun was low, it was a mixture of white and black.

Up and up we went, the details of the Moon's surface growing rapidly smaller as the area of view became correspondingly larger. I have never ceased to be thrilled by the sight of a land mass, whether it be the Earth or the Moon, swiftly dropping away beneath me. I was preoccupied with my thoughts when suddenly Jet asked: 'All OK with you, Doc?'

Quickly I diverted my gaze from the screen to the gauges in front of me. 'Yes, Jet,' I replied.

'First class takeoff,' said our captain.

'Let's hope the rest of the Fleet do as well,' I replied.

'Control calling *Discovery*. Maximum acceleration has now been reached. Motors will be cut in one hour.'

'Message received,' said Jet, 'and thank you.'

Control now called Freighter Number One. 'Stand by for takeoff – fifteen seconds.'

'Good luck, boys,' called Lemmy. 'See you at the rendezvous.'

'*Ten seconds*,' said 'Tim'.

'I wonder how they're feeling?' asked Mitch.

'If they feel anything like I do before every takeoff,' said Lemmy, 'awful.'

'*Five – four – three – two – one –*'

'There they go,' I said almost involuntarily.

'How long before they catch up on us?' asked Lemmy.

'Not for two days,' Jet told him; 'and getting into formation is going to be a bit tricky.'

'Well, we've got six months to practise,' said the radio operator. 'Wouldn't do to arrive at Mars out of line. It would give a bad impression.'

We could now see on the televiewer a long line of uniformly diminishing spots of light which were the jets of the freighter fleet spread out behind us.

We were on our way. The long journey to Mars had begun.

Chapter 3

Two days after leaving the Moon, the Mars Fleet was in formation and coasting through space. Neither the ships nor anything they contained were subject to the laws of gravity now, but this did not worry us. With the aid of our magnetic boots we were able to walk upright around the cabin with no discomfort. For that matter, we could walk equally well up the walls or along the ceiling. Space sickness, like sea sickness, is something one can get used to and finally overcome.

The ships travelled in line abreast, with the *Discovery* a little above the rest of the Fleet and Freighter Number One nearest to the flagship. From the *Discovery* the ships seemed poised in space, motionless; for, in spite of the tremendous speed at which we were travelling, the background of stars against which we viewed the Fleet was so vast, and at such a distance from us, that movement was virtually imperceptible.

Although there were four men in the *Discovery*, there were only two in each of the freighters. There wasn't room for more. The living quarters of the *Discovery* were cramped enough but those of the freighter ships were even worse. Every man travelling in them had been selected for ability, among other things, to live in an enclosed space with one other person for months at a time without cracking up.

Once the ships were in formation – and it took some time for them to get in line – Jet ordered Lemmy to call up each freighter in turn and get in its report. Number One reported that all was well, but with Freighter Number Two it was a different story. When Lemmy called up Rogers, the captain of

Number Two, and asked how things were, the reply was: 'Shocking.'

'Eh?'

'We've been having trouble all the way.'

Mitch, our chief motor engineer, immediately took Lemmy's place at the radio and demanded of Rogers: 'What kind of trouble?'

'The motor lost thrust soon after we left base. Had to turn on the juice a bit or we'd never have made the rendezvous. We used up quite a lot of fuel. At least ten per cent above estimated consumption.'

'Did you hear that, Jet?' asked Mitch anxiously.

'And that's not all,' Number Two continued. 'Our radio receiver's on the blink. We seem to be transmitting OK but reception from Base is down to strength two.'

'Are you hearing us all right?'

'Yes. Strength five. Ship-to-ship system seems to be OK.'

'Then keep listening out, Frank. We'll call you back.'

From where he was seated at the control table Mitch looked up at Jet. 'Well,' he enquired, 'what do we do about that? Frank might be a good pilot, but he's no radio man or engineer.'

'Who's with him in that ship?' asked Jet.

I looked up the crew list. 'Whitaker,' I answered after a few moments; 'a construction engineer.'

'Then there's no chance of his finding either of the faults. We'll have to transfer a radio engineer and motor mechanic from one of the other ships.'

'The nearest motor man is in ship Five,' I said, 'and the nearest radio mechanic, other than Lemmy here, is in Number Seven. Both ships are on the far side of the formation. Transfer would be tricky.'

'We're closer to her than most,' broke in Mitch; 'I'll go, and take Lemmy with me to look over the radio at the same time.'

'Very well,' Jet agreed. 'Get your suits. And take the long safety lines with you.'

After Mitch and Lemmy had donned their space suits we let them through the airlock into space. In the outer shell of the ship, in a panel near the door, were small rings to which Lemmy and Mitch immediately attached one end of their safety lines, the other, of course, being already fastened to their belts. Thus safeguarded, and with the aid of their magnetic boots, they could, if necessary, walk completely round the ship like flies round a pole and would neither fall off nor have any sensation of being upside down.

On this occasion, however, Lemmy merely bent his knees, gave a little push and slowly drifted over towards Freighter Number One. Once there, he fastened a short line to Number One and made himself secure. Mitch then unhitched Lemmy's long line from the ring on the *Discovery* and attached it to his own belt and Lemmy hauled him across. The same procedure was followed for reaching Number Two. Once there the airlock was opened to let them in.

An examination of the many dial readings and Number Two's log book soon told Mitch that to correct the fault in the motor, part of it would have to be dismantled. This it would be impossible to do for some weeks as the motor was still highly radioactive. So it was decided that, as the motor would not be needed again until the Fleet was close to Mars, repairs could be left until later. Mitch then returned to the *Discovery*.

What happened in Freighter Number Two after that I learned from Lemmy later. He was nearing the end of his work on the radio when Whitaker had to go down into the hold to carry out a routine inspection tour. A few minutes later Lemmy's job was completed and the radio operator called up Base to check the receiver. It proved to be OK.

'Well,' said Lemmy to Frank Rogers, 'that's that. If you don't get Control at full possible strength after this, you may return the goods and get your money back.'

'And I suppose you'll be going over to the *Discovery* now?' asked Frank.

'Yep,' replied Lemmy.

'Oh.'

Lemmy raised his eyebrows and looked at the freighterman in surprise. 'You almost sound disappointed,' he said. 'I don't owe you any money, do I?'

'How do you mean?'

'Way you're trying to hang on to me, I thought maybe I did.'

'No, Lemmy; it's just that I thought I might have had the pleasure of your social company for a bit. Somebody to talk to for a while.'

'You've got Whitaker to talk to.'

'No, Lemmy. I can't talk to him.'

'Why? Has he been struck dumb or something?'

'No, it's not that. He just *doesn't* talk. He's about the most unsociable person I ever met.'

'Then why did you crew up with him?'

'I couldn't help it. I was supposed to crew with Vivis, but he was killed – back in Luna City. I'd hardly time to get acquainted with Whitaker before we took off.'

'And after only two days,' said Lemmy, 'you've decided you can't get along with him.'

'I defy anybody to.'

'But what's the matter with him? Doesn't he pull his weight?'

'About the only thing he does do. But he never says a word, unless it's absolutely necessary.'

Lemmy thought for a moment and then said: 'Then how does he spend his time, when he's not on duty?'

'Mostly lying on his bunk. He just lies there, staring at me.'

Lemmy laughed. 'You sure you haven't hypnotised him or anything?'

'I'm not joking, Lemmy,' said Frank, his voice rising hysterically.

'No, mate,' said Lemmy quietly.

'Sometimes,' went on Frank, 'I think he must be in a trance.'

'If he were,' asked Lemmy, 'how could he carry out his work?'

'He does that all right. Only sometimes, I…' Frank paused. 'You don't think I'm crazy, do you, Lemmy?'

'As if I'd think a thing like that,' replied Lemmy, putting his hand on Frank's shoulder.

'Well, sometimes it's as though he's not the only one here.'

'Of course he's not the only one here, there's… eh?'

'Well, it's not *him*, if you know what I mean.'

'No, I don't know what you mean,' said Lemmy slowly.

'I tell you, if I have six months of this, all the way to Mars, I'll go crackers.'

'Look,' said Lemmy firmly, 'why don't you tell Jet about this?'

'He's got enough troubles without having to shoulder mine, too.'

'But we all know living for weeks in a confined space with somebody you can't get on with is not easy. You begin to see something wrong in everything they do; the way they eat, the way they walk, the way they hold their cigarettes if they smoke, the way they watch you smoking yours if they don't. All maddening, irritating little things – but they can drive you off your rocker in no time. You might even start getting violent.'

'I might at that.'

'Then if Jet thinks you've got a good case, he'll get either you or Whitaker transferred to another ship, before any real trouble starts.'

And there the conversation was interrupted by the sound of the airlock between the hold and living quarters opening. Whitaker was returning from his inspection. Lemmy quickly changed the subject.

'Now, Frank,' he said brightly, 'treat her gently and she'll treat you kindly. The way she's behaving now she'd pick up a signal from Jupiter if there was anybody up there to send one, which there isn't. So if you find you're getting nothing, you know where you're getting it from.' Lemmy laughed and heartily slapped Frank on the back.

Lemmy returned to the *Discovery* full of sympathy for Frank but, after hearing Lemmy's story, Jet declared Whitaker's behaviour must be due to space conditions and decided to wait for them to pass off.

Twenty-four days out from Earth, Lemmy was calling Control on a routine check. I was lying on my bunk writing my diary at the time and although he tried to keep his voice low I could hear him quite distinctly.

'Hullo, Control?' he was saying, 'Flagship *Discovery* calling. Come in please.'

After a long pause a faint, quavery voice emitted from the loudspeaker. 'Hullo, Flagship *Discovery*. Receiving you strength two. Over.'

'Have recorded report on last six hours ready for transmission,' said Lemmy. 'Are you ready to receive it?' He turned to me. 'Time lag between replies gets longer every time we call up, Doc. We must be a million miles from Earth at least by now.'

'Two million,' I corrected him.

Eventually the report was passed and then Control asked to talk to Jet. He moved over to the radio.

'Hullo, Captain Morgan,' said Control. 'Message for you. Urgent. Concerning Whitaker, crew member of freighter ship Number Two.'

'Oh?' exclaimed Jet. 'Whitaker, did you say?'

'Yes. James E. Whitaker. Construction engineer, Freighter Number Two. Information needed on him by personnel records office. Date of birth. Place of birth. Nationality. Full personal description and details of all engineering qualifications and where obtained. End of message.'

Jet looked puzzled. 'Hullo, Control,' he called, 'message received. What on earth do you want all that for? Records must have it already.'

'What do they think we are,' interrupted Lemmy, 'an information bureau?'

'Sorry, Captain,' came the voice of Control; 'I don't write these messages, I only pass them on.'

'Very well,' said Jet. 'I'll call you back in half an hour.'

Lemmy switched off the main radio. 'Call up Number Two, will you,' Jet asked him, 'and get Whitaker.'

The engineer replied to Lemmy's call almost immediately.

'Look, Whitaker,' said Jet, 'I'm sorry about this, but I've had a message from Control about you.'

'Yes, Captain?'

'I have to ask you a number of questions about yourself for personnel records.'

Whitaker's strangely flat, dull voice came back without hesitation. 'All information about me can be found in my personal dossier down on Earth.'

'Yes, yes, I realise that,' said Jet a little impatiently, 'but for some reason Control insists on having it again. So are you ready?'

'Yes.'

'Well, first I must have your full name.'

'James Edward Whitaker.' Whitaker pronounced every word as though he had to think about it; slowly, with long gaps between each name.

'Date of birth?'

'12th September, 1940.'

'Nationality?'

'British.'

'Place of birth?'

'12th September, 1940.'

Jet and Lemmy looked at each other in surprise. 'No,' said Jet, '*place* of birth.'

Whitaker's voice now took on a peculiar quality; 'British,' he said, rolling the 'r'.

'What's he talking about?' asked Lemmy.

Jet was not asking any questions now, but Whitaker continued to talk as though he were – and his voice got slower and flatter, with almost an ethereal quality. 'James – Edward – Whitaker,' he said mechanically. '12th September, 1893.'

At this I sat up in my bunk and Mitch, who had been poring over his tables, looked over towards the radio.

''What's happening over there, Jet?' he demanded. 'Is Whitaker crazy or something?'

'1893, he said,' replied Jet without looking round. 'Hullo. Whitaker – Whitaker…' But Whitaker didn't reply. Not to Jet, anyhow.

'12th September, 1893,' he repeated slowly.

'Listen, Whitaker,' said Jet firmly, 'put Rogers on.'

'Rogers is asleep.'

'Then wake him up.'

'He cannot be woken.'

'Wake him up, do you hear?' Jet commanded.

There was no reply.

'Hullo, Whitaker – hullo,' went on Jet. '*Discovery* calling. Hullo – hullo…'

'It's no good, Jet,' said Lemmy. 'He must have switched off.'

Mitch and I had now walked over to where Jet and Lemmy were standing, tense and worried, in front of the radio. 'What's going on, Jet?' I asked.

'I wish I knew,' replied the captain.

'You don't think Number Two's radio has gone wrong again, do you?'

'The ship-to-ship system never was wrong, Doc,' put in Lemmy indignantly.

'Then you're quite sure it isn't our radio that's wrong?'

'Soon see,' said Jet. 'Hullo, Space Fleet,' he called. 'Flagship calling Space Fleet. Number One, come in please.'

The voice of Number One came back immediately. 'Hullo, Flagship. Freighter Number One replying. Hearing you loud and clear.'

'Morgan here.'

'Yes, sir.'

'Did you hear me talking to Number Two just now?'

'Yes, sir.'

'And you heard him reply?'

'I certainly did.'

'Thank you, Number One. That's all for now.'

'Yes, sir.'

'Well, that settles that. There's nothing wrong with us. Switch on the televiewer, Doc. Let's take a look at Number Two.'

I moved over to the control. A few seconds later the televiewer screen glowed and showed the long line of ships stretching out below us. We could see Number Two quite clearly.

She looked no different from any of the other freighters. She was in line, in perfect formation. We all looked at the screen in silence. Then Jet said: 'I'd give anything to know what's going on in there.'

'Then why don't we go across and see?' suggested Lemmy.

'Use your sense, Lemmy,' said Mitch. 'If we went across, how would we get inside? If they don't hear the radio, how do we get them to open the door?'

'If one of us banged on it with a wrench they'd hear that all right.'

'I think it's worth a try, Jet,' I put in. 'We have no other way of contacting them.'

'Very well then,' said Jet. 'Lemmy, get my suit.'

'Shall I get mine, too?' volunteered the Cockney.

'No, stay here, Lemmy. Keep trying to contact them. Doc will see me safely across.'

Chapter 4

From my position close to the door I stood by as Jet made his way across to Number Two, while back in the ship Mitch watched his progress on the televiewer. Meanwhile Lemmy was constantly calling the freighter on the radio, but with no result.

When Jet reached the freighter's tightly closed main door he rapped on it with the wrench. But he had hardly begun knocking when a familiar voice was heard on the intercom.

'Hullo, *Discovery* – Freighter Number Two calling. Urgent. Come in please.' It was Frank Rogers.

Lemmy immediately connected him to Jet and a few minutes later I heard Frank say: 'Hullo, skipper. Have to report that Whitaker is sick. Very ill, I think.'

'What? Then why didn't you answer when we called?'

'Have you been calling? I was asleep and…'

'Asleep!' There was no mistaking the anger in Jet's voice.

'Yes, sir,' said Frank apologetically. 'And when I woke up I found Whitaker flat out. I can't rouse him.'

'Listen to me, Frank,' said Jet sharply; 'if you're awake enough to get to the main door, open it and let me in.'

'Yes, sir.'

'Hullo, Doc,' Jet called to me.

'Hearing you,' I told him.

'Come over here, will you?'

'Sure thing,' I replied, and unfastening the hook of Jet's line from where it was secured to the ring near my feet I hooked it to my belt and, by way of Number One, hauled myself across. When I arrived at Number Two the main door was already open and Jet was waiting for me in the airlock. After the lock

33

had been exhausted and the hatch opened Jet led the way up into the crew's quarters.

'Where's Whitaker?' he asked as he reached floor level.

'There,' was the reply.

'Good grief!' I heard Jet say. 'He's still standing up!'

By this time I, too, had climbed the ladder and stepped into the cabin. While I was removing my helmet I had time to take in the scene. Whitaker was standing near the control table in front of the radio and leaning to one side at an angle of forty-five degrees.

'Did you have to leave him like that, Frank?' asked Jet angrily.

'It makes no difference whether he's standing up or lying down, Jet,' I interrupted. 'He's unconscious just the same. Help me get him over to his bunk.' Although common sense told me Whitaker's strange attitude was due to lack of gravity within the ship, I must admit that seeing him like that – his eyes half-open but lifeless – was uncanny.

Jet untied Whitaker's magnetic boots and between us we got him to his bunk. He appeared to be in a coma. His breathing was quite regular but his temperature was abnormally low.

While I was still examining Whitaker, Jet questioned Frank. 'Now,' he said, 'let's get to the bottom of this. Why didn't you answer us when we called?'

'If I'd known you were calling I would have,' replied Rogers.

'But good heavens, man, the radio's loud enough, isn't it? Do you want an alarm clock, too?'

'Well, no matter how loud it was, sir, I'm afraid it didn't wake me.'

'What time did you go to sleep?'

'About two hours ago.'

'Did you take a pill?'

'No, Jet, but while I was sleeping…'

'Well?'

Frank swallowed, looked at the floor, hesitated a moment and then continued: 'I had the most horrible dream. One of those nightmares when you know that if you don't wake up something terrible will happen to you. I thought I was back on Earth but the funny thing was that…'

'You don't have to give me details of your dream,' broke in Jet impatiently. 'What was Whitaker doing when you went to bed?'

'Sitting at the radio, on watch.'

'Did you notice anything odd about him then?'

'No more than usual. He didn't have a word to say.'

By this time my examination had been completed and Jet moved over to the bunk. 'Well, Doc?' he asked.

'Still unconscious,' I told him.

'Any idea why?'

'No,' I said, 'I can't understand it at all. I can find nothing wrong with him but I can't rouse him.'

'If it's just sleep, it must have come upon him very suddenly.'

'It certainly did,' I replied. 'Anyway, I don't intend to leave him before he wakes again – and that might be hours. Perhaps you'd better go back to the *Discovery*.'

'But that would mean Frank virtually running this ship on his own,' Jet protested. 'You can't share his watches and stay with Whitaker at the same time.'

'I can manage for a few hours anyway, sir,' said Frank, trying to be helpful.

'No, I have a better idea,' said Jet. 'Do you think we could move Whitaker over to the *Discovery*?' he asked, turning to me. 'We could keep an eye on him then without upsetting the watch routine.'

I was a little doubtful as to the wisdom of Jet's suggestion, but Frank received it enthusiastically. 'He doesn't weigh anything, sir,' he reminded us eagerly. 'It would only be a matter of towing him across.'

'Rogers,' I said, 'you almost sound as though you'd be glad to get rid of him.'

'Well… it's not that, sir,' said Frank hesitantly.

'Under the circumstances, Doc,' said Jet, 'if we can move him I think we should.'

'Very well,' I replied. 'Give him an hour. If he doesn't wake by then, I'll consider it.'

The hour passed slowly but at the end of it there was still no sign of life from Whitaker. He lay on his bunk, breathing a little heavily but otherwise not moving. Jet called up Mitch and told him to prepare to transfer to Number Two. Once Mitch was outside the *Discovery*, Jet and I, carrying Whitaker between us, were hauled across and when we reached our own ship Mitch pushed off towards the freighter.

Back in the flagship we removed Whitaker's suit and laid him on Mitch's bunk. We had hardly done this when the engineer called up from Number Two to say he was safely aboard. At that moment there was a moan from Whitaker and Jet hurried to my side.

'He's waking,' I told him. A second later Whitaker's eyes opened. He looked around him in surprise and tried to sit up.

'Here,' I said, 'get this down. It'll make you feel better.'

But he refused the little flask I offered. 'Where am I?' he asked quietly.

'You're aboard the *Discovery*,' I told him.

'How did I get here?'

'Doc and I went over to your ship and brought you back,' said Jet.

'And what was I doing all that time?'

'Sleeping,' I said. 'At least, that's what you appeared to be doing.'

'Can't a man sleep without he has to be hauled from one ship to another?' he asked almost angrily.

'Now take it easy,' said Jet; 'you fell asleep standing on your feet. That's not natural.'

'Under gravity-less conditions?'

'What I mean is, you fell asleep in the middle of talking to me.'

'Oh, yes.' Whitaker paused a moment as he cast his mind back. 'I remember. Records had lost my dossier.'

'I didn't say so. I merely said that they wanted information about you.'

'Do they still want it?'

'Yes.'

'Then get it over with.'

'I'd rather you waited a bit, Jet,' I suggested; 'at least until I've given him a thorough look over.'

'Ask your questions, Captain Morgan,' said Whitaker flatly and apparently disinterested.

'No,' said Jet, 'you'll stay where you are until Doc considers you're fit to get up. Later I'll have you transferred to another freighter.'

'I'm not going back to Number Two?'

'No.'

'But Number Two is my ship. I must go back to it.'

'I'm sorry, Whitaker, but under the circumstances that is impossible. You and Rogers don't get along too well. One of you has to be moved.'

'Then let it be Rogers. He's the one who complains.'

'Whitaker,' said Jet firmly, 'if I decide to move you, you'll move, is that clear?'

'Yes, sir.'

Jet lowered his voice. 'All right, Doc, he's all yours. I'll question him later.'

'Sure, Jet,' I said.

Whitaker 'rested', much against his will, for six hours. At the end of that time the only report I could give Jet was that he was fit and well again, physically at any rate. In due course Jet got the information he required and had it radioed back to Base.

As to the cause of the strange, deep sleep that had so suddenly overtaken Whitaker, I was none the wiser, nor, apparently, was he. But, if I learned nothing else, after spending an hour or more in his company I could appreciate how difficult Frank Rogers had found him. There was some indefinable... well... 'atmosphere' surrounding Whitaker that made me uneasy just to be near him.

When Whitaker was fit enough to take up his duties again and began moving around the cabin, Jet and Lemmy noticed his strangeness, too. Tension in the ship began to haunt and then, less than twenty-four hours after Whitaker had joined us, something happened that drove all of his behaviour from our minds.

A report came through from Freighter Number Five. Every ship took its turn at radar watch and Number Five had just started its two-hour vigil when Grimshaw, one of its crew, made a startling discovery.

'Unless I've gone crazy, sir,' the Canadian was saying excitedly, 'there's something pretty solid in front of us. And it lies right across our path.'

'How strong are the signals?' Jet asked him.

'Very faint, but they're there, skipper.'

'All right, Number Five,' said Jet. 'Keep constant watch will you? I'll get the other ships to see if they can pick up anything.'

A few minutes later we were getting signals on our own radar and as more reports came in it became obvious that the object which blocked our path, whatever it was, was colossal.

'What do you make of it, Doc?' Jet asked me after the tenth series of reports had been received.

'I don't know what to say,' I told him. 'It could be a cloud of meteors or even tiny asteroids. How far are we from it now?'

'Well, I estimate we'll reach it in about twenty-one hours, if we stay on our present course.'

'Then don't you think we should notify Control and see what they have to say?'

'Yes,' said Jet; 'perhaps we should.'

It was more than four hours (by which time Lemmy had retired to his bunk) before we received a reply to our message, and then all Control could say was: 'Unable to say with certainty what the object is. Possibility that it may be one of these things: meteor swarm, comet dust or a cloud of ionised gas. If either of the first two, suggest evasive action be taken as soon as practicable. If ionised gas, you can expect to pass through it safely with no adverse results other than a temporary upsetting of electronic equipment. Please keep us fully informed. End of message.'

'Well,' said Jet, 'with regard to the first two objects they're much the same thing and equally as dangerous. But if it is ionised gas then we can take a chance and plunge straight through it.'

'And how are we to tell which it is?' I reminded him.

'I don't think we will be able to, Doc, until we get fairly close to it – and by then it will be too late to get out of its way. We'll see what Mitch thinks.'

The Australian was sure that the swarm we were approaching was composed of meteors. 'For safety's sake, Jet, I think we should treat it as though it were and take evasive action,' he said.

'That will mean changing course,' said Jet, 'and once we start that we may never reach Mars.'

'If we're battered to pieces by meteors we'll never reach it either.'

'Well, we're not likely to meet the outer layers of that swarm for some hours yet,' Jet went on, 'and that gives us plenty of time to get you back into the ship. If we decide to change course, you'll have to be here.'

'And I shan't be sorry,' said Mitch. 'Being a member of a freighter crew can get darned dull.'

'Very well,' said Jet. 'I'll call you later.' And with that he switched off the receiver and again turned to me. 'Well, Doc,' he asked, 'what is our estimated distance from it now?'

'About half a million miles,' I told him. 'We should reach it in about seventeen hours.'

'Then if we are going to transfer Whitaker and get Mitch back here, we'd better start doing something about it at once.'

'Where do you intend sending him?' I asked.

'I don't know. If he has the same effect on other crews as he has on Frank, wherever we send him could well be disastrous.' Jet thought for a moment and then said: 'He'll have to go to Number Six – with Peterson. He's about the toughest freighter pilot we have.'

I was about to wake the construction engineer and tell him to put his suit on when Lemmy, who occupied the bunk above him, began to moan.

'What on earth's the matter with him?' asked Jet in surprise, looking first at Lemmy and then at me. 'Is he having a nightmare or something?'

Apparently Lemmy was, because he suddenly began to twist and turn in his bunk and to cry: 'No, no-oh, help. Help!'

I moved over to the bunk with Jet close behind me. As I did so, Lemmy gave a piercing scream as though he were in great pain. I took him by the shoulder and shook him.

'Lemmy,' I called. 'Lemmy! What's the matter?'

But he just went on yelling and screaming. Then suddenly his eyes opened wide and he sat up in his bunk and began to grapple with me. After a bit of a struggle I freed myself from his grasp and slapped his face. That brought him round. The yelling stopped and he sat quite still, staring at me.

'Lemmy?' I asked, gently. 'What's the matter?'

He said nothing for a few moments; just stared at me as though he were trying to recognise me. Then, with a little shudder, he said: 'Oh, it's you, Doc. Where are we?'

'Now calm down, Lemmy,' I said. 'You're in the *Discovery*.'

'*Discovery*? But Jet and I were…'

'On the way to Mars.'

'Mars?' It was as though Lemmy had never heard of the word. 'Oh, Mars,' he said suddenly. 'Yes, that's right. And this is Jet, isn't it?'

'Who else?' I asked him.

'Yeah, it all comes back to me now.'

'What happened, Lemmy? Did you have a bad dream?'

'Yes. Yeah, that's what it must have been. It was a dream. It didn't really happen. I mean, I couldn't have left this ship, could I?'

'No, Lemmy,' I said, trying to reassure him, 'you've been lying on that bunk for the last half hour, sleeping.'

Lemmy breathed a sigh of relief. 'Thank goodness,' he said. 'That was about the most horrible dream I ever had.'

'But it was only a dream,' said Jet. 'Now get down out of that bunk. We've got work for you to do.'

'Yes, Jet,' said Lemmy meekly and, donning his magnetic boots, he slung his legs over the side of the bunk and came down the ladder. As he descended to the floor his gaze fell on the still form in the bunk below. Then suddenly he became hysterical again. 'Oh no,' he moaned, 'that's *him*. Jet – that's the same fellow who was...'

'Lemmy,' Jet shouted. 'Pull yourself together.'

'What's he doing here?' asked Lemmy frantically. 'Where's Mitch?'

'Lemmy, shut up,' said Jet. 'Mitch is in Freighter Number Two – you know darn well he is. What are you carrying on like this for?'

Lemmy calmed down at last. With a long look at Whitaker, he said: 'Then who's this?'

'Whitaker, of course.'

'Whitaker?'

'What's the matter with you, Lemmy? Have you lost your mind or something? I had him transferred to this ship two days ago.'

'Yes, so you did,' said Lemmy slowly. 'But he...'

'He was in your dream?' I asked.

'Yes, Doc.'

'Gave you quite a shock to see him lying on that bunk, huh?'

'Yes.'

'Me, too, in a way.'

'How do you mean, Doc?'

'Well, in spite of all the commotion, he hasn't even stirred.'

Realisation of this occurred to Jet for the first time. 'No, he hasn't, has he?' he said slowly.

Lemmy began to get all worked up again. 'I tell you Jet, there's something about that fellah. He's a jinx and he's putting the mockers on the whole Fleet.'

Jet moved over to Whitaker and shook him roughly by the shoulders. 'Hey, Whitaker – Whitaker!' he said, almost shouting.

Whitaker opened his eyes immediately and gazed into Jet's face. 'Yes, captain?' he replied calmly.

'You awake?' Jet asked in surprise.

'Yes, sir.'

'Didn't you hear all that row just now?'

'No, sir.'

'Then you must be deaf.'

'No, sir. Just waiting for you to wake me. To transfer me to Freighter Number Six.'

'That's right,' said Jet. 'Hey, wait a minute – how do you know?'

'Isn't it true, then?'

'Yes, it is, but you were asleep when I decided which ship you should go to. Now, how did you know?'

'It was a foregone conclusion, captain. Peterson's the only person in this whole fleet who'll put up with my company. Unlike Mr Barnet here.'

'I don't want to be rude,' interrupted Lemmy, 'but you're right. The sooner you leave this ship the better I'll like it, and if they transferred you to Number Nine you'd still be too close for me.'

'Lemmy, shut up,' said Jet. 'As soon as you've eaten, you'll both put on your suits and get ready to go outside. Then you'll make your way from ship to ship until you reach Number Six. And you'll take the propulsion units in case you should come adrift. When you get to Number Six, Whitaker will stay there. Lemmy, you will then escort Simmonds from Number Six to Number Two. Leave him there and then escort Mitch to this ship. Is that clear ?'

'Yes, Jet,' said Lemmy, his voice dropping low.

'Right,' went on Jet, 'when you're ready, Doc will open up the airlock and let you out.'

Chapter 5

Number Six was about eight hundred yards from the *Discovery*, being the last freighter in line but two. We watched the suited figures of Whitaker and Lemmy slowly making their way, ship by ship, towards the far side of the formation. They had just about reached Number Five and were now only tiny figures.

'I must say,' I said to Jet as we watched the screen, 'the atmosphere in this ship is a lot easier now Whitaker's gone. There's something very peculiar about him.'

'I know. I felt it myself but I didn't like to admit it.'

'But why should he affect us like that?' I continued. 'Everybody he comes into contact with seems to find something they don't like about him.'

'I think it goes deeper than that, Doc.'

'How do you mean?'

'Lemmy's dream.'

'What about it?'

'One of the things Rogers complained of was that all the time Whitaker was in his ship he hardly dared sleep for fear of the frightening dreams he'd have. And then, when Whitaker comes over to our ship, almost the first day he's here exactly the same thing happens to Lemmy.'

'Frank had nightmares, too?' I asked.

'So he said,' went on Jet. 'But since Whitaker left Number Two he hasn't had one.'

'But how can a man's mere presence cause people to have nightmares?'

'Search me, Doc, but I can't help feeling that Lemmy's hysterics were no coincidence. Ah, the main door of Number Six is opening.'

A minute or so later there came a call from the freighter telling us that Lemmy and Whitaker were outside the ship and that the crew were in contact with them.

A moment later there came the voice of Control from Earth demanding to speak to Jet.

'All right, Doc,' said Jet, 'if you care to take over here, I'll talk to Control.'

'Sure, Jet,' I told him.

Jet moved to the other side of the cabin. A few seconds later the voice from Earth said: 'Hullo, Captain Morgan. Here is your message. Information on Whitaker received. It has been checked against his dossier in Records Section and found to be identical.'

'Well, of course,' I heard Jet mutter, impatiently.

'But further investigation has revealed that the only James Edward Whitaker who answers to the description we have was born in 1893. In 1924, at the age of thirty-one years, he disappeared and was never seen again.'

My attention was focused on the televiewer, but I could easily imagine the look of surprise that must have come over Jet's face.

'What!' he exclaimed. 'But Whitaker is thirty-one.'

Control ignored the interruption. 'Director of Records requests that he be allowed to talk to Whitaker as soon as possible.'

'Hullo, Control,' said Jet, an urgent tone in his voice now, 'your message received although not fully understood. But I can't put you on to Whitaker at present. May I call you later?'

'Very well.'

He called over to me. 'Doc, did you ever hear such preposterous nonsense? Is Whitaker in Number Six yet?'

'No,' I told him. 'He and Lemmy are hardly in the airlock.'

'Then Control will have to wait.'

And wait they did, for it was more than an hour before Whitaker had been safely transferred to Number Six, Simmonds to Number Two and Mitch and Lemmy were back in the *Discovery*. As soon as they had taken off their suits, Jet called a conference to decide what to do about the unidentified object ahead which, according to the latest radar reports, was now uncomfortably close. At last it was agreed that we should press on and risk flying through the swarm of meteors if that is what they proved to be. Jet seemed to have forgotten his promise to Control to put Whitaker on to them, so I reminded him of it.

'What's all this about Whitaker?' asked Mitch, who was seated at the control table estimating, yet again, our rate of approach towards the swarm.

'All Control said, Mitch,' Jet told him, 'was that the only man they could trace who answered to Whitaker's description was born in 1893.'

Mitch's eyebrows lifted in surprise. 'But it doesn't make sense.'

'Don't you think I realise that?'

'When does Whitaker say he was born?'

'1940. But he did mention 1893 when I questioned him before, when he was still in Number Two.'

'But didn't they check up on him before he joined the crew?' asked Mitch. 'During his training period or anything?'

'They must have done.'

'Then if they were ever going to find out anything as fantastic as this, wouldn't they have found it out then?'

'I would have thought so.'

'Records Section must be as crazy as coots, all of them.'

'I'd agree with you, Mitch,' I said, 'but for one thing?

'What?'

'Whitaker's odd behaviour. You took his place in Number Two so you can't know what I'm talking about. But all the while Whitaker was in this ship I had a strange feeling of foreboding. Jet and Lemmy, too.'

'Well, I think you're all jumping to hasty conclusions.'

'Do you? Then what about the enquiries from Control?'

'Mere routine. And that's what started *you* off. Had they asked for information about any other member of the Fleet you would have imagined things about him, too.'

'Maybe, Mitch,' I said, 'and I hope you're right. But we'll soon see.' For, at that very moment, Jet was at the radio, having made up his mind that before Whitaker spoke to Control he would himself talk to Earth again.

The conversation lasted fully ten minutes and when he had finished he came over to us and said: 'Well, gentlemen, I'm afraid I have some more rather startling news.'

'What is it, Jet?' asked Mitch.

'Remember the journalists who came up to the Moon to watch the takeoff?'

'Uh-huh.'

'Well, it seems that when they returned to Earth one of them hit on an idea for a series of articles for his paper. He thought he'd visit the relatives of the crews; wives, mothers, and so on, and collect first-hand material on what it's like to be the wife of a space man – you know the sort of thing.'

'He'd have a job with me,' said Lemmy. 'I'm a bachelor.'

'He'd thought of that, too. If any of the men didn't have wives, he had their parents supply the story. Well, he ran a whole series of articles on us, our histories. Apparently he left nothing out.'

'Go on,' said Lemmy.

'Come to the point,' said Mitch impatiently. 'Where does Whitaker fit into all this?'

'That is the point. He doesn't seem to fit in at all.'

'How do you mean?'

'Well,' went on Jet, 'the first odd thing this journalist struck was that although Whitaker was supposed to hold degrees in astronautical engineering, he'd never been on the roll of the Astronautical College.'

'But he must have been!' I exclaimed.

'He might have faked his diploma,' suggested Lemmy.

'Quite easily,' said Jet, 'but that wouldn't have given him the knowledge he's got. He's a first-class engineer – one of the best we have.'

'Then where did he learn?' asked Mitch.

'Beats me,' said Jet. 'But that's not all the story. This journalist, drawing a blank at the Astro College, decided to seek out Whitaker's relatives and, in due course, he found his way to Whitaker's home in Kensington and asked to see his parents. But he hadn't any.'

'Well,' said Lemmy, 'orphans are not uncommon.'

'No, Lemmy, they're not. But even the parents of orphans don't die before their children are born.'

'Oh no, I grant you that,' said Lemmy, 'but… eh? What was that?'

'The parents of James E. Whitaker,' said Jet slowly, 'died before the Second World War.'

'But that's impossible,' protested Mitch. 'Whitaker wasn't born until 1940.'

'Let Jet finish, Mitch,' I said.

Jet continued. 'But living at the same address as Whitaker had given was a family of the same name. Headed by a man of forty-eight who declared his father's name was James. And this James Whitaker left his home one morning in 1924 and was never seen again. All efforts by the police to find him were a complete failure.'

'Could be a coincidence,' suggested Mitch.

'Could have been, Mitch,' said Jet, 'quite easily. Only Edward Whitaker produced a photograph of his father. Control says it bears a striking resemblance to the one Records have of the Whitaker flying with us. Of course, as soon as he realised there was something odd about all this, the journalist took the whole matter up with Control who then took it up with the police. And police records show that the James E. Whitaker who disappeared was identical in every way, physically, with the Whitaker in Number Six. Even to the colour of his eyes.'

'Green,' said Lemmy positively.

'How do you know?' asked Mitch.

'If he'd looked at you the way he looked at me sometimes when he was in this ship, you'd know they were green.'

'Well, it all sounds very mysterious,' said Mitch, 'but I'm sure there's some rational explanation. Why don't you tackle Whitaker about it yourself?'

'That's just what I intend to do,' said Jet; 'but not while he's in Number Six. When we're safely through that swarm or whatever it is I'll have him come back here where I know our conversation won't be overheard by the rest of the Fleet.'

'I think Jet's right,' I said to Mitch and Lemmy. 'Until we get to the bottom of this business the fewer people who know about it the better.'

'Then let's forget the whole thing for now,' suggested Jet, 'and get back to work. Now, have you got those figures ready for Control, Mitch?'

'Yes,' replied the engineer. 'They're on the table.'

'Good. All right, Lemmy, get back to the radio and get in the latest radar reports.'

'Yes, mate,' replied the Cockney.

So, on the surface at any rate, the affair of James Edward Whitaker was temporarily forgotten.

Jet and Mitch were fully occupied for the next two or three hours checking our position. But for my part, although I did my best to concentrate on my work, my mind kept returning to Whitaker. On one or two occasions I thought I heard his flat, dull voice; and once I even looked up, expecting to find him standing at my elbow. No matter how hard I tried I could not get him out of my thoughts.

So it was for three hours or more, until a shout from Lemmy called us over to where he was working at the radio.

'What's the trouble?' asked Jet.

'Communication with the Fleet is almost impossible,' said Lemmy. 'There's so much static I can't always make out what's being said. Here, *you* listen.'

He called Number Four and then switched over to 'receive'. The speaker immediately produced a loud mushing noise which almost completely drowned Number Four's reply.

'You see what I mean?' said Lemmy. 'How can I keep in contact with that row going on?'

'Any idea what's causing it?' asked Jet.

'Yes – that meteor swarm or whatever it is. It must be chock full of static and the closer we get to it the worse it's going to be.'

Jet was thoughtful for a few moments. 'Well, there's nothing we can do about it,' he said at last. 'We can't turn back now, that's certain. We're so close to that thing we haven't the time. We can only hope that communication will be re-established once we've passed through. Meanwhile I'd better give the ships their orders while they can still hear me. Call them up, Lemmy. I'll talk to each of them in turn.'

In spite of the static and constant requests for repeats of what he had said, Jet managed to convey his orders to the Fleet. They were told that suits would be worn from now on so that, in the unlikely event of a ship being holed by a meteor, its crew would be safe until they could be transferred to another freighter. He added that if the *Discovery* were put out of action, command would be taken by Frank Rogers in Number Two.

When he had finished talking to Number Eight, Jet turned to us and said: 'Well, gentlemen, we'd better put on *our* suits. Then stay at your posts until further orders – and good luck.'

Lemmy looked at Mitch and me, spread his hands in front of him and observed: 'A nice cheerful prospect, isn't it?'

The ships were now sending in their radar reports every ten minutes or so. From the amount of static that arrived with them we knew that the meteor swarm was very close indeed: Jet estimated that it could not be more than twenty-five thousand miles away.

Our own radar screen was now virtually useless. The televiewer was no better; the picture distorted, shimmering and covered with lines. Trying to make out anything on it was like looking through a blinding snowstorm. Nevertheless, Mitch stayed by it the whole time, hoping that it might clear and reward him with a glimpse of the Fleet still in good coasting order. It was estimated that the thick of the swarm was now less than forty-five minutes away.

From my post at the radar I could hear Lemmy vainly calling Freighter Number Six.

Finally, Jet went over to him. 'Having more trouble, Lemmy?' he asked.

'Yes, Jet. Number Six is five minutes late with his report. Ten times I've tried to raise him but I get no reply. Apart from that, everything in the garden's lovely.'

'Any of the other ships reply?'

'I don't know. I haven't called them for some time.'

'Then do it now.'

'Yes, Jet.' And Lemmy bent to the task of calling the ships in one by one.

For a while nothing happened and then, very faintly through the mush, we heard a voice say: 'Hullo, Flagship – hullo.'

Lemmy put his ear to the speaker, trying to detect who it was.

'Hullo, Flagship – hullo. Number Six calling *Discovery*. Need to hear from you urgently.'

Now it was clear that the voice was that of Peterson, fading, surging and distorting. Lemmy replied to him but apparently Number Six didn't hear because Peterson's next call was: 'Emergency! Come in, please!'

Lemmy looked a little startled. 'Emergency?' he repeated.

Jet immediately took over the radio control. 'Hullo, Number Six – Morgan here. Go ahead with your message. We can hear you.'

But no message came. Only a great surge of static, louder than before.

Again Jet called and then a third time. 'It's no good, mate,' said Lemmy. 'With all that row going on, how can you expect to hear anything?'

But, to everyone's surprise, Peterson's voice suddenly came through, quite loud and almost perfectly clear.

'Hullo, Flagship, hullo. For heaven's sake, answer me, do you hear? Answer me!' The last two words were shouted.

'Blimey!' exclaimed Lemmy. 'What's happening to him?'

Jet ignored the question and called the freighter again.

'Hullo, Number Six. We can hear you. What's the trouble? Over.'

More static, but no further word from Peterson.

'There,' said Lemmy, 'he's gone again. He seemed pretty upset, too, didn't he?'

Jet tried once more. 'Hullo, Number Six – Flagship calling. Come in please and send your message.'

This time there was a reply. Very faint, very distorted, but audible and recognisable. Only now it wasn't Peterson's voice. It was Whitaker's.

'Hullo, Whitaker,' said Jet. 'What's the trouble over – the issue?'

'Hullo, Captain Morgan,' said Whitaker, slowly and deliberately. 'There is no trouble. Everything is normal.'

'What do you mean, everything is normal? What was Peterson panicking about?'

'And you're ten minutes late with your radar report,' put in Lemmy, glad to get a dig at the man he disliked so such.

'I have the radar report all ready,' said Whitaker flatly. 'Are you prepared to take it?'

'No, not yet I'm not,' said Jet. 'I want to speak to Peterson. Put him on.'

There was quite a long pause before Whitaker spoke again. 'Radar report number nine,' he said. 'Signals powerful and indicate object now less than twenty thousand miles distant.'

'He's reading it just the same,' said Lemmy. 'He didn't hear you.'

Jet shouted this time. 'I don't want that report for the moment, do you hear? I want to speak to Peterson. Now put him on. At once.'

If Whitaker had heard Jet he gave no indication of the fact. He carried on reading the report as though he had not been interrupted for, when Jet ceased speaking, we heard him say: 'End of message. Will keep listening watch and call again in ten minutes as per routine.'

'He couldn't have heard you,' suggested Lemmy. 'Otherwise he would – '

'I'm not so sure he didn't hear me,' said Jet. 'Hullo, Whitaker. I want to talk to Peterson immediately!'

Whitaker's voice came back coldly. 'He cannot talk to you. He is asleep.'

'That's exactly what he said about Rogers, Jet, remember?' said Lemmy.

'Asleep?' asked Jet. 'At a time like this?'

'I cannot wake him,' said Whitaker. 'He must remain asleep. Orders must be obeyed without question at all times.'

'Orders? What orders?' Jet demanded angrily. 'I've given no orders about sleeping. Wake him up, do you hear?'

We waited for a reply, but none came.

'There's something fishy going on over there, Jet,' said Lemmy. 'Wherever that geyser is there's trouble.'

'Even if he was answering,' said the Captain, 'we'd never hear him with all that row going on.'

Any further attempt Jet might have made to get in touch with Whitaker was prevented by a cry from Mitch who asked him to go over to the televiewer immediately. Jet went over to the motor engineer and left it to Lemmy to try and re-establish contact with Number Six.

Mitch wanted to report that the televiewer was hopeless. It was absolutely impossible to see anything on it. 'That meteor swarm or ionised gas,' said Mitch, 'is now close enough to blanket out all our electronic equipment. I don't see that there's any point in trying to use it any more.'

'Yes,' said Jet wearily, 'I think you're right. It can only get worse now. It will be impossible when we get into the heart of that cloud.' He then addressed us all generally and said: 'We'd better put our helmets on and keep them on until we've passed through that object.'

A few minutes later we were enclosed in our space suits and our helmets fastened. Jet at once called for a radio check on the personal sets, but static was as bad on the main receiver, and reception hopeless.

The only way we could communicate was by placing our helmets together. We could then, by means of the vibration of the air within them, hear each other loudly enough to make ourselves understood. We must have looked rather odd, standing there in the middle of the cabin with our heads touching, but it was the only way we could receive Jet's orders.

'Now listen carefully,' he said. 'For safety's sake, we'll have to keep our helmets on until we've passed through the swarm. Meanwhile, Doc and Mitch, you will go back to the radar and televiewer and keep watch, and Lemmy, you keep calling the Fleet every ten minutes. Is that clear?' We told him, in turn, that it was.

'Then get back to your posts, all of you.'

Chapter 6

W e must have entered the swarm half an hour later. By that time most electronic equipment had gone completely haywire. Very soon it wasn't only the radio and television circuits that were affected. The oxygen, fuel tank, air conditioning, humidity, air pressure, speed and navigational indicators were all jumping about wildly. They went on that way for nearly seven hours. Of course, during this period, we could not contact Freighter Number Six any more than we could contact any other ship, and we were still no nearer finding the reason for Peterson's panicky call nor for the almost rebellious tone of Whitaker's replies to Jet. In fact, cut off completely as we were from all things outside the ship, we could not even be sure that the rest of the Fleet was still with us.

Not only were we, in *Discovery*, a little world apart but each man was himself enclosed in his own small world, confined within the narrow limits of his tightly fitting space suit. And then, quite suddenly, while I was sitting at the radar, gazing at the blank screen, I heard the static noise gradually returning in my earpiece.

Minutes later it was quite loud, and very faintly through the sound I could hear Lemmy's voice calling the Fleet. I saw Jet sit up suddenly at the control table and heard him call: 'Lemmy.' Lemmy wheeled round and looked at Jet. 'Lemmy,' said Jet again, 'I can hear you calling. Can you hear me?'

'Yes, Jet, I can,' came the operator's voice, very faintly.

'Can you hear him, Mitch – and you, Doc?' We could.

'Then we must have made it,' said Jet. 'We must have passed through the swarm.'

'Don't speak too soon,' said Mitch. 'There's the rest of the Fleet to consider.'

'Yes,' said Jet, 'and, Lemmy, now that the personal radios are working, there's a good chance of your being able to contact them. Have a try, will you?'

'That's exactly what I was doing when you heard me calling just now.'

'Then keep at it. Can you call them without our hearing you? It will be chaotic if we're all talking at once.'

'I've already thought of that, mate,' said Lemmy. 'I'll feed my personal radio straight into the ship's transmitter, then you won't hear a thing'

'Good,' said Jet. 'Now, Mitch, how about the televiewer?'

'Well, she's not showing any picture yet, but she's alive all right. I've got the snow storm back.'

'Well, as soon as you can get a picture, check up on the Fleet.'

'Too right I will,' said the engineer.

I asked Jet whether he thought it would now be safe to remove our helmets, but he would not allow us to do so until everything in the ship was in good working order again.

It was a considerable time before Lemmy made contact with Number One. The static was nothing like as strong now and the freighter came through quite clearly. Apparently everything in the ship was nearly back to normal although, of course, for some hours all their electronic equipment had been dead. Unfortunately, their radar and televiewer screen were, as yet, no better than ours. Shortly afterwards, however, our radar screen started coming back to normal. The flashes and wavy lines began to disappear. A shout from Mitch told us that the televiewer was also beginning to behave itself. He was already able to make out, albeit vaguely, the shapes of the ships that formed the Fleet.

'Well,' said the Australian cheerfully, 'that proves it. That thing is behind us. And we passed through it without a scratch.'

'Yes,' said Jet, rather thoughtfully.

'Do you think it was meteors?' asked Mitch.

'I wouldn't like to say for sure,' said Jet, 'but I doubt it.'

'So do I,' agreed Mitch. 'No ordinary meteor swarm could have upset the equipment like that and the chances are that at least one of the ships would have been struck.'

By now Lemmy had made contact with all freighters except Number Six, crews reporting that they were safe and that almost all their equipment was back to full working order. Lemmy reported the matter to Jet and added that none of the other ships could raise Number Six either.

'Is your picture clear yet, Mitch?' asked Jet, turning to the engineer.

'Coming up gradually. Clearing slowly.'

'Well, let me know as soon as it is. Meanwhile you'd all better take your helmets off. I think it's safe now.' To obey was a pleasure for, having been enclosed in our helmets for so long, things had begun to get very uncomfortable.

The first normal voice I heard after emerging from my 'fish-bowl' was that of Mitch, who gave an excited cry and said: 'There! The Fleet's still in perfect formation. We must have stuck together the whole time. In fact, going through that swarm seems to have had no ill effects on us at all. It…' he broke off suddenly. 'Hey, wait a minute,' he said, his voice rising in alarm.

'What's up?' asked Jet.

'Where's Number Six?'

'What?'

Jet and I hurried over to the viewing screen. 'It's not there,' said Mitch as we approached. We both stared at the screen. 'Good grief,' said Jet at last, 'It's gone.'

Every ship was told to search the area all round us with their radar and televiewer apparatus and we settled down to do the same. For what seemed eternity I glued my eyes to the tiny radar screen, straining to see the slightest trace of a signal. And then, finally, Mitch said: 'It's no good, Jet; there's no sign of her – either in front of us, either side of us, up or down.'

'She must be lagging behind,' said Jet, more, I thought, in hope than with any real conviction. 'Too far behind for the televiewer to pick up.'

'Then I'd still be able to contact her by radio,' Lemmy pointed out. 'But I've been calling her for two hours now.'

'You don't think the disappearance of Number Six has anything to do with Whitaker being aboard her, do you, Jet?' I asked.

'It has been at the back of my mind,' he replied.

'There would be nothing to stop his turning on the motor, leaving the formation behind and going on ahead,' suggested Mitch, 'if he wanted to.'

'But why should he want to?' I asked. 'Where could he go?'

'Lemmy, call up Control,' ordered Jet.

The radio operator left us and moved over to the table. But in less than a minute he was back and saying: 'There's no point in my trying to call Control, mate. It's a complete waste of time.'

'What are you talking about?' asked Jet. 'The radio's working, isn't it?'

'Yes.'

'Then get back to it at once and get Control.'

'I'm sorry, Jet,' said Lemmy, 'but I'm afraid you're still talking through your helmet. That ionised gas or whatever it was we came through completely ruined any kind of ship-to-ship communication, didn't it?'

'That's not exactly news.'

'Well, that gas now lies between us and Earth,' went on Lemmy, 'and if no radio wave can penetrate it, then Earth cannot receive us nor can we receive them.'

'Of course we can't,' said Mitch bitterly. 'That cloud cuts us off from home completely. At least until the Earth has moved sufficiently in her orbit to be clear of it.'

'And how long will that take?' I asked.

'At a rough guess,' replied Mitch, 'I'd say two months.'

There was a pause. Finally the silence was broken by Jet. 'Well, gentlemen,' he said, looking at each of us in turn, 'this loss of contact with Base, while serious enough, need not be fatal. They won't give up trying to contact us for weeks – months, in fact – and we shall be talking to them again long before we reach Mars. Meanwhile we'll have to keep going. We'll have a lot more work to do, of course, now we're on our own, particularly in the navigational field; so we'd better get started. Lemmy, call up the Fleet. Have them take bearings on the sun, the Earth and Mars and report their findings as soon as possible.'

'Yes, mate,' said Lemmy.

'Meanwhile, Mitch, you and I had better get to work on the navigational tables. As soon as we've worked out our position and velocity we can eat.'

'Then don't take too long,' said Lemmy. 'I'm famished.'

When Jet and Mitch had completed their calculations they were able to say that our course was near enough correct and we could expect to arrive above the surface of the Red Planet at the appointed time, always supposing, of course, that no other mishap delayed us. We sat down to our meal that night in better spirits than our situation warranted.

The next few days were uneventful. By now the sun was only four-fifths of the size it appeared from Earth but, because of the clear viewing conditions out in space, was a far more beautiful object; a great gleaming, blue-white disc which hung in the sky surrounded by a fiery corona. As for the Earth, it now appeared bluish in colour with reddish-green patches which were the land masses. The whole was covered with irregular white cloud formations and at both poles we could see the incredibly bright ice caps. To the naked eye, the Earth-Moon system looked like a huge double star which expanded and shrank as the satellite encircled its parent planet.

But the most interesting and remarkable object in the whole heavens was Mars. As we observed it through the small navigational telescope, it already appeared much larger than we had ever before seen it. Deep pink in colour, the darker portions of its surface showed up sharply in olive green. Even at this distance we could detect a few cloud masses floating in its atmosphere and the dark, thin lines of the canali were certainly no optical illusion.

And so we coasted on for another month. We had now covered nearly one hundred and nineteen million miles since taking off from the Moon. No contact with Earth had yet been made, nor could we hope to establish it for at least another two weeks. We had resigned ourselves to wait patiently when suddenly, one day, from the loudspeaker above the control panel came the familiar voice of home saying: 'Hullo, Space Fleet – Control calling.'

Lemmy, who had been lying on his bunk trying to sleep, pushed off from the wall and went floating over towards the radio. He had hardly begun to drift when the voice came through again. 'Control calling Flagship *Discovery*. Trying to contact you. Come in, please.'

If Lemmy was quick off the mark, Jet was even quicker and he got to the table before the radio operator. Once there he lost no time and shouted into the microphone: 'Hullo, Control – Morgan calling. Hearing you loud and clear. Repeat, loud and clear. Over.'

Mitch, his face lit up with smiles, was the last to reach the radio. 'Well,' he said excitedly, 'there's a turn-up for the book. I didn't expect to hear that beautiful Australian accent for another two weeks at least.'

'Beautiful, he calls it,' said Lemmy with a laugh.

But before Mitch could reply, Control came through again. 'Hullo, *Discovery* – Control calling. Have urgent message for you. When can you take it?'

'Any time you like,' said Jet. 'Switch on the recorder, Lemmy.'

'Recorder on,' said the operator.

There was a five-second pause, and then we heard: 'Control to *Discovery*. Message will be transmitted in one minute. Stand by, please.'

'Standing by,' said Jet.

The smile disappeared suddenly from Lemmy's face. 'Here, wait a minute,' he said.

'Huh?' said Jet, turning to Lemmy, surprised at the tone in his friend's voice.

'He answered you pretty smart, didn't he?'

'How do you mean?' asked Jet.

'The last time we had a message from Earth was a month ago. The time-lag between calls then was ten seconds.'

'So?' asked Mitch, imitating one of Lemmy's pet responses.

'So by now the lag should be at least twenty seconds – but that answer came back in five.'

'I didn't even bother to notice,' said Jet. 'Are you sure?'

'Of course I'm sure. The times I've spoken to Earth I reckon I should notice a thing like that, shouldn't I?'

'Well, we'll soon see,' said Mitch. 'Get them to call you again, Jet.'

But before Jet could do so, Control were themselves talking to us. 'Hullo, Flagship,' said the familiar voice of the Australian operator, 'are you ready to take the message?'

'Sorry, Control,' said Jet, 'I didn't hear you. Will you repeat that?'

The moment Jet ceased to speak, all eyes went up to the clock above the table to watch the second hand as it jerked round the dial.

'Control to Flagship,' came the voice. 'Repeat, are you ready to take the message?'

'Lemmy's right,' said Mitch. 'It was five seconds.'

'Sorry, Control,' said Jet, 'cannot take message at this moment. Will call you again in a few minutes.' He switched off the radio, turned to us and said: 'What on earth is going on?'

'The Fleet must have turned itself round while we were in that gas cloud. We're going back home,' suggested Lemmy.

'We're heading for Mars,' said Mitch firmly. 'Correct course, correct position, just as we should be.'

'Then,' said Lemmy firmly, 'that can't be Control.'

'Then who is it?' I asked.

'Search me,' said the Cockney. 'I'm no clairvoyant – just a radio operator.'

'It *must* be Control,' said Mitch decisively. 'The short delay must be due to some freakish way the wave travels or something.'

'Use your loaf, Mitch,' said Lemmy. 'How could that be? Lots of things can block a radio wave but nothing can change its speed, not so's you'd notice, anyway.'

'Call them up, Jet. Let's take the message at least,' I suggested.

'Very well, Doc. We can argue about it afterwards. Switch her on, Lemmy.'

'Transmitter on,' said Lemmy.

'Hullo, Control,' said Jet. 'Morgan calling. Now ready to receive your message. Go ahead, please.'

Automatically we all looked at the clock again. Exactly five seconds had passed before we heard the words: 'Control to Flagship. Here is your message. Urgent. Control to Flagship *Discovery*. By order of the Supreme Council, Flagship *Discovery* and accompanying freighters are to abandon all attempts to reach Mars and return to Moon base immediately. Repeat, return to Moon base immediately. End of message.'

'Eh?' was all that Lemmy could say.

'Turn back?' asked Mitch incredulously.

'Hullo – hullo, Control,' said Jet. 'Morgan speaking. Are you crazy? We're nearly half way there. What are the reasons for turning back?'

'There can't possibly be any,' I said.

The voice of Control gave none either – all it said was: 'Emergency operation, Plan B, to be put into effect immediately.'

'Plan B!' exclaimed Jet angrily. 'That means a complete turn around. Return to Base immediately, regardless of what we think our chances are. Plan A would give some choice in the matter; if I thought it safe to go on, I'd go. But if Control orders Plan B I have no choice. Even if we were about to touch down on Mars we'd have to turn back.'

'But they can't expect us to abandon the whole project without giving some valid reason,' protested Mitch.

'You know the golden rule on this trip. Carry out orders first, ask questions afterwards.'

'In an emergency, yes,' replied the engineer indignantly; 'but what emergency is there?'

'This is where I intend to break the golden rule,' said Jet, 'and ask them.' He turned back to the microphone. 'Hullo, Control – Morgan calling. Have received your message but am at a loss to understand it. Expedition is going well. Can you give me your reasons for ordering Plan B?'

'If the Controller gave that order,' said Lemmy, 'he'll be hopping mad at your questioning it.'

'No madder than I am at his giving it,' said Jet.

The voice of Control came back almost at once, loud and clear. 'Your message received. Emergency Operation Plan B to be carried out at once.'

'There,' said Lemmy, 'what did I tell you?'

'Orders must be obeyed without question at all times,' continued Control blandly.

'Yes,' protested Jet, 'but... hey, wait a minute. What did he say?' he asked, looking round at the three of us.

'Orders must be obeyed without question at all times,' I repeated.

'Control never used that expression before,' said Jet.

'But it's not the first time we've heard it,' Lemmy reminded us.

'Whitaker!' I said.

'Yes,' said Jet, 'Whitaker.'

'But that's the voice of Control,' said Mitch. 'I'd know it anywhere!'

'It certainly sounded like Control,' I said.

'Lemmy,' said Jet, 'turn back the tape.'

'How far?' asked Lemmy.

'To the part where Control first called us.'

'Right.'

'What do you intend to do?' I asked, as Lemmy wound the tape back.

'Listen to it all again,' replied the Captain.

And listen to it we did. To every word, from the time when Jet first replied to Control's calls until the statement about orders being carried out without question. When the playback had finished, Mitch said: 'Control. No doubt about it. I'd stake my life on it.'

'It sounds like them, all right,' admitted Lemmy, 'but it still doesn't explain why the time-lag between replies is so short – or why we hear them so loud and clear.'

We played the tape again and listened to it in silence. But this time Mitch suddenly gave a start as the recorded voice said: 'By order of the Supreme Council, Flagship *Discovery* and accompanying freighters are to abandon all attempts to reach Mars and return to Moon Base immediately.'

'That's not the same voice,' the Australian said excitedly. 'Almost, but not quite. Before the actual message, a new voice took over.'

We played the tape a third time.

'It *is* a different voice,' said Jet. 'In the shock of being told to turn back we just didn't notice it. Lemmy, could you get a bearing on that signal?'

'Yes, if you keep him talking long enough I could.'

'All right, get ready to do it. I'll call him up.'

Lemmy sat at the controls and switched in the directional aerial. Five minutes later, Jet said: 'Well, what's the bearing?'

'One degree to starboard,' announced the radio operator. 'Azimuth reading. Altitude nil, depth nil. That means he's almost right slap in front of us, whoever he is.'

Jet switched off the transmitter and turned to face us. 'Well, gentlemen,' he said, 'I think that about settles that. It's not Control. It's someone using the voice of Control in the hope of fooling us into turning back.'

'But who?' asked Mitch.

'Whitaker, of course,' said Lemmy. 'Who else?'

'Then he must have got ahead of us,' I said.

'But what could he gain from that?' asked Jet.

'He's got one of our ships, hasn't he?' said Lemmy.

'But he can't go anywhere in it. Even if he went on to Mars he couldn't land her – she's not built for it.'

'And if he just keeps going,' said Mitch, 'he'll eventually cover a full orbit and in a couple of years he'll be back where we all started from – on the Moon.'

'And we'll be there waiting for him,' concluded Jet.

'There'd be no point in that, either.'

'He must be raving mad,' said Lemmy decisively.

'No, there must be some other reason behind it,' said Jet, 'something much deeper and stranger than we can comprehend; something to do with his being born in 1893, maybe.'

'You don't really believe that, do you?' asked Mitch.

'I'm beginning to believe almost anything so far as Whitaker is concerned,' replied Jet. 'The way he behaved the whole time he was with the expedition and the uncanny effect he had on the crew members of the ships he was in – all of it must add up to something.'

'What?' I asked him.

'I wish I knew, Doc. If I did we might have some idea of what to expect next. Lemmy,' he said suddenly, 'get me Frank Rogers of Number Two on the ship-to-ship system.'

'Yes, mate.'

'Rogers, Jet?' I asked. 'What for?'

'He spent more time with Whitaker than anybody. Maybe he can throw some light on this business.'

Chapter 7

When Rogers came through the airlock that led into the cabin of the *Discovery*, he seemed very pleased at being asked over, which was understandable as, like nearly all the freighter crews, he had not left his tiny little cabin since takeoff from the Moon. However, apart from complaining yet again of Whitaker's strange manner and his persistent, almost sullen silence, Frank could tell us very little, although he did say that the construction engineer had seemed to take a quite remarkable interest in anything that came through on the radio, and added: 'He was always asking if he could take my radio watch.'

'Did you let him?'

'No, of course not; it's against regulations, except in an emergency. Besides, I thought it rather an odd request from a fellow who was always telling me that "orders must be obeyed without question at all times".'

'Seems to be his favourite phrase,' said Jet to the rest of us. 'But when he did get to the radio,' he asked Frank, 'was there anything odd about the way he carried on?'

'Well, I remember one occasion – I came out of the cargo hatch after a routine check and found him tuned into Control and listening to the messages being passed between this ship and base.'

'Oh? Had he been ordered to listen in on Control's frequency?'

'No. He was supposed to be on the ship-to-ship wavelength. And the other odd thing about it was that he'd recorded everything Control had said.'

'Only Control's transmissions, not ours?'

'That's right, Jet.'

'You tackled him about it, of course?'

'Yes, but he said you'd called him up and asked him to keep check watch on Control as reception wasn't too good and you didn't want to risk not hearing anything vital.'

'Well, it is possible,' said Jet, 'but we'll check up. Can you let me have the actual date?'

'When I get back to my ship I can.'

'Good. Then that's all, Rogers – and thank you very much. What you've just told me may well prove very useful.'

Half an hour after he got back to his own ship, Frank came through and gave Jet the date he had requested. At once I checked back in the log and I must admit that what I found there was no surprise to me. I told Jet and a few moments later heard him say: 'Hullo, Frank – can you hear me?'

'Yes, sir.'

'We've looked up the log. Number Four was on check watch.'

'I thought that might be the case, sir,' came back Frank's voice; 'and I took the matter a little farther.'

'Oh. How?'

'I checked back on the recorder to that date, too.'

'Well?'

'The recordings of Control's messages during that transmission are missing.'

'You mean that Whitaker didn't record them after all?'

'Oh yes, he did, sir, but the tape has been cut and that particular section removed.'

'Has it? Well, that proves a lot. Nice work, Frank – and thanks.'

'Thank you, sir.' There was a click as Rogers disconnected his transmitter.

It was quite clear now what had happened. We had, indeed, heard Control – but not from Earth. What we had heard was the recorded voice of Control relayed to us by Whitaker from Freighter Number Six. He had recorded

Control's voice while he was in Number Two and carried the tapes on him. Had Jet not transferred him to Number Six, it would no doubt be Freighter Number Two which was missing now.

Had he known all along that the ionised gas lay ahead and that when we passed through it communication between the Fleet would be impossible, thus affording him the chance to abscond with Number Six? Or had he merely taken an opportunist's chance to make off with her? And, either way, who was Whitaker and what was he up to? Why was there so much mystery about his identity and why did he wish to prevent the Fleet reaching Mars which, we could only conclude, was his intention?

We talked it over for a couple of hours but came no nearer reaching a solution. Every ship was put on a rota to watch on Control's frequency – to report to the *Discovery* the moment anything was heard, whether the call was thought to be a spurious one from the missing Number Six or a genuine one from Control itself. But, in spite of the constant watches, no contact was made with anybody outside the fleet.

Another two weeks went by, two uneventful weeks during which we covered another ten million miles, bringing our total since takeoff to one hundred and twenty-nine million. We were rapidly approaching the half way mark.

The Fleet still kept perfect formation, except for the gap between Freighters Five and Seven that should have been occupied by Number Six. We were travelling at something over thirty thousand miles an hour, but to all appearances the ships still hung motionless in the star-studded, velvet-black sky.

For nineteen days after the mysterious call from Whitaker nothing untoward was noted in the log and then, Lemmy, who for the sake of a change had taken over radar watch from Mitch for a spell, had something to report. 'There's something out in front of us, Mitch,' said the Cockney. 'I'm getting a signal on the screen.'

'What is it?'

'How should I know? But it isn't very large. Minute as sizes go out here.'

When Jet was told of Lemmy's find he ordered all ships to keep watch and make regular reports. Before long we were able to place the mysterious object at no more than four thousand miles ahead of us. Further calculations told us rapidly that we were overtaking it at roughly a thousand miles an hour which would put its speed at approximately twenty-nine thousand. However, we had no hope of making even a moderately accurate guess at the identity of the object until we got closer.

When the gap had narrowed to around two thousand miles, Mitch declared that he thought he could detect the object through the telescope. He wasn't sure, he said, because what he could see was not much larger than a pinpoint and, with all the stars in the background, what he was seeing could well be a star, too. But ten minutes later he was convinced that he had got it, for his 'pinpoint' had grown slightly in size.

Jet called over to me to ask if I'd picked up anything on the televiewer, but I had to admit that I hadn't. By now Jet and Mitch were taking turns at the telescope. The object was getting steadily larger, and just about an hour after Mitch had first picked up the image Jet declared that it was definitely globe-shaped.

It was about then that I managed to detect the object on the televiewer. It was exactly as Jet had said: globe-shaped, and the sun was lighting it up on one side. It was like a tiny planet. Maybe that's what it was, or an asteroid at least.

Soon all the ships were reporting that the object was globular, although nobody cared to make any guess at its size as yet. I heard Lemmy, who had just received the reports in from the freighters, telling Frank Rogers not to let the diameter of the thing worry him; in another hour he would probably be able to put a tape measure round it.

Quite suddenly there was an exclamation from Mitch over at the telescope. 'Strewth!' he yelled, 'I know what this is. It's a ship – a space ship!'

'Eh?' said Lemmy in surprise.

'Yes,' said Mitch. 'It's Number Six! The reason it looks globular in shape is that its crew cabin is facing us and the rest of the structure is blocked out.'

'Let me get at that telescope,' demanded Jet. He peered into it steadily for a few minutes. At last he said: 'Mitch is right. She's still very small but no other object in the heavens could look like that. And we're overtaking her rapidly. In an hour or so we'll be passing her.'

'I'll say we will,' said Mitch, 'at a thousand miles an hour.'

'Not if we slow down,' said Jet. 'We could drop down to her speed and coast alongside her.'

'What – the whole Fleet?' protested the engineer. 'Think of the fuel consumption.'

'No,' said Jet, 'not the whole Fleet. Just us – the *Discovery.*' Then, as Mitch looked at him blankly, he added, almost pleadingly: 'Look, Mitch. Whitaker is aboard that ship. I want to know why he went speeding off on his own, and why he sent us that stupid message that was supposed to be from Control. Above all, I want to know what's happened to Peterson.'

'All right,' said Mitch. 'If that's what you say we do, we do it.'

Leaving the Fleet in the care of Frank Rogers, the pilot of Freighter Number Two, Jet gave us our orders for turning the *Discovery* over, which was necessary before we could bring the motor into play and slow the ship down. It was an extremely tricky manoeuvre but we managed it and soon we were coasting alongside the wayward freighter. We looked at her image on the televiewer but nothing we saw gave us any clue as to what drama might be taking place aboard her.

'All right, Doc,' Jet said to me at last, 'put your suit on.'

'Eh?' said Lemmy. 'Now wait a minute, Jet. You don't intend going over there, do you? Not before you know everything's all right in that ship?'

'What other choice have we, Lemmy?'

'But the door isn't even on this side. Before you reach it you'll have to pass out of our sight!'

'The personal radios will be on. You can talk to us.'

'Well, if you say so,' Lemmy agreed reluctantly. 'But I tell you, mate, I don't like it. It may be a trick just to get you in there.'

'That's a chance we'll have to take,' Jet told him. 'Doc,' he said to me as I finished fastening my suit, 'let's go.'

'Hatch opening,' said Lemmy resignedly, and pressed the control.

There was a click, a hiss of air and the circular door which led to the airlock slowly opened. Our manoeuvre of slowing down the *Discovery* and bringing her alongside Number Six had been carried out so well that less than fifty yards separated the two ships. It was, consequently, an easy matter for Jet and I to drift to the freighter and secure ourselves to it. To reach the main door, however, it was necessary for us to walk round the hull. Jet led the way.

We climbed over the ship and down the other side while Mitch gave us a commentary on how we looked from the *Discovery*. Of course, as we neared the far side we were lost to Mitch's view and he announced the fact the moment we disappeared. Then came an exclamation of surprise from Jet. 'Good heavens, Doc,' I heard him say over the radio, 'the main door's open!'

'What?' said the startled voice of Mitch in my earpiece.

Jet repeated what he had said and then waited for me to arrive alongside him. Together we slowly made our awkward way down towards the door. It was open all right and the light inside the airlock was on.

'Can you find the remote control switches, Doc?' Jet asked me as I followed him into the tiny chamber.

'Yes, I've got them,' I told him.

'Well, see if they're functioning.'

I pressed the button and could feel the vibration as the door slowly closed behind us.

'Well,' observed Jet, 'at least the power packs in this ship are in working order.' As soon as the door was shut I pressed the air contact and the lock filled up. We watched the little gauge near the control panel steadily rise with the air pressure. 'OK, Doc,' said Jet, when it had reached maximum, 'open the hatch.'

The circular door above our heads slowly folded back and we were bathed in a beam of light that shone down from the cabin above. Jet and I looked at each other. We knew all too well that the noise of the hatch opening must have been heard by anyone in the freighter cabin; but nobody came to greet us. 'Let's go up there, Doc,' said Jet at last.

'Watch your step, cobber.' It was Mitch's voice coming over the radio. He could, of course, hear every word Jet and I were saying. Once in the tiny cabin we looked around us. As far as we could tell, the place was empty. There was no sign of Peterson or Whitaker. It was uncanny.

'But they must be here somewhere,' said Jet.

'Not necessarily,' I told him. 'The main door was open. They might have abandoned ship.'

'But why? Unless they wanted to commit suicide.'

'Having Whitaker as a crew mate,' I reminded him, 'might have driven Peterson to do just that.'

'Then where is Whitaker? He should be here at least.'

'Yes, I guess so,' I admitted.

'Hullo, look at this!' said Jet suddenly. He pointed to a number of empty food containers, most of which were strewn all over the table, although one or two were still floating in mid-air.

'What a mess!'

'Check up on the oxygen supply and air conditioning. I'll check the main control panel.'

After a few minutes I was able to say that everything seemed to be in order in my department, but Jet reported the main fuel tanks empty.

'They must have used it up when they put on a spurt to get away from the rest of the Fleet,' I suggested.

'Yes, and somebody must also have slowed the ship down again,' said Jet, 'otherwise we would never have caught up on her. And I'd say that somebody was Whitaker.'

'Maybe,' I said, 'but what was Peterson doing meanwhile?'

'Heaven knows. Let's get over to the radio panel and take a look at the log.' There we found a further mess; recording tape was strewn all over the floor. 'Try and get it back onto the spool, Doc,' Jet said. 'Later we'll play it back.'

While I was sorting out the tape, which was quite a complicated business as it was terribly tangled, Jet called up the *Discovery* on the ship-to-ship system. Mitch's voice replied immediately, indicating that at least Number Six's radio was working well.

'What's going on over there, Jet?' Mitch asked.

'Everything's in chaos,' Jet told him. 'Half-eaten meals on the table, recording tape all over the floor – and no sign of the crew.'

'Do you think they've abandoned ship?'

'If they have they must have been stark, raving mad, both of them,' replied Jet. 'I'll call you later, Mitch. OK?'

'OK,' said Mitch, 'I'll keep a listening watch.'

Jet moved away from the radio to where I was still trying to disentangle the tape. 'Looks like a long job,' he said.

'Yes, I'm afraid so.'

'All right,' he said, 'while you're sorting that lot out I'll do a bit of investigating on my own. I'll look in the personal lockers first. See if they hold any clues.' But Jet had no sooner opened the door of Peterson's locker when he let out an exclamation of surprise. 'Hey, Doc. Peterson's suit – it's gone!'

I moved over to Jet's side of the cabin, a long piece of tape in my hand, to see for myself. Sure enough the locker which should have contained Peterson's suit was empty.

'Maybe they had some trouble outside,' I suggested, went out to fix it – and drifted off.'

'Both of them?'

'Why not, Jet?'

'Because that would more or less put Peterson in league with Whitaker. But the last we heard from Peterson he was yelling for help.'

'Well, maybe. But at the same time everything points to having gone outside for some reason or other. The main door open; the suit missing…'

Jet didn't answer, but moved to the second locker which, of course, was Whitaker's. He jerked the door open, took a glance inside, and then turned and looked steadily at me. 'Just as I thought,' he said, slowly. 'Whitaker's suit is still here. Look, Doc,' he went on, 'I'm going down into the cargo hold. One of them, both of them even, might be there.'

'Right. But make sure the air pressure's up to full before you open the cargo hatch.'

'I'll watch it, Doc,' he said.

Jet was gone for about fifteen minutes, during which I was able to straighten out the bulk of the tape and rewind it onto the spool. I did not play it back as I knew Jet would like to hear it at the same time as I did. So, first ascertaining by the personal radio that Jet was OK, I began a systematic search of the crew's quarters. I examined the motor panel, the radio panel, the log books, the stowage lockers, the mess on the table; in fact, pretty well everything.

Finally I moved over to one corner of the cabin where, set into the floor, was a circular, transparent plate which gave access to the inspection hold. Situated on the wall near the hatch was a light switch. I turned it on and looked through the glass into the hold.

What I saw down there had me yelling for Jet to come back into the cabin immediately. A couple of minutes later he was at my side. 'We'd better open her up, Doc,' he said at once.

'Where's the switch?' I asked. 'I'm not familiar with the controls on these freighters.'

'On the main control panel. Bottom left. Blue section.'

I moved over to the panel, found the switch and turned it on. The inspection hatch cover slipped to one side, and Jet lost no time in descending the ladder which led to the bottom of the hold.

Chapter 8

What I had seen was the body of a man. It was lying on the floor all of a heap and it was difficult to tell whether whoever it was was alive or dead. Jet turned the still form over and supported it in the crook of his arm. It was Whitaker. A cursory examination told me that, although he had been badly beaten up, especially about the head, he was still breathing.

'Let's get him up into one of the bunks,' Jet suggested.

That was quite an easy operation as Whitaker, like everything else in the ship, weighed virtually nothing. Between us we guided him up the ladder, gently floated him towards his bunk, pushed him down on it and strapped him in. While I gave Whitaker a thorough examination, Jet went back to the cargo hold to continue his search. It was some time before he got back. Although he searched the place from top to bottom and had even been down into the tank inspection hold, there was no sign of Peterson.

'Then we'll have to accept the fact that he left the ship,' I said.

'But why?' asked Jet. 'He must have known he'd never be picked up, not in a million years. He must have known he was stepping out to certain death.'

'There are an awful lot of things which need explaining, Jet. Why the cabin is in such chaos and how Whitaker came to be lying down in the inspection hatch with multiple head injuries.'

'How is he, Doc?'

'In a bad way. The base of the skull is fractured and there's a considerable amount of haemorrhage.'

'Is he still unconscious?'

'Yes – and if he ever regains it I'll be very surprised. He'll need constant watching. Shouldn't be left for a moment. And I need supplies.'

'How about the medical locker?'

'It doesn't amount to much more than a first-aid outfit. I'll have to have one of my kits brought over from the *Discovery*.'

'Or take Whitaker over there?'

'No, Jet,' I said, 'he's too ill. To move him that far might well prove fatal.'

'In that case, I'll have Mitch bring across all you need. I was going to ask him to come over, anyway.'

'What for?'

'Well, so far as I can tell, the ship's in full working order, but only Mitch can confirm my belief that the motor is still usable. If it is we can salvage the ship.'

'OK,' I said. 'When you've finished talking to Mitch maybe I could have a word with him.'

'Sure, Doc.'

'So you decided to call up at last,' said Mitch when Jet contacted him. 'Don't you realise the Fleet is now seven thousand miles ahead? If we don't catch up with them soon they'll get to Mars without us.'

'That's just what I'm calling up about, Mitch. Peterson has disappeared. The crew's quarters over here are in a shocking state but the power packs are working; so is the air supply and radio – and the motor's OK so far as I can tell. But I need you to give it a thorough inspection.'

'You want me to come over there, then? OK, Jet. Who'll be coming back – you or Doc?'

'Neither. I've got to tidy up the place.'

'Couldn't Doc do that?'

'He's too busy with Whitaker who's too sick to be moved.'

'You mean you intend leaving Lemmy here alone? Maybe for hours.'

'It won't hurt him.'

It was about two hours later that Mitch came up from the inspection hold to give his report on the motor. Apparently it was all right and there was enough fuel in the reserve tank to give her the necessary acceleration and enable us to overtake the rest of the Fleet.

'That's good news, Mitch,' said Jet. 'We'd better get back to *Discovery* and prepare to turn the ships over.'

'Both of us?' queried Mitch. 'You can't expect Doc to stay and handle a manoeuvre like that alone.'

'There are only two takeoff couches in here,' Jet reminded the engineer, 'and Whitaker is already occupying one of them. And Doc must stay with Whitaker. Firing can be controlled from the *Discovery*. He should manage quite easily.'

Jet, unaware that I had heard every word of this conversation, moved over to where I was sitting by Whitaker's bunk. But before he could speak I said: 'I'm sorry, Jet, but if the motors are fired I can't hold myself responsible. The pressure that Whitaker would be subjected to would kill him for sure.'

'But we've got to catch up on the Fleet sometime soon,' protested Mitch. 'They must be ten thousand miles ahead of us by now.'

'That's for Jet to decide,' I said, 'but as medical officer I must put my point of view.'

'The acceleration wouldn't be all that great, Doc,' said Jet, obviously very worried, 'four gravities at most.'

'Too much,' I said. 'In his present condition I doubt if he could stand even two.'

'Well, that's too bad,' said Mitch flatly. 'Do we put the whole Fleet in jeopardy for the sake of one man who's given us nothing but trouble since we took off, tried to get us to abandon the trip and go back, and killed one of his own crew mates into the bargain?'

'We've got no proof that he killed Peterson,' said Jet quietly.

'Look, Jet,' Mitch argued, 'let's face the facts.'

'I am facing them, Mitch,' replied the Captain. 'If Doc says Whitaker is too ill to stand the pressure, then I must take his word for it. We wait. Either until Whitaker is fit again or until time compels me to overtake the Fleet. And meanwhile you can figure out what that time is likely to be.'

'OK,' said Mitch, resignedly. 'Where do they keep the navigational tables in this ship?'

'Same place as in any other. In the locker under the control table.'

Mitch went over to the other side of the cabin and sat down. At that very moment there came a sigh from the bunk.

'Jet,' I called quietly, 'come over here. I think Whitaker is coming round.'

The sick man moaned.

'What did he say?' asked Jet, as he came over to the bunk.

'I didn't quite catch it,' I replied.

'Leave me alone.' The words were quite distinct now.

'But nobody's touched him, Doc,' said Jet. He put his hand on the engineer's shoulder. 'Whitaker. Whitaker,' he said gently. 'Can you hear me? This is Captain Morgan.'

'Turn back. Turn back,' said Whitaker. 'You must turn back. I can fight them, but you can't.'

Jet turned to me. 'What's he talking about, Doc?'

'I wouldn't try to make sense of it, Jet,' I told him. 'He's delirious.'

'You do not know the power they have.' It was Whitaker again. 'I defy you. Do you hear? I defy you!' The last three words were shouted.

I rubbed his brow gently with my hand and quietly called his name. This seemed to soothe him for, although he continued breathing heavily, he didn't raise his voice. He merely said: 'I must go back. Back to my wife and children.'

'Has he a wife and children, Doc?' Jet asked.

'If he has,' I said, 'this is the first time he's ever them.'

Whitaker rambled on. 'They've gone to the Exhibition,' he said. 'Everybody's going.'

At this moment Lemmy's voice called from the radio. Apparently it was time for routine inspection and for the *Discovery* to call in the Fleet reports. 'Somebody had better come over here soon, Jet,' said Lemmy. 'You can't expect me to keep watch on the radio, radar and televiewer and inspect every part of the ship as well. It's a big enough job for the four of us.'

'They're running a special train from Baker Street,' said Whitaker.

'Eh? What was that, Jet?' asked Lemmy.

'It's all right,' said Jet quickly. 'I'm sorry to have left you alone for so long. I'll attend to it.'

'Will somebody be coming back, then? If so, I'll tell Number One to hold his report until they do.'

'One of us will be coming across in just a few minutes.'

'Right,' replied the Cockney. 'Incidentally, Jet, how's Whitaker?'

'They must turn back. I must tell them to turn back.' Whitaker was shouting again now.

'Still in pretty bad shape, I'm afraid.'

'Oh,' came Lemmy's sympathetic voice. 'Well, I'll get the main door open, Jet. Be all ready for whoever comes across.'

It was decided to send Mitch back. After he had gone, Jet and I settled down to watch over Whitaker, but he had relapsed into a deep coma and said nothing more. So Jet set about clearing up the mess in the cabin. It took him about four hours before things looked shipshape again. Then he carried out the routine inspection of Number Six and passed the report over to Lemmy. Finally he prepared a meal and, with both of us sitting by Whitaker's bed, we ate it in silence.

After Jet had cleared the containers away I realised how tired he was looking. 'You must be completely exhausted,' I told him, 'why don't you get some sleep?'

'I am a little tired, Doc,' he admitted. 'But how about you? You've had no more sleep than I.'

'But I haven't been doing any physical work, Jet. Just sitting here and watching Whitaker.'

'I wonder what did happen between him and Peterson, Doc. If only he'd come out of that coma he might be able to tell us.'

'I wouldn't bank on that just yet,' I warned him. 'He's been too quiet for my liking for a long time. Now go to bed. I'll wake you in four hours.'

'OK, but if Mitch or Lemmy call, wake me up, will you?'

'If it's anything important, I will,' I assured him.

'OK,' said Jet. 'Goodnight then,' and with that he climbed the little ladder which led to the bunk above Whitaker's. He was asleep almost before I had got his safety straps into position.

I had hardly settled down by Whitaker's side before he began to speak again. First he announced his name; his full name. 'James Edward Whitaker,' he said. He repeated this a couple of times and then added the year in which he was born. Not 1940 as we had all been led to believe; but 1893. Then, to my great concern, he began to rave. He shouted, he twisted and turned and he threw his arms about. Try as I would I could not quieten him. If he had not been strapped into his bunk his contortions would have sent him floating round the cabin to crash against one of the walls and, perhaps, injure himself even further.

I felt sure that Whitaker's yelling and screaming must waken Jet before long and then, to my surprise, I realised that Jet was making almost as much noise as Whitaker. Like him, he was tossing and turning on his bunk and, although his eyes were tightly closed, the perspiration stood out in little beads on his brow. He twisted and turned as though trying to free himself from the straps that bound him to his bed.

I tried to waken him but to no avail. Then, once more, I tried to waken Whitaker, with no more success. I began to sweat a little myself. It was as though Jet, by some inexplicable means, was suffering in sympathy with Whitaker; as though he, too, were bearing the pain and delirium of the injured man. I have heard of such cases before; of husbands who suffered from toothache or even abdominal pains while their wives were in labour; of twins who felt an injury sustained by their brothers or sisters even though they were far apart; but this was the first time I had had first-hand experience of such a thing.

There was absolutely no doubt that there was a strong connection between the ravings of the two men for, besides acting in much the same way, they often seemed to be talking to each other. Most of the words they spoke were incoherent but occasionally they became crystal clear, as when Whitaker was announcing his date of birth and Jet suddenly said: 'But that's ridiculous. That would make you seventy-eight years old and you don't look a day older than thirty.'

Then came snatches of conversation, some connected, some disconnected, such as: 'Have you been to the Exhibition? They're running special trains from Baker Street. Look at that star. That's Mars. Isn't she beautiful? It's not red really, you know. It's pink and olive green. If only we had a telescope powerful enough we could see the cities on her.'

'Cities?' It was Jet now.

'Didn't you know?' Then Whitaker began to sing – a song I'd never heard before. Some nonsense about it being night-time in Italy and Wednesday in some other place. He sang it heartily and laughed when he finished.

'Are we going to this Exhibition, Whitaker, or aren't we?'

'Yes. That's why we've come here. In you get, Mr Morgan. We'll show you an Exhibition such as you never realised existed.'

At this point Jet's voice took on a tone of fear: 'Where are you taking me?' he yelled. 'Take your hands off, do you hear? Let go of me!' Jet's delirium was increasing. He shouted louder than ever, at times he even screamed. I climbed up the ladder and tried to calm him. I took hold of his shoulders but he immediately began to struggle with me and I received a heavy clump on the side of the head. I quickly retreated down the ladder again, feeling sick and dizzy. With his eyes still closed Jet went raving on like a lunatic.

It was then I realised that Whitaker had quietened down. He lay on his bunk, motionless. He had stopped breathing. I felt for his pulse: there was none. I put my ear to Whitaker's chest but could not hear his heart beating. Whitaker was dead.

Jet's screams of protest were louder than ever now. I decided to make yet another effort to rouse him. I climbed the ladder, took him by the shoulders and shook him. I slapped his face and then called his name in his ear.

'Jet!' I yelled. 'Wake up; wake up, do you hear?'

That seemed to do the trick. His eyes opened and although for a few seconds he still struggled to loose himself from my grip, he soon realised who I was and where he was. But his face was ashen grey and he was trembling violently.

'What on earth were you yelling like that for?'

'A dream, Doc,' he said breathlessly. 'I had such a fantastic dream.'

'A dream?' I asked him.

'Yes,' he said. 'I dreamt I was back in London – but not a London I knew. A London of the past. The buses were open-decked at the top and everybody was going to an exhibition somewhere. Some buildings I recognised and in other places were older buildings where new ones now stand. And Whitaker was there. Seems he was taking me to catch a train at Baker Street, but he took me to Regents Park instead where there were about a dozen other men – all with faces and voices exactly like Whitaker's. And then they began to attack me – and then you woke me.'

'You were yelling your head off,' I told him.

'I'm sorry, Doc,' he said. 'Did I disturb him?'

'Whitaker, you mean? Nothing will ever disturb him again.'

'He's dead?'

'Yes, Jet.'

'Are you sure?'

'Perhaps you'd like to look for yourself?'

Jet undid his safety straps, put on his magnetised boots and descended to the floor. When he was down I switched on the reading light above the lower bunk then stood to one side as Jet leaned over to stare down into Whitaker's face. Jet gave a violent start and a cry of horror. 'Good heavens, Doc, you might have warned me.'

'Of what?' I asked him in surprise.

I moved closer to the bunk to get a better view of the still form lying there. Then I, too, let out an involuntary exclamation and my heart gave a sudden jump.

'Is that him?' Jet asked.

I stared at Whitaker's face for a few moments before trusting myself to reply. It was so altered, and the shock of seeing it so, so great, that it took me some time to regain control of my senses.

'It's him all right,' I said finally and in a shaky voice I hardly recognised as my own. 'Can't you see the likeness?'

'Yes,' said Jet, "but he's – he's so old.'

And, indeed, there on the bunk before us was the body of a frail old man. His face was lined, his form withered, his hands honey and the veins standing out. Yet the face was unmistakably that of Whitaker. In death he had reverted to his true age and his body showed it in every physical way.

'Control was right,' I said slowly, still greatly shaken. 'Whitaker was seventy-eight years old, but it took his death to prove it.'

Chapter 9

The death of Whitaker and the subsequent change in his physical appearance was the most severe shock we had received since leaving the Moon. What did this strange, fantastic transformation mean? How had Whitaker managed to retain his youth for so long? And where had he been between 1924 and the time he joined the expedition as a reserve crew member?

Had there been some strange power in control of Whitaker that compelled him to do things against his will? A power that prolonged his life until the intervention of sudden death cut off the controlling medium, allowing the wear and tear of forty-seven years to overtake him in a matter of minutes? If there was an answer to all these questions, neither Jet nor I were able to supply it. The fact remained, Whitaker was dead. There was no longer any point in lagging behind the rest of the Fleet.

So the two ships, the *Discovery* and Number Six, were turned over and their speeds increased. Twelve hours later we overhauled the remaining freighters and took up our places in formation. Whitaker we left behind, having 'buried' him in space.

One of the first things Jet did when he got back to the flagship was to play over the recording tape that I had salvaged. It consisted mainly of routine calls from Control to the *Discovery*. Whitaker had obviously taken them down during his radio watches, probably while Peterson was asleep. Clearly these were the tapes he had played in the hope of fooling us that he was Control before giving the order to turn back. But why he had done it, we still hadn't the least idea.

Nothing we found gave us any indication as to why Peterson had abandoned ship, for we could only assume that he, too, was dead. Somewhere, in between the orbits of Earth and Mars, his body, still enclosed in his suit, must even now be drifting on a course that will take him for ever round the Sun. If not for ever, then for thousands of years, until he comes close enough to some heavenly body to be drawn to it by gravitational attraction, finally to crash upon its surface.

I wondered what the next tragedy would be, for, up to now, our trip seemed, as Lemmy put it, to have the 'mockers' on it and to be cursed with one unfortunate occurrence after another. Happily for us, however, the next event was a very welcome one; Lemmy made contact with Control. The cloud of ionised gas through which we had passed must have moved out of line with us and Earth and once more our signals were able to reach home.

Lemmy called up Mitch and me in Number Six and told us the good news. No doubt about its being Control this time for reception wasn't very good and the time-lag between call and reply amounted to more than half a minute.

So elated was Jet at being able to talk to home once more that he allowed all ships to tune in to Control's frequency and listen to Base's transmissions. After the normal routine calls and reports had been made, Jet asked Control for the news bulletin. This was an item to which we all looked forward and, before we lost contact with home, it was relayed to the Fleet every twenty-four hours. Not only did we hear the latest international news but also the results of recent sporting events which made us all feel very much less cut off than we had been hitherto. We began to look forward again to the time when we would reach the Red Planet.

Mitch and I now made up the crew of Number Six, but there were occasions when one or other of us had to go over to the *Discovery* to help out Jet and Lemmy with some of the major duties which were peculiar to the Flagship. We were getting very close to Mars when I received one such summons from Jet.

I arrived in the *Discovery* to find Jet sitting at the Control table on watch while Lemmy examined the surface of Mars through the navigational telescope. The radio operator turned to greet me as I entered and asked if I would like to take a close look at the planet. Not knowing as yet what Jet wanted me for, I declined.

'It's beautiful, Doc,' said Lemmy, 'really beautiful. To call it the Red Planet is a mistake, if you ask me; there's as much green as red – and so bright!'

'Now don't go getting too ecstatic, Lemmy,' I said jokingly, 'or the crews of every freighter will be wanting to come over here and take a look as well.'

'Two weeks from now,' said Jet, 'every ship will be less than a thousand miles above the Martian surface. We'll be able to see it much clearer then than we do now – even with the telescope.'

'I can hardly believe we're that close,' I said, almost to myself.

'And the nearer we get, Doc,' Jet said, 'the stranger I feel.'

'You, Jet?' I exclaimed. 'After twenty-seven trips to the moon?'

'I can't explain it, Doc. That's why I've asked you to come over here. Let's go to my bunk and sit down.'

I gathered from this that Jet was not too happy about Lemmy's hearing what we were saying. I followed him over to the bunk, but Lemmy didn't seem to be particularly interested in us and kept his eye glued to the telescope.

Once we had settled ourselves, Jet said: 'When we set out on this journey, Doc, I was looking forward to six months of uneventful, perhaps even dull, routine while we were coasting here, but this trip has been anything but that and I have a feeling that our exploration of Mars is not going to be quite what we expect, either.'

'In what way?' I asked him.

'I wish I could tell you. I can hardly wait to set foot on Mars and yet, at the same time, I'm full of apprehension about it.'

'Oh? Why?'

'I've been checking up. You remember I told you that in my dream Whitaker kept talking about an Exhibition?'

'Yes.'

'Well, from the impression I got of the London I was dreaming about I guessed the period to be some time in the 1920s. So I asked Control to find out if an Exhibition had taken place during that decade and, if so, whether it was possible to reach it by train from Baker Street.'

'And had there been an Exhibition then?'

'Yes. The Empire Exhibition of 1924 – at Wembley.'

'Good grief!' I exclaimed.

'I had no idea such an Exhibition had ever been held.'

'Well, it was a little before your time,' I reminded him.

'After that, I asked them to check up on the song – the one that Whitaker sang. Apparently it was a popular song of the same year, 1924 – the year in which he disappeared.'

'But that's fantastic, Jet. What did Control say about it? Weren't they curious to know why you wanted the information?'

'I told them I needed it to settle an argument.'

'Do you think it was wise not to tell them everything?'

'Yes, I do. Suppose I did tell them about Whitaker making that phoney call and trying to get us to turn back, isn't there a chance that Control might tell us the same thing? On the face of it, somebody, something – using Whitaker as a go-between, maybe – seems to have been trying to do exactly that, and somebody on Earth might consider that the risk of carrying on is too great and order us to return.'

'They'd be more likely to scoff at the whole thing and put it down to imagination.'

'That, Doc,' said Jet with a laugh, 'is a polite way of saying I'm unstable, mentally unbalanced.'

'Oh, I wouldn't go that far,' I began, but Jet cut me off.

'I'm not so sure that Control wouldn't. Nor the rest of the Fleet.'

'Surely, Jet,' I argued, 'you don't think the crews imagine that you...'

'Why shouldn't they? Only three of us have been really seriously affected by Whitaker: Frank Rogers in Number Two, Lemmy and myself – and both Lemmy and Rogers seem to have got over it long since.'

'And you haven't?'

'I'd have thought no more about it, Doc, but for the information I got from Earth less than an hour ago.'

Our discussion was brought to a close by Lemmy's leaving the telescope and walking over to where Jet and I were sitting. 'Well,' he said as he approached, 'it won't be long now, and I won't be sorry.'

'What won't be long, Lemmy?' I asked.

'The landing on Mars. I can't wait to get my feet on terra firma again. Pity about the atmosphere down there, Doc. I'd give anything to have a good, deep breath of fresh air.'

'You'll have to do without that, Lemmy,' I told him with a laugh. 'The oxygen content of the Martian atmosphere is far too low. One breath of it would probably kill you.'

'Too low to support life, do you think, Doc?'

'Almost certainly.'

'I wonder! I'll lay you six to four that there's a couple of Martians sitting down there at this very moment looking up at the Earth and telling each other that there couldn't possibly be any life on our planet because the oxygen content of its atmosphere is too high.'

Lemmy chuckled at his own joke but his merriment was cut short by Jet's saying: 'Would you mind seeing Doc safely across to his ship, Lemmy? In a couple of hours we'll be refuelling Two and Six and I want everybody at their posts.'

I left the *Discovery* and returned to the freighter, quite disturbed, I must confess, by what Jet had told me. I racked my brains to see how it could possibly all tie together, but eventually had to give up; first because, try as I might, I could find no answer to the enigma and second because, less than half an hour after reaching my own freighter, the order came from Jet to get Number Six ready for the fuelling squads.

Two weeks later we 'met up' with the Red Planet absolutely on schedule, increased our speed and went into free orbit round the globe about a thousand miles above its surface. At this height we were above the planet's atmosphere and could therefore have gone on encircling indefinitely had we chose. In fact, that is what most of the Fleet would be doing until we started back to Earth. But three of the ships, namely the *Discovery* and Freighters Number One and Two, were to attempt a landing.

The *Discovery* was, of course, constructed especially for this purpose. Its two large wings would enable it to glide down through the Martian atmosphere. But the freighters had to be modified. First the massive girders were taken apart and the spherical cabins removed. The main bodies of the ships had been carried in the girders, together with the wings. Now the construction engineers, encased in their suits and attached to their job by their long safety lines, were floating around the ships and reassembling them. They were to act as tenders, and carry stores and materials down to the Martian base for the use of the crew of the *Discovery* and the other men selected to make the landing.

Some two days after we arrived over the planet the job was done. The time to go down had arrived.

While Lemmy, Mitch and I positioned our control panels, Jet went forward to the tiny pilot's cabin from which he would guide the *Discovery* down to the surface. As soon as he was safely settled in his seat he called us up on the inter-communication system. 'Now,' he said calmly, 'I'll just run over the procedure again for luck. Once the motors have been fired, we should enter the Martian atmosphere within a few minutes. We use its resistance to reduce our speed until it is low enough for us to attempt a landing.'

'I only hope there's enough atmosphere to make the necessary difference,' said Mitch.

'That we'll find out,' said Jet. 'If there isn't, we'll attempt a tail-first landing such as we normally make on the Moon. Now, are you all set?'

We were. Jet then called up the pilot of Number One. 'Hullo,' he said, 'we'll be on our way in just a few moments. You will wait ninety minutes and then follow. Is that clear?'

'Yes, Jet,' replied Rogers.

'And in the event of your not landing on the prearranged spot you are fully acquainted with the procedure for locating us?'

'Yes, Jet.'

'Thank you, Frank. Then we'll be off.'

'OK. And good luck, skipper. Good luck to all of you.'

'Same to you,' yelled Lemmy. 'We'll see you down there.'

'OK, Mitch, it's all yours,' said Jet lightly. 'Turn on the motor and I'll take her down.'

'Stand by for firing,' said Mitch, his voice shaking with excitement. 'Contact!'

We felt the motors burst into action and almost at once the Fleet fell behind us as, nose down, we headed for the Martian surface.

Ten minutes later we were in the atmosphere. As we touched it, the ship bounced, like a stone thrown along the surface of a pond. By now the motors had been cut and we were depending on the gravitational pull of Mars to take us down and on the atmosphere to slow us up. An hour and a half later we were gliding, as smoothly as you please, about ten miles above the planet's surface.

'Now on the last lap,' came Jet's eager voice in my ear, and approaching the pole fast. 'I can see the snow shining in the sun – if it is snow.'

'We're going just a little too fast,' said Mitch anxiously. 'Air speed three hundred and fifty, Jet.'

Jet let out another parachute brake.

We knew that behind us, but as yet over another part of the planet, was Freighter Number One. 'We expect to make our landing soon,' I heard Lemmy telling Frank over the radio. 'Approaching the ice cap now.'

'I'll keep a lookout for you. Have you seen any Martians yet?' asked Frank.

'No,' said Lemmy. 'Jet keeps me so busy with the radio I don't get time to go near the televiewer. For all I'm seeing of what's outside I might as well be in a submarine.'

'Well, I've got a good view from the pilot's cabin here,' said Frank enthusiastically, 'and it's a wonderful sight, Lemmy. Everything is pink, like it was perpetually bathed in the light of a beautiful sunset.'

'Is that right, Doc?' Lemmy called over to me.

'Yes, Lemmy,' I told him. 'That's as good a description as any.'

'I wish you'd take over the radio for a spell,' he begged, 'and let me have a look.'

'Come on, then,' I said, 'but make it quick.'

Lemmy and I changed seats.

'Televiewer's pointed directly below us,' I told him. 'But don't forget we'll be landing soon and every man will have to be at his own post.'

Jet, who was busy piloting our ship, did not talk except to ask Mitch for height and speed checks, but Lemmy kept up a running commentary on what he could see of the Martian surface in the televiewer. He asked innumerable questions and then, quite suddenly, said: 'Oh, blimey!'

'What's the trouble, Lemmy?' asked Mitch, looking up from his little table.

'Doc, come over here, quick. Look!'

I left my seat and moved over to the televiewer, scanning it over Lemmy's shoulder. 'What is it?' I asked him.

93

'There was something down there. A light – a brilliant, orange light.'

'What!'

'Yes. Like the reflection from a huge mirror. Only came on for a second and then it went again.'

'Where did you see it, Lemmy?' I asked.

'There – see? Where those two dark green lines cross. Where that big purple patch is.'

'That's the Lacus Solis,' I told him.

'I don't care what it is. I saw a light there.'

'May be water,' I suggested, 'reflecting the sunlight?'

'But I thought you said it was unlikely there was any water on Mars.'

'Well, maybe there is after all.'

'But it was so sudden, Doc, and so bright.'

'What did you think it was?' called Mitch sarcastically. 'A Martian signalling landing instructions?'

'Now there's no need to be sarky,' retorted Lemmy. 'It might be important.'

'I think it's more important that you get back to the radio and let Doc carry on with the observing as he's supposed to.'

'Yes, Mitch,' said Lemmy dejectedly, and he got out of my seat and moved back to his own.

I looked intently at the Lacus Solis, often known, because of its shape, as 'The Eye of Mars'. It is frequently visible in telescopes down on Earth and has always been an interesting point of observation for earthbound astronomers. But very soon the Lacus Solis moved out of the picture and the edge of the ice cap, now only a few thousand feet below us, came into view.

'Where are we now, Doc?' Lemmy called.

'Just over the cap.'

'Is it ice?'

'I don't see what else it can be.'

'I knew I should have packed my skis.'

'Hullo, back there.' It was Jet's voice.

'Yes, Jet?' asked Lemmy.

'Landing is imminent. You'd better strap yourselves in.'

We did as we were told and the picture in the televiewer showed the ground coming up ever closer.

'Height five thousand feet,' announced Mitch. 'Speed two hundred and twenty. Think you can get her to stay upright, Jet?'

Jet laughed. 'I think so. She's behaved herself very well up to now.'

'Then put her down gently,' said the Australian. 'I'd hate her to pile up after coming all this way.'

'Do me a favour, Mitch,' said Lemmy. 'Can't you think of anything more cheerful than that?'

For the next ten minutes nobody said anything, cheerful or otherwise. I think we were all holding our breath as we rapidly descended towards the white glare below us. Soon our height was only a few hundred feet and our speed down to little more than one hundred and fifty miles an hour. We were almost at landing speed.

I did my utmost to relax but found myself tense and gripping the sides of my seat. Mitch was monotonously reeling off the figures from the height indicator. Lemmy, like me, sat motionless and silent.

'About to make the run-in,' announced Jet. And then: 'What on earth is that noise?'

I saw Lemmy cock his head to one side as though trying to catch any unfamiliar sound. I, too, listened, but Mitch, intent upon his work, didn't appear to have heard Jet's question. But for the low hum of the power-packs there was no sound in the ship.

'Can't you hear it back there?' asked Jet again.

'No, Jet,' I yelled, 'I don't hear anything. What kind of noise is it?'

'It's like the buzzing of a thousand bees. It's as though they were right inside my head. You must hear it.'

But none of us did – neither Lemmy, Mitch nor I.

Jet gulped. 'Putting her nose down,' he said. 'Oh, good heavens!'

'What is it?' I asked. 'What's the trouble?'

'I don't know, Doc. I feel most peculiar. I think I'm going to black out.'

'Oh, no!' exclaimed Lemmy.

We were down to less than two hundred feet now.

'I feel so sleepy.' Jet sounded as though he were trying to stifle a yawn.

'One hundred feet,' announced Mitch.

'Jet,' I called, greatly alarmed, 'are you going to make it? Shall I come up there and...'

My words were cut off by the sudden impact as the landing wheels struck the surface. The ship lurched, bounced, and rose up again.

'Watch it, Jet,' cried Mitch sharply. 'What are you trying to do?'

'Sorry,' came back Jet's hesitant voice. 'We bounced. I'll try again.'

Now our port wing dipped down in a steep angle. I saw Mitch clutch at the air in an effort to support himself; had he not been strapped into his seat, I'm sure he would have fallen out of it.

'For Pete's sake!' he called. Then, turning to me: 'What's come over him, Doc? He doesn't seem able to control the ship.' He began to unfasten his safety belt but I stopped him.

'No, Mitch,' I yelled. 'Stay where you are.'

'But there's something wrong up front. Jet's in trouble.'

Jet certainly must have been. 'Unless I land her now,' he said, haltingly, 'we'll never make it.'

'No, take her up again!' shouted Mitch. 'Switch on the motor.'

'I daren't – I – haven't the time. Stand by for crash landing.'

I heard Lemmy give a groan. A split second later the ship touched down, swerved sharply to port, lifted her starboard wheel and then, by some miracle, put it back on the deck again. She swayed a little, began to lose speed, straightened up and then gently rolled to a standstill.

Chapter 10

L emmy groaned. 'You all right?' I asked him.

'Yes, Doc. I think so.'

'Then what were you moaning for? I thought you'd been hurt.'

'No, Doc. That was a sigh of relief at finding myself all in one piece.'

'How about you, Mitch?'

'I'm OK, Doc. But what about Jet?'

Obviously Jet was not OK, for he did not respond to our calls.

Lemmy was the first out of his chair. He undid his safety straps, took a couple of steps in the direction of the pilot's cabin and immediately sank to his knees.

'What are you doing down there?' Mitch asked him.

'I don't know,' replied the Cockney, looking up at us rather pathetically and obviously not daring to move. 'I seem to have lost the use of my legs. What's happened to them Doc?'

'Lemmy,' I told him, 'for six months, while travelling through space, we have been living under gravityless conditions and now, the moment gravity returns, you leap out of your chair and try to run. Your legs just aren't used to it.'

'Oh, is that all?' replied the Cockney with relief. 'For a minute I thought I must have been hurt in the crash.'

'Get up slowly,' I said, 'take off your magnetised boots and, when you start walking, go easy.' Mitch was the first to reach the pilot's cabin. He opened the power-operated door to reveal the figure of Jet slumped over the controls. Between us, Mitch and I lifted him out of the cabin while Lemmy reconverted one of the chairs to a bunk.

Jet had a nasty-looking, bluish lump on his forehead and had evidently struck it on the instrument panel during touchdown. Apart from that, he did not seem to be hurt but, to my surprise, his skin was extremely cold to touch.

I sent Lemmy over to the medical locker for a dressing to put on the wound and Mitch began to remove Jet's boots. As he did so, Jet gave a low moan and opened his eyes.

'Hullo, Jet,' I said. 'How are you feeling?'

It took him a few moments to realise where he was. 'What happened?' he asked.

'We made an emergency landing. You bumped your head and were knocked out cold.'

'Is the ship all right?'

'Yes, Jet,' said Mitch. 'It wasn't much of a bump.'

'What was wrong, Jet?' I asked. 'Why did we have to crash land?'

'I couldn't help it. I was blacking out. All I remember was that frightful noise and the louder it got the hazier everything became. Didn't any of you hear it?'

'No, Jet. We didn't.'

'But it was so loud, and I'd stake my life that it had something to do with my losing control. What could it have been?'

'It could have been anything,' I said as I applied the dressing which Lemmy had now brought. 'Maybe the descent was too fast for you; the change in atmospheric pressure too sudden.'

'But the pilot's cabin is airtight; the pressure in the ship remains constant at whatever speed we come down. And what about the noise? I'm absolutely convinced it was that which induced the blackout.'

'Or whatever induced the blackout also induced the noise.'

'And I feel so cold.'

'Lemmy is making some tea. It will warm you.'

I must say Jet's condition puzzled me. There was really no accounting for his blacking out and certainly no accounting for the 'noise' he had heard nor, most important of all, for the drop in his temperature. The only similar case in my experience was Whitaker's. His temperature also had been extremely low when we found him, asleep on his feet, in the freighter, only a day or two after takeoff.

However, I said nothing of this to Jet who, after drinking the tea, seemed to recover very rapidly. Soon he was up on his feet again and, but for the bruise on his head, was perfectly normal.

We were all, of course, consumed with curiosity to see what the world looked like outside and, as soon as Jet was able to join me, he and I went into the pilot's cabin while Lemmy and Mitch took their first look at Mars from the navigation hatch.

I cannot say that the sight which met our eyes was one of great beauty, but it was certainly startling. The ground was a brilliant white sheet as far as the eye could see. The skid marks of the ship had left deep dark furrows in the ice, if it was ice, showing that it was of no great depth; perhaps a foot or so, no more. But the most amazing thing was the sky. It was mauve, and the sun, which hung near the horizon, a deep orange. The ship threw a long, deep shadow across the ice.

Lemmy seemed rather disappointed with the view. The only thing that surprised him was the sky. 'I thought it would be blue,' he said. 'Will it be this colour all over the planet?'

'Almost certainly,' I told him. 'It's because of the thin atmosphere.'

Having taken our first glimpse of this strange new world, our next move was to set foot on it. We donned our space suits and went outside, taking along a collection of instruments of various kinds with which to carry out our preliminary tests. The first thing I did on setting foot on the Martian ground was to scoop up a handful of the ice. It was hard and brittle like tiny crystals and, as I let it run through my fingers, it glistened in the sun like a shower of minute diamonds.

During our first hour on Mars we did a lot of work. We measured the pressure of the atmosphere, both at ground level and, with the aid of a balloon, up to five thousand feet. We dug up small samples of the blue-black soil which lay below the ice and boxed it to take back to Earth with us. We took temperatures of the atmosphere, ice and soil and photographs of ourselves standing by the ship.

A few minutes before sunset we downed tools and cheered as Frank's ship made a perfect landing and came to a standstill not fifty yards from where our own ship was parked. Jet then ordered us all inside the *Discovery* again, for we knew only too well that the temperature at the pole during the Martian night would be far too low for any of us to stand, even in our heated suits.

Next morning we were up before dawn, eager to get another look at the strange Martian world. It did not take long for the sun to warm the thin atmosphere and soon Frank and his crew were busily unloading the land trucks from the ferry. We worked hard all day, helping them equip the Land Fleet for our exploration, but the task was not finished until nearly sunset. We were to have headed towards the Martian equator as soon as the trucks were ready but, even though we knew they would be ample protection against the cold, Jet decided to spend one more night in the ship and start out at daybreak the next morning.

Frank, meanwhile, was to return into free orbit and load up his ship for a second landing. He was also to bring down other crew members who would remain at Polar Base while Frank, after equipping his own fleet of land trucks, would follow in our tracks.

As there was still an hour's light left, Frank decided to take off immediately. We watched him from the *Discovery*, a great red belch of flame emitting from his exhaust as he sped along the ice and then rapidly climbed through the thin atmosphere into the mauve void above. An hour later we received a call to say he had rejoined the rest of the Fleet in free orbit and that cargo from the remaining freighters was already being transferred into Number One for her next trip down to Martian soil.

Next morning we left the great ship which had been our home for so many months to transfer to the land trucks. We wore our protective clothing while we were 'in transit', but once inside the hermetically sealed cabins of the tractors we were able to remove our suits and stow them. There was room in each of the driving cabins for two men. Jet and I were in one truck and Mitch and Lemmy in the other. We were, of course, in touch with each other and the Fleet by radio and, by leaving the radios on, could all take part in general conversation.

'Well,' I heard Mitch say to Lemmy as we got under way, 'this is it. Man's first exploration of Mars is about to begin. Take your last look at the *Discovery*; you won't be seeing her for some months.'

'And how many miles do we cover on this trip?' asked Lemmy.

'Oh, about seven thousand,' said Mitch, unconcerned.

'Well, let's hope the trucks stand up to it,' said the Cockney. 'What do we do if we have a breakdown? Ring up a garage and ask them to tow us in?'

Mitch laughed. 'Frank and his mechanics will be only a couple of days behind us, Lemmy,' he said. 'If we have a breakdown we just sit tight until they roll up.'

And so we set out, across the great, glaring white wastelands of the south polar ice cap towards the warmer climes of the temperate zones near the equator. The transport trucks, looking almost black against the gleaming white of the ice, resembled two lines of beetles slowly wending their way across a barrel of flour. Each caravan comprised three trucks. In the lead was the tractor with its roomy, airtight cabin in which sat the driver and navigator. In tow was the living quarters vehicle, a huge, tank-like machine which, in its base, carried food, water, surveying tools, spare clothing and other personal equipment. On its upper deck, hermetically sealed to an oblong platform, were living quarters, looking like transportable Eskimo igloos. Then came the cargo truck, carrying fuel, oxygen tanks and other equipment too bulky to be stored beneath the living quarters.

Soon the great spaceship had been left far behind. Finally it disappeared from view over the horizon and all contact with the rest of the Fleet, except by radio, was gone. We were alone, just the four of us, two in each caravan, slowly ploughing our way across the great white desert.

We covered one hundred and fifty miles that first day. At sunset we stopped the trucks and camped for the night. Darkness fell and with it came the bitter cold. It was so cold outside that the heaters had to be turned on at full pressure to keep us from freezing, even within our double-skinned living quarters. While the two caravans stood under the black, diamond-studded sky, we slept. Next morning we were on our way again and by noon had covered another seventy miles. We ate our midday meal, checked with the Fleet and heard that Frank was already on his way down to Polar Base with his newly loaded freighter.

After lunch, Jet and I went outside and dug up some more samples of the soil below the ice. We put these in little boxes, stowed them in the rear of the caravan and then climbed aboard the tractor to continue our journey northwards. We made another hundred miles by sunset and a further eighty by the following noon. Frank told us now that he was ready to follow in our tracks just as soon as Freighter Number Two, the third and last ship to make the descent, had touched down with the remainder of the necessary supplies.

On the third day we were still travelling across ice but were anxiously scanning the horizon. We knew it could not be long before the limit of the cap was reached and we sighted the drier soil of the Mare Australis.

Towards the middle of the afternoon we noticed that the horizon directly in front of us was covered with a long range of low hills. This was rather a surprise to us as we had expected the ground to be perfectly flat up to the Mare Australis at least. Yet the hills appeared to be at least one hundred miles in length and approximately two thousand feet tall at their highest point. We estimated that we would reach them about sunset, and would almost certainly have to camp on their summits. However, this did not worry us unduly as we did not expect to find a precipice on the other side. Also, of course, the added height would give us an extended view of the terrain beyond and, with luck, we might well be able to take a good look at the Mare Australis before we descended to the plain and began to make our way across it.

It was just after we had sighted the hills that we received an urgent call from Frank Rogers back at Polar Base. 'It's Number Two, skipper,' said Frank anxiously. 'She's in trouble.'

'We were thinking it was about time she passed over us,' said Jet. 'What's wrong?'

'I wish I knew. I was in radio contact with her on the ship-to-ship system until five minutes ago, but now I can't get any reply to my calls.'

'What was her position when last you heard from her?'

'Fifty miles directly north of you.'

'Then keep calling her. Meanwhile we'll see if we can pick her up.'

We switched over to Number Two's frequency and heard Frank calling her. Suddenly we heard McLean, Number Two's pilot, saying, very faintly: 'Hullo, Base – Number Two calling. Trying to contact you. Please answer me.'

It was obvious that Frank was not hearing him. Jet called up Number Two himself and received a reply immediately. For some unknown reason Number Two's radio was not carrying as far as Polar Base.

'Hullo, Land Fleet,' the pilot was saying, his voice strained and nervous. 'I can't control the ship. I'll have to make a forced landing.'

'What's the matter with the ship?' demanded Jet.

'Nothing, Captain, it's us.'

'What's wrong?'

McLean seemed to find it difficult to speak. 'There's a – weird noise. Seems to be right inside my head. I – can't keep awake. It's – it's so cold – I – I – don't think we'll ever make Base. I'm going to put the ship down. It's the only way I can hope to save her. I – I – feel – so – sleepy…'

'Listen, McLean,' said Jet urgently, 'you must not go to sleep. You must stay awake, do you hear?'

'We're almost on the deck now,' came the weak reply. 'About to land, but the ship – is – difficult – to…'

Then there was silence. Jet called McLean again. 'Hullo, Number Two – hullo,' he said desperately. He called a second time and a third. Then, turning to me, he asked: 'How far north of us did Frank estimate she was?'

'Fifty miles,' I replied.

'Then if we increase speed to twenty miles an hour we should cover that distance before sunset?'

'That doesn't mean we'll find her. Not before dark, anyway.'

'But there's a chance.'

'Yes, and there's a chance of burning up the motors, too,' came Mitch's voice in my ear, 'the load we're dragging behind us.'

'That's a risk we'll have to take,' said Jet curtly. 'If that ship is wrecked, her crew will be in dire need of help.'

'OK.'

'All right, then, turn on the juice.'

Chapter 11

Both caravans ploughed steadily on through the powdery ice, leaving two black lines of caterpillar tracks behind them. We had, for our own safety, to proceed with caution and, at the same time, we had to find the wreck of Number Two – before nightfall, if possible.

Jet called up Frank at Polar Base and told him that, in view of the situation, he was to start out after us immediately. 'You'll be quite safe if you follow our tracks,' Jet said. 'Now, how soon can you leave?'

'Within the hour.'

'Good. Then we hope to see you sometime tomorrow. Keep in radio contact all the way – and good luck.'

'Thank you, sir.'

For the next hour we rode in silence, our eyes glued to the horizon for any sign of Number Two. But there was no sign of life at all, not a blade of grass, no trace of moss and certainly no suggestion of anything like an animal. To all appearances Mars, in this region at any rate, was a dead, deserted world.

It was already growing dark when we reached the lower slopes of the hills and began a steady climb upwards. Fortunately the gradient was not steep. When we reached the summit, both trucks together, only a faint trace of daylight remained in the sky. Even so, there was enough light to enable us to survey the scene.

And what a scene it was.

Stretched out, thousands of feet below us, was a great, purple plain. The hills rolled gently down towards the flat land and, at their feet, the ice gave way to the purple soil. We had reached the limit of the ice.

'Blimey,' came Lemmy's voice over the radio, 'talk about the heights of Abraham!'

'Never mind the scenery,' said Jet impatiently, 'look for the ship.'

But the light was fading so rapidly that even had the freighter been within visible distance I doubt very much whether we would have seen her. Soon it was completely dark.

'Well,' said Mitch at last, 'we arrived too late. Had we got there half an hour earlier, we might have stood a chance of locating her.'

'Maybe she's not even down there,' I suggested.

'But she must be, Doc,' said Jet. 'According to Frank she was fifty miles directly north of us before she crashed.'

'But that was several minutes before she crashed, Jet. She could have drifted miles off the course in that time.'

'All we can do,' said the Captain, 'is go down there and search.'

'In the dark – and with absolutely no clue as to the direction in which she lies?' I protested. 'We don't even know whether the ground down there will support the trucks.'

'But what about the ship and her crew? Every minute we waste might mean the difference between life and death.'

'Maybe,' I said, 'but there's no point in throwing our own lives away. Had we seen her I'd agree to make an attempt to reach her. But to wander down there in the dark might be suicide.'

'Doc's right,' came Mitch's voice. 'We can start out again in the morning as soon as it's light. We can't even see the plain any more. Nothing but pitch darkness and the stars and…'

He was interrupted by an excited cry from Lemmy. 'Hey, Doc, Mitch, Jet – look!' he exclaimed. 'A light!'

'What?'

'Yes, down there – see it?'

A couple of minutes later we could all see it but, as Mitch observed, it was no bigger than a pinpoint.

'That must be the ship,' said Jet. 'At least one of the men must be all right and he's switched on the landing light in the hope of guiding us to his position. We must let him know we've seen him. Let's put on our light, Doc.'

'No – wait, Jet,' I told him. 'That light. It's moving.'

'What!'

Almost immediately Mitch's voice came over the radio to confirm my opinion. 'It's distinctly travelling towards the west,' he said.

'Good grief,' said Jet, 'then that can't be the ship. And if it isn't, then who is it? *What* is it?'

We watched the light for about fifteen minutes, during which time it diminished in brightness and finally disappeared. We waited for ten minutes in the hope that it would reappear – but it didn't.

'It seems to have gone for good,' said Jet. 'What could it have been?'

'Goodness knows,' I replied. Then a sudden thought struck me. 'It might have been the boys of Number Two,' I suggested. 'Maybe they've taken the land truck out of her and have put on their headlight and are trying to find their way to Polar Base.'

'Maybe,' said Jet thoughtfully. 'In that case, the place where we first saw the light must be where the wreck of the ship is. So all we have to do now is head straight for that point.'

'You mean go down there in the dark after all?' I asked him.

'Yes,' he answered. 'If we find the ship it will be easy to pick up the tracks left by her land truck and we should overtake her crew by morning.'

'Very well, if you say so,' I told him. 'But I think we're taking a great risk.'

'We'll reduce speed to ten miles an hour and keep our highlights on all the way,' Jet continued, as though I had not spoken. 'With luck, Number Two's land truck might even see them and find us before we find them.'

Jet called up Mitch and told him of his plan. And then, with our headlights blazing, we switched on the motors and slowly began the descent down the ice-covered slopes towards the plain below.

Half an hour later we reached the base of the hills, and great irregular patches of black began to appear in the ice-covered ground.

'The ice is giving out fast,' remarked Jet. 'Shouldn't be long before we leave it behind entirely.'

We continued our course for two hours but no sign of the ship was seen. By now we estimated that we must have reached the point where we had first seen the light and that to go on any farther might mean going too far. Jet ordered the trucks to halt while we swung our headlights in every direction, hoping to pick out the ship in the inky darkness. But there was still no sign of it.

'Well, it looks as though we've drawn a blank,' said Mitch. 'What do we do now?'

'There's nothing for it but to camp here for the night and wait until morning,' replied Jet despondently.

'If you ask me, we'd have done better to have stayed up in those hills,' said Lemmy. 'Then at least we would have had the advantage of height when we make the search in the daylight.'

I was of the same opinion but, for Jet's sake, did not say so.

It was agreed that Jet would take the first watch, so Mitch and Lemmy went back into their living quarters to get some sleep, leaving their radio on so that they might be called when their turn came.

It hardly seemed worth my going back into living quarters to sleep for only two hours, so I stayed up with Jet and snoozed in my driving seat. When Jet woke me, he had nothing to report, and neither had I when the time came to call Mitch.

I was woken in the morning by the excited voice of Lemmy coming through the intercom speaker, saying that he had sighted the wreck. Jet and I rushed out into the driving cabin to look for ourselves and there it was, about two miles ahead of us, tipped up on its nose. The port wing, which was badly crumpled, was touching the ground.

Jet ordered the trucks to be started up immediately and we drove to within a few yards of where the ship was standing. There seemed to be no sign of life aboard her and, even though we called many times, we could get no reply on the radio.

As soon as the sun was high enough in the sky to raise the temperature outside to a safe level, we donned our suits and let ourselves out. The first thing we did was to walk round the ship and inspect it for damage. With the exception of the crumpled wing she seemed to be quite intact but, much to our surprise, the cargo doors in the belly of the ship were open.

'She's a bit of a mess, isn't she?' said Mitch. 'She must have hit the deck pretty hard.'

'Yes,' said Jet. 'It's a miracle that any of her crew were still alive and able to leave her.'

'What makes you so sure that they did?' asked the engineer. 'There are no tracks of any land trucks around here that I can see, except our own.'

'Then how can you account for the cargo flaps being open?' asked Jet.

'The impact might have done it. Might have set the mechanism off and they just opened automatically.'

'I think we'd better go inside, Jet,' I suggested. 'Her crew must be in there after all.'

The easiest way into the ship in its present position was through the open hatch, but as this was some twelve feet above the ground, we could only reach it by standing on the roof of one of our trucks. From there, Jet led the way, taking a flashlight with him in case the ship's lights didn't function.

Before actually entering the hold, Jet shone his torch round. The beam fell upon the outer door of the airlock leading into the cabin. Jet gave an involuntary exclamation of surprise when he saw that the inner door was open, too. 'That means there can be no air in the cabin,' said Mitch.

'Oh, blimey,' said Lemmy. 'No wonder they don't answer our calls.'

'Come on,' said Jet, 'keep close to me.' And with that he entered the freighter.

Within a few minutes we were all in the cabin. It was empty.

'Well,' said Jet, with finality, 'they must have left the ship. What else could they have done? Probably the main airlock is out of action and, when they discovered that, they decided to go out through the cargo hatch. Though why they should leave the airlock open beats me. Now let's make a thorough search. Doc and I will stay here. Lemmy and Mitch, you go back into the cargo hold and see what you can find there.'

We split up to do as Jet directed, but after only a few minutes Mitch came running back. 'Well,' he said, as he entered the cabin with Lemmy close on his heels, 'it's as I thought. The land truck is still in its stowage, so wherever the crew of this ship went, they walked.'

'But they wouldn't be crazy enough to go outside without a land truck,' said Jet. 'Certainly not at night. They'd be frozen to death.'

'It was still daylight when they crashed,' Mitch reminded us, 'and if they left then they could have walked quite a way before nightfall.'

'The ground outside would have been soft and wet from the melting ice,' I said. 'Anybody walking out there would be bound to leave footprints. Let's see if we can find any.'

'Yes, come on,' said Jet.

Once outside we searched the area around the cargo hatch, but the only footprints we could find were our own. Our task was made more difficult by the fact that much of the ground had been churned by our land trucks. It then occurred to me that, except for their size, all the boots worn by crew members were identical in construction.

'We'd better look over parts of the ground we're sure we haven't walked on,' I suggested, 'and then if we find any prints we'll know they aren't ours.' They all agreed that that made sense, so again we split up and began our search anew.

It was Lemmy who first found something. He called us over to his side of the ship in great excitement. 'Come on,' he yelled, 'I've found 'em.' We all hurried over to where the radio operator was standing, gazing down at some footprints that led away from below the cargo flaps towards where the ship's tail would have been had the craft not been standing up on her nose.

We followed them, and about half a mile from the wreck they disappeared. In their place we found three deep circular impressions of some four feet in diameter. They marked out the corners of an equilateral triangle, the sides of which would be about twenty feet in length.

We all gazed in puzzled silence for a few minutes and then Jet said: 'Well, gentlemen, I think we all know what this is – it's the light.'

'The light?' asked Lemmy, in a hoarse whisper.

'Yes. Or whatever was carrying the light. It must have come here to investigate the ship after it had crashed. Maybe it even caused the crash.'

'You mean somebody's been here, messing around with our ship?' asked the Cockney.

'Exactly.'

'But what about our crew? What's happened to them?'

'It's pretty certain that they, or their bodies if they were dead, have been taken and transferred to some other kind of machine.'

'But where have they been taken to?' asked Lemmy. 'And who took them?'

'That's what I intend to find out. That light, when we last saw it, was moving directly west from here.'

'Yes, Jet. And pretty fast, too,' I reminded him.

'Very well. From now on we travel westwards.'

'You mean you're going after that thing?' asked Mitch.

'Yes.'

'But how are we going to find it? A flying machine doesn't leave any trails.'

'If we don't find it,' Jet replied, 'we'll come back here and continue our journey towards the equator as originally planned. Now come on.'

We ran back to the trucks and, once inside, took off our suits and settled down in the driving seats. Then, at top speed, we headed westward.

Neither Jet nor I spoke a word to each other, but we both thought very hard; at least, I know I did. Here was something quite unexpected: definite proof that life existed on this strange planet. An intelligent life; a life, apparently, very similar to our own.

Chapter 12

The ground over which we travelled was a sea of purple mud. Portions of it clung to our tractor treads in thick clods but it must have been fairly hard underneath for we didn't sink very far into it. There was not a hill or mound of any kind in sight now, and the purple soil stretched clear to the horizon, uninterrupted and undisturbed.

Towards the middle of the afternoon, I noticed that the land to the north-west had a pink tinge about it and Jet suggested it must be the south-eastern tip of the great Argyre Desert.

During our long trip since dawn neither Jet nor I had mentioned the flying machine which we were pursuing. We both realised that the chances of our overtaking it were so remote as to be virtually non-existent. We were like a car – a very slow one at that – trying to overtake a fast aeroplane.

The silence was broken by the voice of Frank coming over the radio. 'Hullo, Land Fleet,' it said, 'Rogers calling.'

'Hullo, Frank,' replied Jet. 'We can hear you.'

'This is to report that we have now topped the hill and are about to descend down the other side. We can see Number Two from up here – through the glasses at any rate.'

'When you get to her,' said Jet, 'look her over straight away. Give me a report on the chances of salvaging her cargo and getting it back to Polar Base.'

'Yes, sir.'

'You can enter her by the cargo hatch. We left the ladder extended so you wouldn't have any trouble getting up. We also left the air supply to build up so that you can spend the night inside if you wish.'

'Thank you, sir.'

'Keep in regular contact, Frank, and be sure to be under cover with all hatches tightly closed at least an hour before sunset. And make no attempt to leave the ship or your trucks between then and sunrise, no matter what happens.'

'You're darned right I won't, skipper!'

'Now our position at the moment is, approximately, longitude eleven degrees thirty-four minutes, latitude minus fifty-three degrees twenty-two minutes. We are heading directly westwards along the latitudinal line. Call again as soon as you reach the ship, Frank. And good luck.'

The afternoon wore on as we sped on our way through the purple mud. At last the sun sank below the horizon. Twilight descended and rapidly turned to a glorious, star-studded night. When it was completely dark, we made camp, but before going back into the living quarters, Jet called up the other truck. 'Now listen, Lemmy,' he said, 'I want you to keep watch while we get something to eat. If you see any sign of that light call us up immediately. Is that clear?'

'Yes, Jet.'

'As soon as Mitch has finished his meal he will relieve you, and then Doc and I will take over in this truck.'

My turn for watch came four hours later. Jet was asleep on his bunk as I made my way through the connecting airlock between the two trucks and into the driving cabin of the tractor. It was quite dark in there. We had decided not to put on any lights that could be seen from the outside. Having eased myself into my seat, I let my eyes get used to the darkness until the stars in the sky seemed to hang like brilliant, multi-coloured lamps just above my head. Then I called up Mitch to tell him that he could go back to bed.

'How about it?' I asked. 'Did you see anything?'

'No, Doc, not a thing.'

'Any word from Frank?'

'Yes, he decided to spend the night in Number Two. He and Grimshaw have kept a constant watch from there but they've seen nothing, either.'

'Well, get some shut-eye, Mitch. I'll give you a call if I see anything.'

'Thanks, Doc.'

I could imagine Mitch crawling through the airlock into the living quarters truck, thankful that it would be another six hours before he would again be called upon to keep the lonely vigil. I scanned the sky from east to west and from north to south as far as the window of the cabin would allow. I saw nothing but the stars.

The time went by incredibly slowly. After what seemed an eternity I looked at my watch and saw that I had been keeping sentinel for only twenty minutes. I had to force myself to stay awake.

Suddenly my attention was drawn to the horizon in the north-west, to a bright blue 'star' which had appeared above the black line that marked the spot where the purple plain met the sky. Slowly, very slowly, it rose and, as it rose, grew larger.

I switched on the microphone and spoke quietly into it. Jet could not have been sleeping very deeply, for he answered my call immediately.

'Hold on, Doc,' he said, 'I'll be right out.'

I had to call Mitch and Lemmy a second time before I received a reply from them.

I don't think it took Jet above two minutes to reach me and by that time the light was very much bigger and heading in our direction. Soon it had grown from pinpoint size to something like three or four feet in diameter. It was now a bright orange colour and varied in strength.

Then, at colossal speed, the light passed over our heads and was behind us. Both Jet and I spun round in the tiny cabin and tried to follow its path, but the back of the cabin obstructed our view.

'If it stays on that course,' I heard Lemmy say, 'it won't be going anywhere near Number Two.' But it wasn't staying on course. Quite suddenly it veered round, changed its line of flight and swept round in a huge arc. I thought at first that it was going to encircle us but it flew due east, in a direct line towards Freighter Number Two.

'Call up Frank, Lemmy,' Jet said urgently. 'Warn him that the thing is coming.'

'Right, Jet. Hullo, Frank – Lemmy here.'

Frank, his voice distant, answered immediately. 'Hullo, Lemmy – Rogers speaking.'

'We don't want to put the wind up you, chum, but that light we told you about…'

'Well?'

'It passed over us a moment ago and it looks as though it's heading straight for you.'

'Oh, *is* it?' said Frank, emphasising the verb.

'Yes, mate,' went on Lemmy. 'Keep a sharp look out and if you hear anybody knocking on that door, pretend you're out.'

'Don't worry, Lemmy,' said Frank. 'We're sealed up tighter than sardines in a tin.'

'Good for you.'

'Did they see you, Lemmy?'

'We don't see how they could have missed us. Passed right overhead, but they didn't even hesitate.'

'OK, Lemmy. If it comes this way I'll let you know the minute I sight it.'

'Thanks mate – and don't go doing anything hasty.'

The ship, or whatever it was, must have been travelling at about a thousand miles an hour, for approximately twelve minutes later Frank called up to say that he could see the light heading straight for him.

Jet immediately took over the radio and talked to Frank direct. 'Hullo, Frank. Where are you keeping look-out – from the pilot's window?'

'No, Jet. Through the televiewer.'

'Where is the light now?'

'Directly in front of us. Elevation about forty-five degrees – no, now it's descending very gently. It's almost down. It's touched the deck and – the light's gone out.'

'Can you see a ship of any kind?'

'Not really, Jet. It's so dark out there.'

'Have you got the lights on in the cabin?'

'Yes, Jet.'

'Then put them out.'

'But they can't be seen from outside, sir.'

'I realise that, Frank. But the darker the cabin the better your chance of seeing things on the televiewer.'

'Very well, sir. Hold on a moment.'

'I wouldn't like to be in Frank's shoes right now,' said Lemmy quietly; 'not with that thing sitting on his doorstep.'

Frank was now calling again, and he sounded very excited.

'Hullo, Frank,' said Jet.

'Things are happening, sir. That thing out there is definitely circular, and a pale green, oval-shaped light has appeared in the lower part of it.'

'Some kind of door, you mean?'

'Possibly.'

There was another, shorter pause and then Frank, hoarsely whispering so that we could hardly hear him, said: 'Oh, Jet… somebody… something is coming out!'

'What do they – it – look like?' asked Jet.

'It's difficult to tell. All we can see are faint shadows. The green light is so pale – like luminous paint. It's only because parts of it are being obscured occasionally that I know anything is there at all. There's one, two, three – yes three shadows passed across it. Apparently towards the ground.'

'Listen, Frank.'

'Yes, sir?'

'They must be going to approach the ship, but almost certainly they are not aware that you are in there. They probably expect to find the cargo flaps still down as they left them yesterday.'

'Then they have a big surprise coming, haven't... oh – what's that? What the...?'

'What is it, Frank?'

'There's a click coming from the control board. The cargo flap relays are working, sir – somebody outside is pressing the switch.'

'But they can't get in, can they, Frank?'

'I hope not, sir. That switch won't open the doors, that's for certain – we've broken the remote control circuit. Oh, they've stopped now – they must have given up. Look, sir, it's so dark outside that it's impossible for the televiewer to show a bright picture, but if I went out into the pilot's cabin and looked through the window I might see much more.'

'Very well, Frank. But be careful. Switch off the televiewer and the control board lights before you go, in case they should be seen when you open the pilot's cabin door.'

'Yes, sir.' There was a pause. 'About to enter the pilot's cabin. Now.'

We heard the hum of the motors over the radio as Grimshaw opened the door for Frank. 'I'm in the pilot's cabin now, skipper,' came Frank's voice.

'Can you see any better?' asked Jet.

'Yes, just a little. The green light is an opening into that sphere.'

'How big is it? Can you tell?'

'Not without knowing exactly how far away she is. At a rough guess I'd say between six and ten feet, but...' Frank stopped as though he had seen something that startled him.

'What is it, Frank?'

'It's the crew,' Frank whispered. 'I can just see them. Vague shapes. They just passed under the port wing and are heading back to the sphere.'

'Frank,' said Jet nervously, 'What do they look like? How big are they?'

'It's difficult to tell. They're all bunched up together and their silhouettes seem to mingle. If only there was a little more light!'

'Keep watching them, Frank. When they reach the door they should show up clearly against it.'

'Yes.' There was a pause during which we all waited expectantly. But when Frank spoke again it was merely to say: 'If they *are* heading for their ship, Jet, they couldn't have reached it yet. It must be a lot farther away that I thought.'

'Can you still see them?'

'No, skipper. They've been completely swallowed up by the darkness. Oh, wait a minute. They've reached the light now. They stand out as clearly as... oh, one's about to climb back in and I... oh, my...' There was a clatter in our headphones as though Frank had dropped his microphone. Jet called two or three times to ask what had happened. There was no reply for some seconds, and then at last Frank said: 'It's all right, skipper. The light – the big one – it came on again and I threw myself to the floor.'

'Oh, blimey,' said Lemmy. 'Now we'll never know what they look like.'

'But I saw them, skipper,' went on Frank. 'For a split second I saw them.'

'Then what did they look like, Frank?' Jet asked urgently.

'Just like you and me, Jet. Just normal human beings.'

I heard Jet catch his breath. 'Frank, are you sure? You are straining your eyes in the darkness. They could have played you tricks.'

'I'd stake my life on it,' went on Frank. 'When the big light came on it showed them up so clearly. I couldn't have made a mistake.'

'Did you see the ship take off again?'

'No. While the light was on I thought it best to lie low. A couple of minutes later she was gone. The last I saw of her was a diminishing light in the sky. It must be heading back your way.'

It was. It arrived in about ten minutes. But this time it kept a perfectly straight course and passed over our heads to disappear below the horizon in the direction of the Argyre Desert.

It wasn't long before Jet was calling Frank again, asking every possible question about what Frank had seen. How were the men dressed? How tall were they? Was he sure that they were normal human beings?

Finally, Frank was allowed to get some sleep which, I felt sure, he needed – for on top of his disturbed night he faced an early start back to Polar Base with as much of the salvaged cargo as he and Grimshaw could carry in their land trucks.

The first rays of the morning sun had hardly lightened the sky when our two caravans set out. We travelled steadily in a straight line towards where the light of the strange ship had disappeared over the horizon the night before.

Three hours and sixty miles later the soft, damp, purple soil of the Mare Australis gave way to the pink dust of the Argyre. By noon the Mare had been left far behind. Now the two trains of vehicles ploughed through desert, each trailing a miniature dust storm behind it.

For the first time since landing on the planet, the sun's rays shining through the windows of the driving cabins were hot enough to allow us to travel through the day without the need of heaters to keep us warm.

The desert scene was unbelievably beautiful. The sand was pink and, unlike the flat plain of the Mare Australis, gently undulating. Slowly, as the day wore on, a copper-coloured sun made its way across the mauve northern sky. At noon we rested, refreshed ourselves and stretched our legs by walking ankle-deep in the sand, for sand it certainly seemed to be. By then we were well into the desert, surrounded on every side by low, pink hills, without the tiniest living plant to relieve the monotonous, if colourful scene.

In our first day across that great desert, we covered nearly two hundred and fifty miles and then, under a canopy of the blackest sky, studded with the brightest stars, we settled down to sleep. We kept a constant watch but no sign of the mysterious ship was seen. Not long after we had made camp we had a call from Frank, telling us that he had now reached Polar Base again and had taken a considerable part of the cargo of the wrecked freighter with him. He reported, too, that all was well with the rest of the Fleet still travelling above the planet's surface in free orbit.

Next morning we were on our way again, hoping to make the far side of the desert before nightfall. Jet didn't allow us to let up for a moment. While one man drove the truck, his companion navigated and, in between times, scanned the horizon with the powerful binoculars in the hope of sighting the strange sphere or some sign that would lead us to its base. But there was none; nothing but the pink stand stretching on endlessly.

It was two hours before sunset and I was driving. Suddenly the motor began to vary, and our speed with it. 'Maybe we had better stop,' said Jet reluctantly, 'and let Mitch look her over. We can't afford to have the trucks breaking down at this stage.'

Jet called up Mitch and told him to halt, and a few moments later we had drawn up alongside. We all got out of the trucks and Mitch immediately began to carry out an inspection of the motor. It didn't take him long to find the trouble but, he said, it would take him at least an hour to put it right. Under the circumstances, there was nothing to do but wait.

I suggested that perhaps as the motor had 'gone on the blink' we should make camp here for the night anyway, but Jet was determined to press on so long as there was daylight left. We had halted at the bottom of a high sand dune and, while Mitch was tinkering with the inside of the tractor, Jet walked round in small circles and occasionally stopped and looked up to the ridge which lay ahead. At last he said: 'Look, Mitch, while you're tending to that, I'd like to climb to the top of this dune and see what's on the other side. I won't go out of sight.'

And with that, and calling to Lemmy to follow him, Jet started climbing up the slope. Fifteen minutes later I could see the minute figures of him and Lemmy silhouetted against the sky. We were, of course, still in radio contact and I could hear every word that Lemmy and Jet were saying. So could Mitch, but he was so busy tinkering with the tractor's motor that I doubt if he even noticed.

Suddenly I heard Jet's voice in my ear. 'Good heavens!'

'What is it, Jet?' I asked. 'What can you see?'

'The other side of the hill leads down to a valley, a great, wide valley, and it's full of plants like giant rhubarb.'

'Rhubarb plants?' I exclaimed incredulously.

'This must be one of the canals,' said Jet excitedly. 'Did you hear that, Doc?' he called.

'Yes, Jet. I heard it.'

'It must be at least fifteen miles wide and… oh, my goodness!'

'What is it, Jet?'

'Right in the centre of that valley is a great, colossal, pyramid!'

Chapter 13

My first impulse was to go running up the dune to make sure that Jet wasn't seeing things. But he announced that he was already on his way back. When he and Lemmy reached us Jet was so excited he could hardly speak.

'A great pyramid?' I asked.

'Yes, Doc, and just as soon as Mitch has got that motor repaired we'll all go up there and take a look.'

It wasn't long before we were on the move once more. I must admit my heart was pounding as we climbed to the top of the dune where we came to a halt. Below us, as Jet had said, was one of the 'canals' of Mars. So far as I could estimate it was some fifteen miles in width and it stretched from east to west in a straight line. In the middle of the canal, almost directly in front of us, was a pyramid. It was about a mile square and rose in a series of huge steps or terraces each about fifty feet high.

The valley was filled with curious red and blue plants which were, as Jet had said, rather like sticks of rhubarb with a huge single leaf at the top of each stem. They were about six feet in height and the leaves were as big as umbrellas. The plants grew quite close together, not more than two feet separating one from another and the sticks were, I should think, about four inches in diameter.

The leaves of the plants overlapped and, looking down on them, as we were from the sand dune, they seemed to form a solid blue carpet on which one could have walked. 'How tough do you think those plants are, Doc?' Jet asked me. 'If we drove the trucks at them, do you think we could plough a way through?'

124

'I don't see why not,' I said. 'We could try, anyway.'

'How about the soil?' asked Lemmy anxiously. 'Is it firm, boggy or what?'

'We'll soon find out,' said Jet. 'Come on, switch on the motors and let's go.'

Slowly and cautiously we descended towards the rhubarb jungle. When we were nearly up to the plants we reduced speed to two miles an hour. I held my breath as we got closer. I saw Jet grit his teeth and compress his lips as we drove straight into the jungle. We didn't feel a thing. There was no bump, no resistance. We sailed smoothly on, the rhubarb bending downwards before us like aspens before a bulldozer.

Jet breathed a sigh of relief. 'Well, it looks as though we're going to get through, Doc,' he said. 'We'll increase speed to five miles an hour maximum.'

The pitch of the motor rose as Jet accelerated.

It took us an hour to reach the base of the pyramid and, once there, we halted the trucks alongside its lower wall and Mitch and Jet put on their suits and went outside. Pushing their way through the 'rhubarb' was apparently an easy matter. All they had to do was to bend them to one side. In fact, if they bent them too hard the stems snapped. Of course, it was difficult for Lemmy and I to see what was going on, but we had a running commentary on the exploration.

'Well, this wall is solid enough, Doc,' I heard Jet say.

'What's it made of?' I asked him.

'It's difficult to tell.'

'Is it of a brick formation?'

'If it is, then it must be covered with some kind of plaster. The surface is quite smooth.'

'Is there a way into it or through it?'

'Not that we can see, Doc. But we'll walk right round the base. There may be an entrance at one of the other sides.'

'You don't intend to leave Doc and me sitting here alone in the trucks, do you, Jet?' came Lemmy's voice.

'No Lemmy. You and Doc follow us round. Drive at a walking pace.'

'Wouldn't it be better if you rode in the trucks? You can't go hacking your way through rhubarb all around this city.'

'We don't have to,' said Jet. 'There's a path some three feet wide runs the whole length of the wall.'

'All right, Lemmy,' I said, 'get going. I'll fall in behind you.' And off we went.

It was quite easy to keep level with Jet and Mitch because occasionally we got glimpses of them through the vegetation. It took them nearly twelve minutes to walk the length of one wall.

We were just about to turn the corner and start up the next side when Mitch gave an excited cry and shouted: 'Hey, Jet. Look at this – on the ground.'

I heard Jet exclaim: 'You sure it's not yours?'

'No, Jet. Look – mine's still attached to my belt.'

I couldn't stand to wait until they chose to tell me what they had found and so I asked them.

'A safety line, Doc,' replied Jet. 'Exactly the same as we wear.'

'It must have been dropped by one of the crew of Number Two,' said Mitch; 'either accidentally or as a sign to us.'

'They must be here, then,' I observed.

'If they are,' said Lemmy, 'why don't they show themselves?'

'I don't know,' said Jet. 'Perhaps they can't. We must find a way into this place. Let's keep going. If there's no kind of opening to be found when we've walked right round it, we'll think up some way of scaling the wall.'

We had hardly gone a farther fifty yards when Jet called a halt. 'All right, Lemmy and Doc,' he said. 'Stop the trucks, put on your suits and come out.'

'Have you found something else, Jet?' I asked him.

'I'll say we have; right here, near the corner wall. A flight of steps, leading up to the bottom terrace.'

It took me next to no time to put on my suit and join Lemmy, Mitch and Jet outside. The stairway was very narrow, very straight and sloped at an angle of about 45 degrees. These steps were worn, as though they had been used by countless generations of people. 'Whoever they were,' said Lemmy, when I mentioned the fact, 'they must have got fed up with this place and left. Otherwise we would have seen some sign of them by now, wouldn't we?'

'Maybe,' said Jet, 'or maybe they're keeping out of sight purposely.'

We reached the top of the terrace and walked the whole length of it. It was at least a hundred feet wide and through the cracks in its floor a few rather stunted plants were growing. To one side was the drop down into the jungle, to the other was another wall similar to the one we now walked along. But there was no entrance into it as far as we could see. We walked to the spot above where Jet and Mitch had found the safety line but could see nothing that gave us any clue as to why it had been dropped or by whom. 'Well, there's nothing here,' said Jet at last; 'but maybe there's another flight of steps that will lead up to the next level.'

'And what about our trucks?' asked Lemmy. 'Are we going to leave them down there in that rhubarb jungle with nobody to look after them?'

'That's a point,' said Mitch thoughtfully. 'Maybe we haven't seen anybody around but that doesn't mean that there is nobody.'

Jet agreed. 'One of us had better keep an eye on them whilst the rest of us continue the exploration. Lemmy, you'd better stay.'

'Me?' protested Lemmy, a tone of apprehension in his voice.

'If anything happens or if you see anything, just call us up. And, if necessary, we'll come back.'

'You going to walk right round the terrace then?'

'Yes.'

'All right, if you say so. I'll start heading back to the trucks.'

'No need to go right down to them,' said Jet as we separated. Wait at the head of the steps and we'll pick you up there or give you directions on how to reach us if I want you to join us.'

'Yes mate,' said Lemmy miserably. He didn't like the idea at all.

We walked along the next terrace which lay, of course, at right angles to the one on which we had left Lemmy. We had just turned onto the third wall when we heard Frank Rogers calling. 'We're now approaching the position Jet gave us and should be passing over you in a few minutes from now,' Frank was saying.

'Right, Frank boy,' replied the radio operator. He seemed much more cheerful now he had something to do. 'The place we call the city is right smack in the middle of the canal. Have a good look round. You might see something that we can't.'

'We'll do our best,' came back the pilot's voice. 'We'll be travelling pretty fast. But we'll take some photographs, too.'

'I'll remember to smile when you come by.'

Frank laughed and signed off. Lemmy called us and asked where we were. We told him. Soon we would be halfway round the pyramid and then every step we took would bring us closer to him.

He seemed quite cheered at the prospect. 'But don't leave it too long, Jet boy,' he said. 'I get lonely standing here with nothing but a flight of steps and thousands of sticks of rhubarb for company. And another thing...' He stopped and we all looked up into the sky. We could hear Frank's ship approaching. A few seconds later it had flashed over our heads, like a great dark bird.

'Well, that was Frank,' said Lemmy, 'and what a racket he kicked up, too. Let's hope he got some good pictures.'

'I had no idea, Jet,' I said, 'that the ships could make such a noise in this thin atmosphere.'

'Noise? Yes, I can hear the noise, Doc.' It was Lemmy's voice. He sounded a little scared.

'Hullo, Lemmy,' I said, 'what was that?'

'That noise. Can't you hear it?'

'Lemmy,' said Jet, 'we were talking about the noise of the ship. What other noise can you hear?'

'I'll tell you, Jet,' he replied, sounding quite panicky now, 'I can hear a noise. It sounds like it's right in my head...' As Lemmy's voice tailed off, he gave what sounded like a long yawn.

'Lemmy,' said Jet firmly, 'do you hear me?'

If he did, Lemmy ignored him. Instead he said: 'Oh, what wouldn't I give to have forty winks right now? I'm so tired.'

'Lemmy, what's the matter with you? Answer me,' demanded Jet. 'You're supposed to be on watch, you can't go to sleep.'

'Of course I can sleep,' said Lemmy. 'Didn't you hear that fellow just tell me so?'

'Lemmy, for heaven's sake, pull yourself together. Hullo – hullo...'

But Lemmy wasn't answering. We all called him in turn but no reply came.

We half-walked and half-ran back towards where we had left Lemmy. I don't think we could have gone any faster, for running in a space suit is virtually impossible. As we ran we occasionally heard Lemmy speak, as though he were holding a conversation with someone.

It was twenty minutes before we reached the top of the flight of steps where we had left the radio operator. And all that time we were calling Lemmy's name, for we could still hear him talking. But he appeared not to hear us. 'All right,' he was saying, 'but it's only because I'm tired. I wouldn't do a thing like this normally.'

Lemmy's present behaviour reminded me of how Jet had been the night Whitaker died. I had wondered what would have happened to Jet if I hadn't woke him when I did. I was convinced then that it was the proximity of Whitaker that had affected Jet. Was there someone near Lemmy now who was making him behave in the same way?

As though in answer to my thoughts we suddenly heard Lemmy calling for help, his voice rising almost to a scream. 'Hold on Lemmy. We're coming!' I cried. But no reply came from the operator, not even the nonsensical chatter of what had sounded so like a one-sided conversation.

After what seemed an eternity we arrived back at the steps but there was no sign of the radio operator. We ran along the terrace on which we had left him and then, realising the futility of that, returned to the steps. While Jet descended them in case Lemmy had, after all, returned to the trucks, Mitch and I peered through the leaves of the jungle below us in the hope of detecting some movement which might show us that Lemmy was passing through it. But there was nothing. Not a breath of wind disturbed the atmosphere and the leaves lay silent and still as though made of wax.

'He's not down here,' came Jet's voice. 'He's not in either of the trucks. He must still be up on the pyramid somewhere. Wait for me,' and a few minutes later Jet came hurrying up the narrow stairway to where we were standing.

'Where on earth has he got to?' I asked. 'He couldn't have gone very far away in the short time that we left him.'

'And what was happening that made him carry on like that?' asked Jet. 'We've got to find him.'

'Sure we have,' said Mitch, 'but where do we start looking? If he's still walking about, we might go chasing each other round and round this terrace all night.'

'You go back the way we came, Mitch,' said Jet. 'Doc and I go round the other way. Then if Lemmy is anywhere on this level, we're bound to meet him.'

'Right,' said Mitch, and with that he turned his back on us and began to retrace his steps the way we had come, while Jet and I started off along the top of one of the walls we had not yet explored.

'He must be up here somewhere,' said Jet anxiously as we hurried along.

'Or even higher up, Jet,' I suggested.

'But how could he get up there?'

'There was a way up from ground level to this far. I suppose we can reasonably expect a way to lead up higher.'

We reached the far corner without seeing any sort of opening. Before turning we looked back the way we had come in case Lemmy should have reappeared, but the terrace was empty. We turned the corner onto the terrace we had not yet seen. We hadn't gone fifty yards along it before we came across another flight of stairs, identical to the ones which led up from the ground.

'There, what did I tell you?' I said almost triumphantly. 'He must have come up this way.'

'But why?' asked Jet. 'He was ordered to keep an eye on the trucks, and Lemmy's not one to leave his post.'

'I don't think he was disobeying orders, Jet,' I said.

'What? How do you mean?'

'I believe he was obeying someone else's orders. Just as Whitaker was.'

'Oh, nonsense, Doc. If anybody was giving him orders they must have done it by radio and we would have heard them, too, wouldn't we?'

'Yes, that is a point,' I agreed.

We began the ascent of the narrow stairway. When we reached the upper terrace we found it hardly any different from the one we had just left. We looked to the right and then to the left, but could see only the ubiquitous rhubarb plants. 'Well,' said Jet, 'there's certainly nothing along here. Let's go back and look along the other one.'

Some presentiment of danger made us hurry to the corner. Jet was slightly in the lead and as he turned it he gave a cry. When I reached his side I could see why. About fifty yards ahead of us, lying close to the wall, was Lemmy. He was flat on his back and bending over him was a man, loosening the catch of Lemmy's helmet and about to take it off.

'Hey, what the hell do you think you're doing?' cried Jet, oblivious of the fact that as the man was wearing no space suit and therefore was not in radio contact with us, he could not possibly hear what Jet was saying. And yet, at his cry, the man looked up, saw us running towards him and took to his heels. 'Get after him, Doc, for heaven's sake,' yelled Jet. I'll attend to Lemmy.'

I did my best, but in my clumsy clothing I was no match for the man who was wearing nothing but what appeared to me to be a crew suit. I soon gave up the chase and, as I did so, the man turned and looked at me. My heart gave a jump. I recognised him at once as McLean, missing pilot of Number Two. But it wasn't the fact that I knew him that filled me with horror – it was the realisation that McLean, although a human being like myself, was walking and breathing in the Martian atmosphere, without breathing apparatus of any kind.

Chapter 14

Fortunately we had arrived in time to prevent Lemmy's helmet from actually being removed and, so far as breathing was concerned, he was quite safe. Jet snapped the catch back into place and between us we lifted the radio operator, who was unconscious, and carried him along the terrace and back down the steps towards the truck. On the way Jet called Mitch and told him to meet us back at the land fleet.

As it turned out, Jet and I were first to arrive. We let ourselves into the truck by the remote control buttons and, after passing through the airlock, removed our and Lemmy's helmets and suits. 'Mitch must have been a lot farther away than we thought,' I said, as we laid the still unconscious form of Lemmy on the bunk.

'Yes,' said Jet thoughtfully, and he went across to the radio and called up the engineer. Mitch replied immediately. 'Hullo, Jet,' he said, 'I'm still on the terrace, but I'll be with you in a couple of shakes.'

'OK. You can let yourself in, can't you?'

'Sure I can. Don't worry about me.'

I made a thorough examination of Lemmy. He was unconscious, his breathing was very shallow and his temperature sub-normal; symptoms by now all too familiar to me, although I could still find no explanation for them. 'What has happened to him, Doc?' asked Jet when I gave him my report.

'Search me,' I replied, 'but just before we lost contact with him he mentioned hearing a peculiar noise – just as you did when we landed, and as the pilot of Freighter Number Two did before she crashed. But McLean also said he saw a light.'

'Yes,' said Jet quickly, 'McLean. What on earth was he doing up there on the terrace, Doc? And how did he manage to breathe when he wasn't wearing a helmet? All our tests of the Martian atmosphere have proved beyond doubt that it is impossible for a human being to live in it – the oxygen content is too low.'

'That doesn't mean it can't support any kind of life,' I reminded him. 'Those rhubarb plants outside seem to thrive very well.'

'Yes, Doc, but they're plants. Even on Earth plants grow at altitudes almost too high for human beings to live comfortably.'

'Then the only possible explanation is that somehow, somewhere, McLean's body has been conditioned to live in the Martian atmosphere. To do so, his body temperature must be extremely low; and here we find Lemmy, with McLean bending over him, and Lemmy's body temperature is extremely low, too. And so was Whitaker's – and yours, Jet, after we crash landed. It's becoming quite clear to me now,' I went on. 'Whitaker was a man already under some very powerful influence that somehow contrived to get him into one of our ships in the hope that he would wreck the whole project. That's why there was no record of his having been to the Astronautical College.'

'But Whitaker was a normal human being, Doc.'

'No – not normal, Jet. No man who's been missing for forty-seven years and then turns up as a member of our space fleet, looking as young as he did in 1924, is normal. It's my belief that the reason you, Lemmy and Rogers had nightmares when Whitaker was around was that he could more or less hypnotise any member of the crew with whom he came in contact. That's what he must have done with Peterson; that's how he was able to make off with one of our ships.'

'Well, that sounds plausible enough, Doc. But where had Whitaker been during the forty-seven years he was missing?'

'Up here, on Mars.'

'What?'

'Yes. Walking around, breathing the Martian atmosphere just as McLean is doing now.'

'You mean McLean has already been 'conditioned', as you call it – become another Whitaker? And that Lemmy, if we hadn't found him in time, would…?'

'Yes. At least, that's how it seems to me.'

'Well,' went on Jet, 'let's assume that is true; but how did Whitaker get up here?'

'He was kidnapped and brought here.'

'In 1924 – when space travel was no more than a wild dream?'

'The ship that visited the wreck of Number Two and carried off her crew was no wild dream.'

'You mean it was a space ship, capable of reaching Earth?'

'I don't know,' I said a little impatiently, 'all I do know is that Mars is a planet at least as old as the Earth, maybe millions of year older. If it has no animal life now, it almost certainly did once. How else can you account for that city out there? If you ask me, that place is thousands of years old, built when life on Earth was in its early stages of evolution.'

'You mean,' said Jet, almost sarcastically, 'that there were advanced civilisations up here? Probably still are?'

'Mars is a dying planet, Jet,' I reminded him. 'If there ever were creatures up here even remotely like human beings who could think, reason and build, they must have long since died out, or most of them. But any that are left must have the advantage of millions of years of civilization behind them. And who knows what that could enable them to do?'

There was a groan from the bunk. Jet turned towards Lemmy. 'He's coming round, Doc,' he said.

'He'll feel very cold when he does. Perhaps you'd better make him a hot drink.'

By the time Jet returned with the tea, which was Lemmy's favourite beverage, it was obvious that the Cockney was slowly but surely recovering. 'Well Jet,' I greeted him, 'I don't think it's going to be long before Lemmy is talking to us again, which is pretty encouraging. It's less than half an hour since we brought him in.'

'What!' exclaimed Jet. 'Half an hour? Then where's Mitch? He said he would be with us in just a few minutes.'

I had forgotten all about the engineer. 'Call him up, Jet, for heaven's sake.'

Jet went over to the radio, but there was no reply from Mitch, although Jet called him for fully five minutes. Jet hesitated a moment then walked resolutely towards the locker where his space suit was stowed.

'What are you going to do?' I asked him.

'I must go out there,' he replied, 'and look for him.'

'No, Jet – wait,' I began.

'I haven't time to wait, Doc. Anything might have happened to him. He might already be in a far worse position than Lemmy was.'

At this point Lemmy spoke his first intelligible words since we found him. They were: 'Lokshen soup and bagels.'

'Eh?' said Jet coming over to where Lemmy and I were. 'What did he say?'

'He's still delirious,' I said.

'Then you look after him, I'll put my suit on and get ready to go out.'

'No, Jet. I'm sure Lemmy'll be OK once he wakes up. Then we can leave him here while you and I go and look for Mitch. If you go out alone, how do you know that you'll come back?'

'I'll keep in radio contact. You don't have to worry. You'll know that I'm OK.'

'Lemmy was in radio contact with us, wasn't he? But he wasn't OK and Mitch was supposed to be in contact, too, but…'

I was interrupted by Lemmy calling: 'Let go! Let go! I won't take it off. I shall die! Let go of my arm, do you hear? Let go, you old…' Lemmy was waving and kicking his arms about, just as Jet had done the night Whitaker died. I tried to hold him down but had to yell for Jet to come and help me.

With two of us trying to restrain him, Lemmy became more vehement than ever. 'Let go of me – let go!' he yelled.

'He's awake, Doc,' said Jet in surprise. 'His eyes are open.' I could see they were, but Lemmy didn't seem to recognise either of us and he fought harder than ever. 'Let go of me, do you hear?' he kept saying. Then: 'My helmet – where's my helmet? You give me back my helmet. I shall suffocate…'

'You don't want your helmet, Lemmy,' Jet said. 'You're in the living quarters. You don't need your helmet.'

Suddenly Lemmy stopped struggling. He looked first at Jet and then at me, and said: 'Oh – Jet – and Doc. I thought you were Mr Vanberg.'

'Who?' I asked.

'Vanberg. The fellow who lived upstairs.'

'Lemmy,' I said, reaching for the tea, 'drink this. It's nice and hot and it'll do you good.'

'I can do with it,' he replied with a little shudder. 'I'm all cold inside. I need something to warm me. What wouldn't I give for a nice bowl of lokshen soup right now!'

'Tea is all we have that's hot, Lemmy. Now drink it.'

'Yeah,' said the Cockney, taking the flask from my hand. 'Ta.' He took a few sips and then said: 'Where am I, did you say?'

'In one of the trucks, in the caravan.'

'That's funny,' said the radio operator. 'I thought I was back in London, just off the Commercial Road.'

'You must have had a bad dream, Lemmy,' I suggested.

'No, Doc – it was no dream. It was real. So clear in every detail. It was Sunday morning and, as I said, I was back home in London, in the market. It was crowded with people, as it always is on Sundays, but I couldn't talk to them. They couldn't hear me. I don't think they could even see me. But a voice from nowhere kept talking to me, telling me to go on to

Bernstein's where I could get some soup and bagels and some smoltz – which I'm very fond of.'

'But if you were dressed up in your space suit, how could you have eaten it?' queried Jet.

'That's what I'm telling you, mate; this voice kept telling me to take my helmet off. But I wouldn't.'

'That voice you heard – did you recognise it? Or see the person it belonged to?'

'No, Jet, I didn't see him, but the voice was familiar all right.'

'Whose was it, Lemmy? Think – think hard.'

'Well, if it was anybody's at all, I'd say it was McLean's. But it wasn't his normal voice, if you know what I mean. He sounded almost like Whitaker.'

'McLean's!' said Jet in triumph. 'That's what I thought you'd say.'

'But how could it be McLean's? We haven't seen him since Number Two crashed.'

'Look,' interrupted Jet, 'there's some strange power at work here. You were induced to think you were home, where you'd been happy. Somewhere where you felt safe and everything was normal. And then, having been hypnotised into this state, somebody – someone using McLean's voice maybe – tried to get you to remove your helmet.'

'But what for?'

'I can't be sure, Lemmy. But I have a good idea. You don't know it, but while you were under that illusion you somehow found your way up to the next terrace. And that's where we found you – with someone who looked very much like McLean bending over you and about to unfasten your helmet and take it off.'

Lemmy's startled comment was interrupted by Jet who, still consumed with anxiety for Mitch, said to me: 'Let's go.'

'Go? Where are you going?' Lemmy asked anxiously.

'Mitch should have been back nearly an hour ago,' said Jet, 'but he hasn't returned. We must go out and look for him. Doc insists it's safer for two of us to go, which means you'll have to remain here.'

'But what if that noise comes back?' exclaimed Lemmy. 'What if it starts hypnotising me again?'

'You must fight it as you fought against taking off your helmet in your dream. When we're gone, break the airlock circuit so that the door cannot be opened from the outside. And open it to nobody but us or Mitch, if he should come back before us. We'll keep in constant radio contact.'

'And what if anything happens to you?' Lemmy asked.

'We're hoping it won't. Now we're aware of what can happen, maybe we can fight it, too. All right, Doc. Put on your suit and we'll go.'

What had happened to Mitch? We discovered later that he, too, had been affected by the same mysterious hypnotic power from which we had only just succeeded in rescuing Lemmy.

Against his will the Australian was led away from the terrace of the pyramid and, when he recovered his senses, it was to find himself out on the dunes of the desert. There was no sign of the city, the canal, the jungle, the trucks; no sign of Jet, Lemmy or me, either. No sign of any kind of life. But he was still dressed in his suit and so decided, quite naturally, to try and contact us by radio. He began to call. 'Hullo – hullo, Jet, hullo, hullo…' And in his receiver he heard a reply. 'Hullo, there.' But it was not the voice of Jet.

Mitch looked across to the next dune and saw the figure of a man. He was dressed in high boots, trousers, a flannel shirt and an Australian bush hat.

'Where did you spring from?' the engineer said, startled.

'I might ask you that,' said the strange figure. 'Come on over. I've got a fire going and the billy's on the boil. You'd like a cup of tea, wouldn't you?'

'Yeah,' said Mitch, 'I'd like it fine.'

'Come on then.'

Mitch made his way over to the man who took him down into a small valley where a fire was burning. Stretched out in front of it were two or three blankets and nearby lay a tucker bag. 'Sit down, cobber,' said the stranger. 'Make yourself at home.'

Mitch thanked him and sat down. It was almost dark; deep twilight, and the fire lit up the leathery face of the stranger with a bright orange glow.

Suddenly from the distance came a mysterious, blood-curdling wail. Mitch started. 'What's that?' he asked.

'Dingoes,' said the man calmly. 'They're starting up early tonight. You hunting scalps?'

'Eh?'

'Dingo scalps for the Government bounty. I've got a swag bag full of 'em.'

'No, I'm not hunting dingoes,' said Mitch. 'I'm lost, I need help.'

'Where do you have to get to?'

'The city. I must get back.'

The stranger laughed. 'City!' he repeated derisively. 'The nearest settlement to here is Oodnadatta – two hundred miles to the south. And city is a fancy name for that place. But, apart from it, there's no city within five hundred miles of here, unless you count Marugee, and that's in ruins, anyway.'

'Is it in a valley?' asked Mitch eagerly; 'a long, wide, valley?'

'That's the place.'

'How far is it?'

'Oh, a couple of miles.'

'Then show me the way to go – the others will be looking for me,' said Mitch anxiously.

'Well if you insist,' replied the stranger, 'but, if you ask me, you don't seem in a fit state to be walking any place.'

In spite of his opinion, the stranger stood up and, with Mitch following, led the way towards the valley. They reached it in about twenty minutes and, from the hill top, Mitch looked down on Marugee. 'That isn't the place,' he said, his voice breaking with disappointment.

'You said a ruined city, in a valley, didn't you?'

'Yes, but the one I'm looking for is at least a mile square and built up in steps like a great pyramid. And the valley is full of plants – like rhubarb. You brought me to the wrong place.'

'There's no other place to take you. Now, you'd better come on back to my camp and take a rest. It'll be dark directly, and you'll be getting cold.'

Mitch shivered. 'But the city,' he said, 'I must find the city.'

The stranger took his arm and led him down the slope and back towards the camp. 'You can find it tomorrow,' he said with finality.

When they got back, the stranger ordered Mitch to sit down and then put a blanket round his shoulders. 'There's Matilda in the bag,' he said conversationally. 'Tastes pretty good roasted over the red ashes. Would you like a bite?'

'No thanks,' said Mitch, 'just the tea. That's all I need.'

The stranger stirred up the embers of the fire. 'What are you doing out here? What's your line?'

'Astronautics,' said Mitch. 'I'm an engineer.'

'Astro-what-ics?'

'Astronautics. I travel among the stars.'

The stranger eyed Mitch thoughtfully for a moment, and then said: 'I see what you mean. Thirty-two years ago I felt much the same way myself. That's when I came out here to live in the desert, with only the dingoes and stars for company. When did you decide to leave it all behind?'

'Leave what behind?'

'The noise, the fight, the jungle – the grind of city life.'

'We took off last April.'

'Wasn't easy, was it? Something deep inside you said you should resist the desire and go back. But you won't regret it. Look at me; thirty years I've been tramping over this desert, and still as young and fresh as when I started out. You wouldn't think I was sixty-two, would you?'

Mitch certainly didn't think so. 'You don't look a day over thirty,' he said.

'Exactly. This is the place to keep you young. Out here with the sand, the mulga, the eucalyptus, the dingoes and the stars. What more could a man want?' As if in answer the dingoes started up their mournful chorus again, but this time Mitch, listening to them, thought he could detect the voice of Jet calling to him.

'Hey, listen,' he cried, jumping up excitedly, 'did you hear that? That was Jet.'

'Sit down,' said the stranger calmly. 'It was the dingoes. There's nobody here but you, me and the dingoes. Now, in that bag there's a box of tea. Pass it out, will you?'

Mitch fumbled awkwardly into the bag. 'Is this it?' he asked.

'Thanks. How do you like it? Strong?'

'Look,' said Mitch desperately, 'before we go any further I'd like to ask you a few questions.'

The stranger ignored him – and the cries of the dingoes increased. 'Do you like plenty of sugar?'

'Never mind the sugar,' said Mitch angrily. 'I'm talking to you.'

'Sorry I've got no fresh milk.'

'What's the matter with you?' screamed Mitch. 'Can't you even listen to what I'm saying?'

'Sit down, Mitch,' said the stranger firmly. 'Sit down and save your breath.'

Mitch sat down suddenly. 'Sit down, Mitch?' he repeated, fear clearly discernible in his voice. 'How do you know my name? And what are you doing here anyway? What's happened to me? Where is this place?'

'This is the Northern Territory,' said the stranger deliberately.

'Northern Territory. Where?'

'Australia. Where else?'

'Australia! On Earth?'

'Where the heck did you think it was? On Mars?'

Mitch was really scared now. 'But this is Mars, isn't it?' he pleaded. 'Isn't this the Red Planet?'

'Yes – and I'm a kangaroo.'

'What are you trying to do? Drive me crazy?' Mitch said, his voice rising hysterically.

'Me? Drive you crazy? You walked into my camp, two hundred miles from the nearest town, without so much as a billy to brew your tea, tell me you're lost, and that you live in a pyramid and can't find your way home.'

Mitch went to great lengths to tell the dingo-hunter who he was. 'My name is Stephen Mitchell,' he said hesitantly, struggling to convince himself as he spoke. 'I'm an astronautical engineer. Seven months ago I left the Moon on an expedition to Mars. A week ago I landed on the southern ice cap and, with three other members of the ship's crew, began to explore this planet. And now I find myself here and you tell me this place is Australia – back on Earth.'

The stranger took a step towards Mitch and, looking down at him, his face grim, said: 'Look, Mitch, it's my opinion that you've spent too long in the sun. Not many miles from here there's a cattle station run by a farmer and his wife. Tomorrow I'll take you there and they'll call up the flying doctor and get him to look you over. Now, lie down and take it easy. Or do I have to put you to sleep with the butt of this rifle?' He stopped and picked up the weapon from the ground as he spoke.

Mitch, now more than half convinced that he was mad, was immediately subdued. 'No,' he said softly, 'there's no need for that. Maybe I am the crazy one.'

'The swag bag's unrolled,' said the stranger. 'Lie down on it.' Mitch obeyed him without a murmur. 'That's it,' said the stranger. 'Now go to sleep – and don't give me any more trouble.'

Once again the weird, compelling music started up in Mitch's head. But this time he made no attempt to resist it. He felt it was beyond his power to do so. He let it take hold of him and lull him into a deep sleep. As he gradually lapsed into unconsciousness he could hear the stranger still talking, his voice seeming to come from a long way off and mixing with the eerie howls of the dingoes. 'Tell yourself you're not going to give me any more trouble,' he was saying. 'Understand?'

'Yeah,' said Mitch wearily.

'And that you'll do exactly as I tell you from now on.'

'Yeah, yeah – anything you say,' said the engineer.

'Good on yer.'

'I feel so tired – awful tired.'

'Then go to sleep. And remember, tomorrow everything will be all right.'

The dingoes howled even louder. It seemed to Mitch that they completely encircled the camp; hundreds of them, each calling his blood-curdling wail to a moonless sky. And through it all came the voice of the dingo-hunter saying: 'Tomorrow everything will be all right, tomorrow everything will be all...'

And Mitch knew no more. Everything went black.

Chapter 15

In the meantime, unaware of what had befallen Mitch, Jet and I searched every wall of both terraces but there was no sign of our engineer. We were getting desperately worried when we received a call from Lemmy, back in the truck, to say that Mitch had at last been sighted.

'Where is he?' asked Jet eagerly.

'Just walking along the path that runs along the lowest wall,' replied Lemmy.

'Have you spoken to him yet?'

'No, mate,' said Lemmy, 'but if his radio's working he must have heard me call you. Half a mo, I'll try him now. Hullo, Mitch,' we heard Lemmy say, 'are you receiving me? Hullo…' He went on calling for a while then finally gave it up and said: 'It's no good, Jet. He doesn't seem to hear me.'

'Oh. How far away is he?'

'Only about a couple of hundred yards. Hey – wait a minute…'

'What is it, Lemmy?'

'He's waving his arms about, like he was a tick-tack man at the dogs. Oh blimey – and no wonder.' The tone of Lemmy's voice changed to one of relief. 'He's trying to tell me his radio is out of action. I'd better go back to the main cabin, Jet, and get ready to let him in.'

'Very well,' replied the Captain. 'Doc and I will get back as quickly as we can.'

Lemmy had left the truck's transmitter on and, as we made our way along the terrace, we could hear him muttering to himself as he moved about the cabin. Quite suddenly we heard a hard metallic knocking. 'What's all that banging?' Jet asked.

145

'That's Mitch knocking at the door,' replied Lemmy. 'He doesn't realise he can let himself in – he must think the circuit's still broken. I'd better open up for him, and then...' Lemmy's speech was interrupted by the sound of the main door circuit coming alive. 'Oh, he's doing it himself after all,' went on the radio operator.

Then we heard the airlock mechanism working. 'Well, he's about in,' said Lemmy cheerfully. 'Just coming through the airlock. And here he is.' Lemmy's voice was warm and sympathetic. 'Hullo, Mitch,' we heard him say, 'where have you been all this time? You've had us worried.'

'Hullo, Lemmy,' came the reply. Jet and I both stopped dead in our tracks. The voice that answered Lemmy did not belong to Mitch.

There was a pause and then we heard the same flat voice say: 'What's the matter, Lemmy? Surprised to see me?'

And Lemmy's frightened reply: 'You? Oh, no!' Then there was a click as though somebody had turned off the truck's transmitter.

'That wasn't Mitch,' said Jet in alarm; 'that was the voice of McLean! Come on, Doc.' We reached the steps in about ten minutes and quickly descended them to the rhubarb jungle below. We crashed our way through the plants and reached the door of the truck to find, as we had feared, that it was tightly closed. We called Lemmy two or three times but got no reply.

Under normal circumstances, it was possible to open the truck by the remote control set in the outer hull. However, it would not operate if the inner airlock door was not closed and the chamber exhausted. This must have been the case now for, no matter how many times Jet and I tried the outer control, we could not get the mechanism to function. We were absolutely helpless.

While Jet remained at the door, still trying to get the control to open it, I ran round the truck two or three times and banged on it in odd places, futilely calling to Lemmy to let us in.

Then came an excited cry from Jet. 'Doc,' he called. 'I can hear the airlock exhausting. Somebody's coming out.' I hurried round to where Jet was waiting and arrived just in time to see the main door opening. But nobody came out, so we stepped inside, quickly closed the door after us and waited impatiently until the air pressure within the lock equalled that inside the truck. Then we opened the inner door.

The cabin looked as though a tornado had hit it. Lying on the floor, face down, was the suited figure of McLean. His helmet has been removed and was alongside him. Near the control panel, apparently unconscious, was Lemmy, his face all bloody. We ran over to him immediately and Jet called his name.

Lemmy opened his eyes and looked up into the Captain's face. 'Oh, hello, Jet,' he said weakly. 'You made it. Thank goodness for that.'

'What happened, Lemmy?' Jet asked. 'You're in a terrible mess.'

'I've been in a bit of a rough house, mate. With McLean. I hit him over the head. I had to. He would have killed me otherwise.'

By now I had gone over to the unconscious figure and turned him over on his back. 'It's McLean all right,' I announced, 'and you certainly gave him a pasting, Lemmy.'

'Have I hurt him much, Doc?' asked Lemmy, clambering to his feet and coming to where I was bending over the still form on the floor.

'I don't know yet,' I said. 'Let me get my suit off and I'll take a look at him.'

'And how about you, Lemmy?' asked Jet. 'How do you feel?'

'Just a bit dizzy, mate, that's all.'

'All right. Go and lie down on one of the beds. As soon as I'm free of this diving suit I'll clean up your face.'

While Jet tended Lemmy's wounds and I attended to McLean, we learned the full story of what had happened. When Lemmy saw the suited figure walking along the path, he immediately concluded that it must be Mitch. This was understandable as it is not easy to recognise anybody from a distance when he is in a space suit. However, he soon learned who it really was when McLean let himself through the airlock, removed his helmet and, standing between the door and Lemmy, faced the radio operator.

At first Lemmy was almost pleased to see him and asked where the rest of the crew of the Number Two were. 'Evans was killed in the crash, Lemmy,' said McLean in a curiously flat voice, not unlike Whitaker's.

'And the others?'

'They are quite safe.'

'But where are they?'

'I will take you to them,' said McLean. 'Put on your suit, Lemmy, and come with me.'

But Lemmy, as he put it, wasn't having any. 'Oh no,' he said, 'we'll see what Jet has to say first. He gives the orders around here.'

'Orders must be obeyed without question at all times,' said McLean. 'Put on your suit and come with me.'

'You take off your suit,' said Lemmy, 'and wait till Jet gets here. Now stand away from that radio, I want to talk to him.' But McLean made no move.

'Get away from that radio, McLean,' ordered Lemmy. 'If you are McLean. Because, although you look like him, you certainly don't sound like him.'

'None of us are ourselves any more.'

'Well, I don't feel like anybody but myself. Now, are you going to move out of the way or do I have to move you?' McLean did not reply; merely stood watching Lemmy, his arms folded.

'And where's Mitch?' demanded Lemmy. 'What have you done with him?'

'Mitch is quite safe, but he will not be returning. Neither to you, to the Fleet, nor to Earth. Now put your suit on and come with me.'

'Not only am I not coming,' said Lemmy grimly, 'but now you're here, McLean, you're staying. Nobody is leaving this truck unless Jet says so. Here! What are you trying to do?'

Lemmy broke off and stopped dead in his tracks as McLean, staring at him fixedly, moved slowly towards him.

Lemmy brought up his right fist in an uppercut that caught McLean squarely on the jaw. McLean went down, but was soon on his feet again and then the two men locked together in a struggle that almost wrecked the cabin. Lemmy knew that Jet and I must be hurrying towards the truck and that we couldn't get in unless the inner door of the airlock was closed, so he struggled desperately to get to the control. Time after time McLean prevented him till, at last, Lemmy made a supreme effort, broke from McLean's grasp, and snatched a large spanner from where it hung on the wall. McLean rushed at the radio operator but, as he did so, Lemmy brought the spanner down. McLean dropped in his tracks.

McLean lay on the bunk on which I had placed him for nearly an hour. Strangely, in all that time his eyes were open, fixed to a point on the ceiling. He appeared not to be conscious, yet when I called his name, he stirred slightly. I called him a second time and again he stirred. 'McLean,' I said, 'can you hear me?'

His voice came back at once, flat and dull. 'I can hear you.'

'Then why do you lie there?'

'What are your orders?'

'He's not unconscious at all,' said Jet.

'I'm darned sure he isn't,' I replied. 'But he seems to be in some kind of deep hypnotic state.'

'And what does he mean – what are your orders?'

'I don't know, unless whoever sent him to us gave him orders – orders that he has now forgotten. And he just lies there waiting for new ones.'

'Then give him some and see what happens,' suggested Jet.

'McLean,' I said, 'sit up.'

He sat up without hesitation.

'Now lie down.'

He lay back on the bunk again and stared at the ceiling. I looked at McLean thoughtfully. 'It seems to me,' I said slowly, 'that whoever it was that tried to hypnotise Lemmy has hypnotised McLean.'

'And wherever Mitch is,' asked Jet, 'is he in the same state – and able to walk around in the Martian atmosphere and breathe as easily as though he were down on Earth?'

'Almost certainly,' I told him. 'We can no longer doubt that there is some power in this planet that is able to control our bodies almost as completely as our own minds can. But, before they can condition us to survive out there in the Martian atmosphere, they must first of all get us into a deep hypnotic state. But it is a well-known fact that no matter how deeply a subject may be hypnotised, it is extremely difficult to get him to do things he would not normally do. Hence the fight Lemmy put up in his dream.'

'But McLean, Doc – and Whitaker – they…'

'They must have been easy meat mentally,' I interrupted before Jet could get the question out, 'once they were caught. It seems they put up no fight at all. They merely obeyed orders.'

'It seems, then,' said Jet, 'that whoever induces this hypnosis can get our men to do anything they want without even seeing them?'

'I don't know,' I protested.

'But, if it's true, they can keep us or whoever they have in their control for years.'

'In the case of Whitaker,' I reminded him, 'forty-seven years.'

'And how many people are there on this planet, I wonder, living in a dream and not knowing about it?'

'I hate to think but, unless we are very careful, there'll be a few more soon.'

'Us, you mean?'

'Yes, Jet. Unless we can find some way of combating it.'

'But how can we? We don't even know what we're fighting.'

'This much I do know,' I told him, 'there is nobody more difficult to hypnotise than an unwilling subject. If we are all determined to fight this thing, maybe we can render ourselves immune to it. Up to now, everyone who has come under the influence of this telepathic, hypnotic power has had prior warning. In your case, when you blacked out just before we landed here, there was that strange, sleep-inducing sound. McLean heard the same sound just before Number Two crashed. And now look at him. Three days ago he was a normal man – a member of our expedition working for us and with us. Now he isn't in control of his mind. Does nothing unless ordered to.'

'Then what we must find out is who gives him his orders. Who sent him here to get Lemmy to leave this truck and go with him? Where would he have taken Lemmy? And, above all, where's Mitch?'

'Lying there on the bed, Jet, is the only man who might know.'

Jet looked thoughtfully towards where McLean still lay on his back, staring at the ceiling.

'I suggest,' I went on, 'that we keep McLean here until morning at any rate. Then, if he's sufficiently recovered to walk out of this truck, we'll let him – and follow. He may lead us to Mitch.'

Jet agreed and then suggested it was about time we got some sleep – one of us always to remain on watch. But the night was uneventful. By the time the sun was rising we were all awake. While Jet prepared a hasty breakfast, Lemmy took his second turn at watch in the driving cabin and I took another look at McLean.

He seemed in much the same state as the previous night. I watched him for fully five minutes but he didn't move a muscle. Then suddenly he sat up, giving a little groan as he did so. I thought at first that perhaps he was coming out of his hypnotic trance and returning to normal, but when he climbed down from the bunk and began to make his way towards the airlock with the steady, even, almost ghostly tread of a sleepwalker, I realised he was still as much conditioned as ever.

'Where are you going, McLean?' I asked.

He continued walking and did not even look in my direction as he replied: 'My orders are to return to the ship.'

'The orders have been changed,' I told him. 'You are to remain here. Do you understand? You are to remain here.' He stopped, half-turned towards his bunk and then stopped again.

'Sit down at the table and eat,' I commanded. He did so, and mechanically began to consume the food Jet placed before him.

'Well, that seems to have done the trick,' said Jet.

'If it lasts,' I told him.

'How do you mean?'

'There must be a great conflict going on in his mind. Somehow, from somewhere, he's been receiving orders to go back to where he came from – to 'the ship' – wherever that is.'

'Well, it can't be far away,' said Jet, 'Or he wouldn't have attempted to walk to it.'

We had decided that, as soon as we had all eaten, we would follow wherever McLean might lead us, when, a few minutes later, an excited yell from Lemmy sent Jet and I running to him.

'That ship,' said Lemmy, pointing excitedly to the top of the pyramid, 'it's been up there all the time. And now it's pulling out.'

Jet and I followed Lemmy's gaze and, sure enough, poised motionless at the top of the pyramid was the sphere. A few seconds later it was heading, at incredible speed, in a south-westerly direction. 'Now why should it take off just now,' I asked, 'when, in all probability, McLean was about to lead us up there?'

'I should think that's all too clear,' said Jet. 'They've given up waiting for McLean.'

'Well, Jet, what do we do now?' I asked.

'Go after that ship, of course. I'd stake my life on the rest of the crew of Number Two, and Mitch, being in it. Lemmy can drive this truck while you stay here, Doc, and keep an eye on McLean. I'll go into the other one.'

I ordered McLean to his bunk and an hour later we set out, the two lines of trucks crashing their way through the jungle of curious plants. Soon we had climbed out of the valley and were again making our way across the south-western half of the Argyre Desert, the pink miniature dust storms kicked up by the treads of our tractors marking our passage. Before long the strange pyramid city was lost to our sight below the horizon, leaving us completely surrounded by gently undulating sand dunes topped by a huge inverted mauve bowl that was the Martian sky.

We knew our chances of catching up with the spherical ship were slim and our chances of releasing its captives, if Jet was right, even slimmer, but we pressed on, spurred by the realisation that unless we recovered our comrades soon, we might well find them all in the same state as McLean.

Indeed, as I looked down at the inert, unresponsive form in the bunk below me, I could not help wondering if it were not already too late.

Chapter 16

We had been travelling steadily for ten hours and had covered nearly two hundred miles. The terrain was getting slightly more hilly and the sand even pinker but now, instead of the barren desert, small, sparse, prickly plants were growing among the dunes. They were rather like cactus – miniature saguaro. Occasionally, at the front of some of the dunes, we passed clumps of bushes looking very like that species of cacti known in the south-west of America as brittle bush. In fact, the whole terrain was rather like that of the more barren regions of Arizona. We travelled in a straight line towards the south-west. It might have been quicker for us, on occasions, to have gone round the little hills but we purposely climbed them because of the view we obtained from their summits.

The sun was already nearing the horizon when, from the top of one dune, we saw something directly ahead of us. About a mile away was a collection of buildings. They were very simple in construction, consisting of no more than four walls and a flat roof, and to the west of them was a wire fenced-off corral.

Jet, from his truck, had seen them too, and we compared details, over the radio, of what we could make out through our binoculars. 'We've got to get a closer look at that place,' said Jet at last. 'We'll use the dunes as cover and drive as near as we can without being seen. Then we'll approach on foot.'

We got within about a third of a mile of the house before we deemed it necessary to park behind a high dune. Then Lemmy and I put on our suits and, after taking a quick look at

McLean, went outside. 'Is McLean OK?' Jet asked as I walked up to his truck.

'Yes,' I told him. 'I disconnected the airlock in the living quarters. He couldn't possibly get out even if he wanted to – and we can only get in through the driving cabin now.'

It took us fully five minutes to clamber to the top of the dune. Once at the summit we lay down and peered cautiously over the rim towards the 'farm' which lay just below us. We could see now that the pen or corral was full of peculiar animals. They were about half the size of pigs and were dark brown in colour. They had long snouts, like anteaters, and rather wide paws with three horny toes sticking from them. Their long ears flopped down over their foreheads but, whenever they heard a sound, one or both cocked straight up. 'Blimey – what are they?' asked Lemmy. 'I've never seen anything like that in the Zoo.'

'Whatever they are,' I said, 'they prove one thing: that there is, at least, animal life on Mars.'

'And what animals,' said Lemmy. 'Enough to drive a bloke on the wagon for the rest of his life. Do you think they're dangerous?'

I was about to reply when a low cry from Jet froze us all to the spot. 'Hold it – lay still. There's somebody on the other side of the large building.'

'Hadn't we better duck down out of sight?' asked Lemmy.

'No,' said Jet. 'There's less chance of his noticing us if we don't move.' I could see the figure clearly now. I don't quite know why but it came as a great surprise to me to discover he was a normal man, about five foot seven in height, fairly well built and wearing clothes rather like those of the pioneers in American history books. They were, in fact, made of skins, probably the same skins as worn by the animals in the pen. He carried a rifle – quite a modern-looking weapon – in the crook of his arm.

Like McLean, the man wore no space suit nor seemed to need any kind of breathing apparatus. Suddenly he put his hand to his mouth and whistled. A few moments later there came running round from the other side of the house another peculiar beast. It had a flat body and three pairs of legs. Two waving antennae protruded from its forehead.

'Blimey, what's that?' asked Lemmy. 'Looks like an overgrown beetle.'

'But behaves just like a dog,' said Jet. 'Look at the way it follows him.'

It was true. When, to our surprise, the man bent down and patted the odd little creature on the head, it seemed to enjoy the fussing and rubbed itself against the man's legs as a cat would. That over, the rifleman stood up, shaded his eyes from the sun and scanned the sky.

'Oh no,' said Lemmy. 'He'll be turning in our direction in a minute. He's bound to see us.' I didn't see how he could help it but, at that moment, the man dropped his hand from his eyes and turned his head sharply towards the house.

'Looks as though somebody called him,' I suggested.

We all lay perfectly still as the skin-clad figure walked up to the door, gave it a push and disappeared inside with his 'dog'.

Lemmy breathed a sigh of relief, 'Now let's get back to the trucks,' he said. 'I'll feel a lot safer there.'

'You can go back if you wish, Lemmy,' replied Jet, 'but I'm going down there – to introduce myself, as you might say.'

'Down there?' asked Lemmy.

'We'll never find out anything sitting up here and just watching from a distance.'

'Maybe not,' I said, 'but you're not going down there alone, Jet. I'm coming with you.'

'Me, too,' said Lemmy, changing his mind in the instant. So we stood up and slowly but determinedly walked down the sand dune towards the house. We had to pass quite close to the corral and, as we got up to the fence, the peculiar anteater-like creatures came running towards us. Lemmy instinctively shied away from them, but Jet remained at the fence and even rubbed his hand over their backs which they seemed to enjoy.

'They must have thought we were going to feed them,' he said. 'These animals are quite tame.'

'Well, let's not bother with the animals until we're sure their owners are tame, too,' suggested Lemmy.

We walked up to the house and stopped outside the door. It seemed to be woven from some kind of thick raffia and hung on leather-like hinges. A simple lift catch held it shut. Jet closed his fist and hammered on the door. To our ears, enclosed in our helmets, the knocking sounded very weak. We assumed that the noise was much louder outside in the Martian atmosphere and could easily have been heard by anyone within the house. But whether or not that was so, nobody came to the door.

'Let's go in, Jet,' I said at last. 'I don't think anybody intends to answer.' Jet lifted the catch and slowly pushed the door open. Lemmy blew through his lips and said: 'This place feels so cold – like a tomb. What kind of people could possibly live in here?'

'From what we saw up on the sand dunes, Lemmy,' I reminded him, 'ordinary human beings like ourselves.'

'Then for ordinary human beings they seem to have an extraordinary taste in furniture. What's this contraption supposed to be?' Lemmy was standing by a very crudely made table. It was fashioned from the same straw-like material as the door. I put my hand on it and tested its strength. It was a little rickety but seemed fairly solid otherwise.

'And I suppose this is meant to be a chair?' said Lemmy

Here again was a rough seat woven from the same kind of material.

'And just look at the state of those walls,' I said. 'This place is virtually a ruin.'

'And yet it seems clean,' Jet pointed out, 'and tidy.'

We moved across the room to another door and knocked on that. This time there was an answer immediately. We heard what sounded like the shrill piping of a cricket. The more we knocked the louder it became.

'Sounds like they keep a canary,' said Lemmy, 'or is that Martian language for "come in"?'

Jet put his hand to the latch and lifted it. He opened the door a little way and the shrill piping sound became louder. Then he pushed the door open wide and there, standing barring our path, was the strange, beetle-like creature we had seen outside.

Jet took a step forward and at once the 'beetle' began to back away from him. 'Come on,' he said, 'I don't think this creature will give us any trouble.'

'In you go, Lemmy,' I said, giving him a push. 'Let's see where the door at the end of this passage leads to.'

When we reached it, Jet knocked as before. And as before, there was no reply. Jet tried again and this time we heard a strangely familiar voice say: 'Who's there?'

'That sounded like Mitch,' said Jet, incredulously.

'It can't be,' I said. 'How could he have got this far?'

Jet tried the latch but found the door to be locked so he knocked again and yelled: 'Mitch – Mitch – let us in.'

'For Pete's sake,' came the immediate reply, 'cut out that banging.' The voice was unmistakably that of Mitch. 'If you have anything to say,' he went on, 'say it. If not, go away and leave me alone.'

Jet rattled the latch violently. 'We've got to get in there, Doc, and get him out.'

'If you ask me,' put in Lemmy, 'it doesn't sound as though he wants to come out.'

Before I could prevent him, Jet put his shoulder to the door. I was afraid he might damage his suit, but the door gave way almost at once. It opened on to a dimly lit room into which a small window allowed only a little daylight to enter. On the opposite wall was a crude bed with Mitch lying on it. He lay much as McLean had lain on the bunk of the living quarters truck, staring at the ceiling. He hardly seemed aware of our presence.

'Land sakes, Jet,' I exclaimed, 'I think we're too late. Look at him – no helmet, no suit – and he doesn't even recognise us.'

Jet looked at the still form a moment and then said: 'Mitch, don't you know us?'

Mitch turned his head in our direction. 'You took your time coming, didn't you?'

'Took our time?' I protested. 'We didn't even know you were here.'

'Did you bring the ambulance with you?'

'Ambulance?' I asked.

'You must have done. Well, if we're going, let's go. I won't really be sorry. That sheep farmer and his wife are scared of me. They think a little sunstroke has driven me crazy.'

'Sheep farmer?' I said. 'What are you talking about, Mitch?'

'That couple that took me in. They're certainly sheep they have in the pens outside, aren't they?'

'No, Mitch,' said Jet, 'they're not sheep. They're…'

'I didn't want to scare 'em,' Mitch went on, as though Jet hadn't spoken. 'They were good enough to me. Made up this bed with nice clean sheets and…'

By this time Lemmy was also standing by the couch and gazing down at his crew mate. 'Sheets, did he say? That bed's nothing but a heap of old furs – skins from those animals outside.'

'Well,' Mitch continued, 'why don't you sit down? It'll take me a couple of minutes to get dressed.'

'And where do we sit?' asked Lemmy.

'There are chairs enough, aren't there? Two armchairs by the fire and a sofa in the window.'

We looked around the room and saw three objects which, with a lot of imagination, could perhaps have resembled the furniture Mitch had described.

'Armchairs yet,' said Lemmy under his breath. 'I could make better myself out of an orange box.'

'Yes, we will sit down, thank you,' I said to Mitch gently, 'but over by the window. It's rather warm in here.' I indicated to Jet and Lemmy to follow me and we seated ourselves as best we could on the long, plank-like object which Mitch believed to be a sofa.

'What on earth has happened to him, Doc?' Jet whispered.

'He must be crackers,' said Lemmy.

'No, Lemmy,' I corrected him, 'just changed.'

'To what?'

'I don't know yet.'

'He's not another Whitaker, is he?' asked the Cockney.

He had voiced my own fear, but I merely replied: 'Whatever he is, he sees things quite differently from how they really are.'

'But why did he think we might have brought an ambulance with us?' asked Jet.

'Because he believes he's sick and we've come to take him away,' I replied. 'And so long as he thinks that, that's what we will do. We'll take him to the trucks with us. At least we'll have him back again, and then…'

My suggestion was interrupted by the shrill barking of the dog-beetle at the door.

'What's worrying that dog?' called Mitch.

'Dog!' said Lemmy. 'He thinks it's a dog, too.'

'What's he kicking up that row for?' went on the Australian. 'Have you got somebody else out there?'

'No, Mitch,' I said, 'there's only us.'

'Well something's worrying him.'

'Oh blimey,' said Lemmy suddenly, 'and no wonder.' He was gazing out of the window. 'Look out there,' he said. 'That ship we've been following – that sphere. It's just landed outside.'

Jet and I followed Lemmy's gaze and saw that what he had said was true.

'What was that?' asked Mitch from the other side of the room. 'A plane just landed, did you say?'

'Yes, Mitch,' said Jet, hardly knowing what to reply.

'But didn't you just land here?'

'No, Mitch – we came in the trucks.'

'But the farmer told me you'd be flying here.' Mitch was out of bed now and was dressing himself in his crew suit – the undergarment which we all wore beneath our space suits.

'How could he?' I called back. 'That farmer, as you call him, couldn't even have known we were coming.'

'Who are you?' asked Mitch, approaching us. 'Aren't you the flying doctor?'

'You might call me that,' I said cautiously.

'From Alice Springs?'

'Look, Mitch,' I said firmly, 'finish dressing and come on.'

'Where to?'

'Back to the trucks, of course,' replied Jet, putting his hand on the engineer's shoulder.

'Take your hands off me,' said the Australian, pushing Jet away. 'I'm not coming with anybody until I know just who you are.'

'We are Doc, Jet and Lemmy,' I said, 'of the Mars space fleet. You're one of our crew.'

'The Mars space fleet?' repeated Mitch dazedly.

'Yes, Mitch. We landed here on Mars nine days ago in the Flagship *Discovery* – you, too.'

Mitch took a couple of paces backwards and looked at us with fear in his eyes. 'You're crazy, the whole lot of you. This is Australia.'

'Australia!' exclaimed Jet, taking a step towards the engineer.

'Keep away,' said Mitch, his voice rising dangerously.

'Mitch,' I pleaded, 'you must believe us.'

'Keep off – or I'll hit you with this chair.'

'Mitch,' said Jet, advancing towards the Australian, 'we're your friends. We want to help you.'

'Come a step nearer and I'll let you have it!'

Jet came to a halt not a yard from Mitch. He dared not approach any closer for the Australian was standing with the chair poised above his head. If he brought it down on Jet's helmet and broke it, Jet was liable to be suffocated by the Martian atmosphere which, for all we knew, might be poisonous to us, although, I must admit, Mitch seemed to be breathing it quite easily. 'Mitch, for the last time,' begged Jet, 'you must come with us. You belong to us. You are one of us.'

'I'm not going with anybody,' said Mitch decisively, 'until I know exactly who you are.'

The dog-beetle was making more noise than ever now, and then, quite suddenly, we heard footsteps coming along the passage. My heart sank. Whoever had come out of the sphere which had just landed was now in the house and there was no escape for us. 'The window,' said Jet urgently. 'We can get out of there.'

'Yes,' I said, 'but what about Mitch?'

'If he won't come, there's nothing we can do about it. Let's get back to the trucks. Maybe we can think up a plan for rescuing Mitch later. What else can we do?' he said, turning to me in despair.

'Very well,' I agreed, and headed for the window.

But I had hardly reached it when a voice behind me said: 'Stay where you are!'

Chapter 17

Five figures stood in the doorway. The man who had spoken was of moderate height and build, with a thin, leathery face, indicating that he spent much of his time outdoors in the sun. He wore an Australian-type bush hat, a loose shirt, trousers held up by a wide leather belt and tight-fitting boots which came halfway up his calves. Behind him were the farmer, a woman I took to be his wife and behind them, to my great surprise, were Dobson and Harding, two of the men missing from the crashed Freighter Number Two. None of these people wore space suits or breathing apparatus of any kind. Dobson and Harding stood staring vacantly before them, and it was obvious that they, too, were in a conditioned state, similar to that of McLean and Mitch.

The farmer pointed towards us. 'That's them, Doc. Appeared from nowhere. Frightened the wits out of my wife and then began to search the house without so much as a by-your-leave.'

The leathery-faced man stepped into the room. 'Who are you?' he demanded in a strong Australian accent.

'We might well ask you that,' replied Jet, shouting in his helmet to make himself heard.

'That's easily answered,' said leather face. 'I'm the Flying Doctor in this part of the Territory. I received a report that there was a man here suffering from over-exposure to the sun. So I came to pick him up.'

So this was the man Mitch was expecting; indeed a Flying Doctor.

'If I may say so, Doctor,' I said, as courteously as I could, 'he's not suffering from over-exposure to the sun.'

The Flying Doctor ignored my remark. 'Who are you?' he demanded.

'Matthews is my name. Doctor Matthews.'

'A doctor of medicine?'

'Yes. Of space medicine in particular.'

'Of what?'

'Space – astronautics.'

'That's a branch of medicine I've never heard of. What are you doing here? Where did you come from?'

'We came looking for our Chief Engineer,' said Jet, 'Stephen Mitchell – the man you say has had an overdose of the sun. But he was fit enough when he left us.'

The Flying Doctor turned to Mitch and asked: 'Have you ever seen these men before?'

'Not that I can remember,' Mitch replied.

'Mitch,' I said gently, 'what do you remember? How did you get here?'

'That's the funny thing. Everything that happened before today seems vague and uncertain.'

'In your condition,' said the Flying Doctor, 'what else do you expect? The sooner I get you into bed and under proper medical care, the better.'

I was not going to have Mitch taken away from us so easily. So I turned to the Doctor and said: 'Sorry to disagree with you again, but that's not the reason. Yesterday he was one of us and, like us, he couldn't even walk around on this planet without a space suit. And now look at him.'

'A space suit? So that's what those get-ups you have on are supposed to be? And where do you reckon to be from?'

'The Earth,' said Jet.

The Flying Doctor laughed heartily.

That annoyed Lemmy who demanded what the heck he thought he was laughing at.

'The Earth, you said,' replied the Flying Doctor, grinning broadly. 'Had you said Mars or Venus or some other planet, maybe I wouldn't see any reason to laugh. But this happens to be the Earth and as for your being creatures from another planet, you don't look any different from the rest of us.'

'Earth, is it?' said Lemmy sarcastically. 'And I suppose you'll be saying next that those weird creatures outside in that pen are sheep, and that that beetle sitting there is a dog?'

'If they're not sheep and that's not a dog, then I've been living under an illusion for years. Now listen to me, all of you. I'm going to shut you in this room while I decide what to do with you. I shall post one of my attendants outside the door and another below the window and give them orders to yell if you make any move to escape.' He turned to the farmer and his wife. 'Now come on, John, and you, Mrs Bodie – and you sir,' indicating Mitch. We'll leave them here to think things over for a bit.'

Mitch seemed relieved to be free of us, for he eagerly accompanied the others through the door which was closed behind them but not locked.

'Well,' asked Lemmy as soon as they had gone, 'who's crazy? Us or them?'

'Not us, Lemmy,' said Jet. 'Not for one moment must you imagine it's us.'

'It's just me, then,' said the Cockney. 'I can't even be sure that you and Doc are yourselves any more.'

'Let us begin by assuming that we are mentally stable,' I said.

'Yes, let's assume it,' said Lemmy uncertainly.

'In that case, it must be the others who are unbalanced in some way. Look at this place; it's ancient, derelict and in a state of decay, yet to these people – and Mitch – it is a comfortable home. To them things are not what they seem. They think they live normal, earthly lives, surrounded by normal, earthly animals, on a cattle station in the Australian bush.'

'But where did they come from in the first place, Doc?'

'We can only conclude that they came from Earth, Lemmy, as Whitaker did. And, having been brought here, they were made to think that they are still on Earth. They carry on exactly the life they were leading before they left it.'

'And when did they leave it?'

'Goodness knows,' I replied. 'Probably years ago, as Whitaker did.'

'But, Doc,' asked Jet, 'who brought them up here? And what for? Why go to all the trouble of conditioning them to induce them to believe that they're back on Earth anyway? What's the point?'

'We may never know the answer to that one, Jet. The fact is, up to now, they've had to go down to Earth to pick up their victims. But we have come to them. They already have Dobson and Harding and now, apparently, they have Mitch.'

'And we're next on the list,' said Lemmy. 'That's why that so-called Flying Doctor came. Next thing we know he'll be hypnotising us and that'll be our lot.'

'No, Lemmy; I don't think so. He's just as bewildered about us as that farmer is. I'm sure he believes himself to be down on Earth, too, and that to him we are the peculiar ones.'

'In that case,' observed Lemmy, 'he's going to have a job figuring out how we got here. Mitch, too, for that matter.'

'Well, it's my guess,' said Jet, 'that he'll report it to somebody. He'll probably be under the impression that he's telling the police or some other authority, but in actual fact it'll be the people who are capable of and responsible for this conditioning business.'

'And then,' said Lemmy, 'they'll come and get us.'

'They might,' Jet agreed, 'but I'm hoping that before they get around to it we'll have figured out some way to get away from here.'

'What a hope!' said Lemmy. 'With Dobson outside the door and Harding below the window.'

'Well, one of us at least must get back to the trucks,' I said. 'We've got to contact Polar Base and tell them what's happening – guards or no guards.'

'Here,' said Lemmy suddenly, as an idea struck him, 'do you think Dobson out there will remember us?'

'I doubt it,' I said, but Lemmy was already at the door and opening it.

'Hey you,' he called. 'Hey! I'm talking to you.'

As though from a long way off we heard Dobson reply. 'Orders are that you stay in that room. You are not to leave it until told.' His voice was remarkably like that of Whitaker.

'Oh, maybe I was wrong after all,' said Lemmy. 'That might look like Dobson but it doesn't sound like him.'

'McLean didn't sound like himself either,' said Jet. 'In fact he sounded very much as Dobson does now – the same, dull, expressionless voice.'

'And if you ask me, Jet,' I said, 'he's in much the same condition as McLean was. In a deep hypnotic sleep, not even in control of his own actions.'

'Go back into that room and close the door.'

'And he doesn't want us to be in control of ours either, by the sound of things,' said Lemmy.

'Dobson,' said Jet. 'I'm Jet and this is Doc and this is Lemmy…'

'Unless you return at once, I shall raise the alarm.'

'Close the door Jet,' I said exasperated. 'This isn't getting us anywhere.'

Jet closed the door and the three of us went over to the window and sat on the 'sofa' to discuss the situation. But we had hardly reached it when the door opened to reveal the Flying Doctor.

'All right, gentlemen,' he commanded, 'on your feet. You're coming with us – and we're taking off immediately.'

'Where to?' demanded Lemmy.

'Orders are to take you with us – and orders must be obeyed without question at all times.'

'Blimey,' said the Cockney, 'he's at it now.'

'Where's Mitchell?' I demanded. 'What have you done with him?'

'He's already on his way out to the plane.'

'Plane, you call it,' said Lemmy. 'That thing out there is the funniest plane I've ever seen.'

'Now come along. We have no desire to harm you, but if you feel inclined to be troublesome just remember Mr Bodie will be walking behind you with his gun.'

We had no choice but to obey.

Once out of the house, we began walking towards the 'plane', the Doctor leading and the two conditioned crewmen bringing up the rear. None of us said a word. As we turned the corner of the house, the farmer appeared, and fell in behind Dobson and Harding. There was, it seemed, no chance for us to escape.

Suddenly I heard a whisper in my earpiece. It was Lemmy. 'Whatever I do, Doc,' he murmured, 'ignore it.' Then, in a loud voice, he said: 'Oh, I feel all weak – I think I'm going to faint.' The Flying Doctor turned round sharply and looked at him. 'I feel all dizzy,' went on Lemmy, beginning to reel round like a drunken man. 'I can't walk another step. I must sit down and rest.' And with that he gave a moan and slumped to the ground.

The Flying Doctor started back at once to where Lemmy was lying. Dobson and Harding halted and stared directly before them.

But it was the farmer who reached Lemmy first. Going down on one knee, he turned him over onto his back. Suddenly Lemmy's arms reached up, grasped the man by the neck and pulled him down. Bodie was so surprised by the move that he offered no resistance whatsoever and the moment he was down on top of Lemmy, Lemmy curled his legs around the farmer's and held him in a vice-like grip. Immediately the Flying Doctor ran back and began trying to free Bodie and, in that same moment, I heard Lemmy yell: 'Go on, Jet – now's your chance. Run for it!'

Jet needed no second bidding. In a flash he was running across the sand dunes as fast as his space suit would allow. The

Flying Doctor started off in pursuit but my foot, placed in his way, brought him crashing down to the ground. Dobson and Harding still stood motionless as though nothing had happened at all.

I grappled with the Flying Doctor, rolling over and over in the sand with him. My only thought was to keep him from following Jet. This I managed to do in spite of the cumbersome movements imposed on me by my suit.

Lemmy seemed to be having a similar success with his opponent, but suddenly I heard him say: 'Look out, Doc – the farmer's got away from me.'

I caught a glimpse of the man scrambling to his feet and running over to where the rifle had been dropped. Then he stooped down, picked up the weapon, put it to his shoulder and pointed it at the now small figure of Jet who was climbing the sand dune about fifty yards away.

There was a crack as the rifle fired but the shot went high for, just as the farmer pulled his trigger, Lemmy, who by now was also on his feet, dived at the man's knees and brought him down. Once more the two men were locked in a grim struggle.

The Flying Doctor was yelling at me to let him go for I had him firmly held in a ju-jitsu grasp, but I had no intention of releasing him yet. Then he called to Dobson and Harding to help. The two men came running over and, within a few moments, the Flying Doctor was on his feet and I was dragged to mine. Seconds later Lemmy was also overpowered.

'All right, Lemmy,' I called. 'I don't think there's any need to fight any more. Jet must have reached the trucks by now.'

Jet must have heard me, for over the radio came his voice saying: 'Yes, Doc, I'm outside the airlock and I'm just going in. Are you all right?'

'Yes,' I told him. 'We suffered no damage that I can see. Get inside that truck as quickly as you can and make sure that it can't be opened from the outside.'

The Flying Doctor must have realised the significance of what I was saying for he made no further attempt to pursue

Jet. Instead he ordered Lemmy and I to continue walking towards the sphere which, reluctantly, we did. This time the Flying Doctor walked behind us with Dobson, Harding and the farmer, who had his rifle levelled at our backs.

We entered the spherical ship by a circular door and, after passing through a short corridor, found ourselves in a cylindrically shaped cabin. Its diameter, however, was little more than half that of the overall diameter of the ship, so between the inner and outer shells, I imagined, must be the mechanism by which the ship was propelled.

No sooner were we inside the strange craft than the Flying Doctor pressed a control and the outer door closed. He then closed the inner door and ordered Dobson and Harding to their posts. They took up positions before a couple of control panels and the Flying Doctor told them to get the ship under way. There was a soft whine, a feeling of gentle vibration and then a definite pressure downwards which told us that we were climbing very rapidly.

The Flying Doctor indicated to Mitch to sit down in a chair on the opposite side of the cabin to that occupied by Dobson and Harding. Then, stepping over to the central pillar, he pressed a small control and part of the column slid back to reveal a ladder leading up inside.

'Now, Doctor Matthews,' said the Flying Doctor, 'if you'll kindly climb this ladder I think you'll find the upper cabin much more to your liking – and you, Mr Barnet.'

Lemmy at once appealed to Mitch. 'Mitch,' he said, 'this bloke is trying to separate us – to get Doc and me to go to another part of the ship while he keeps you here.'

Mitch didn't even bother to look up. 'What's wrong with that?' he asked. 'Do you think I want to travel with a couple of crazy loons like you?'

'Mitch boy,' said Lemmy, spreading his hands in front of him, 'I'm Lemmy and this is Doc – your old crew mates from the *Discovery*, of *Luna* and…'

'I've never clapped eyes on either of you before,' said Mitch flatly.

'Now listen, Mitch,' said Lemmy, 'Doc, Jet and me risked our lives trying to find you…'

'I tell you I don't know what you're talking about.'

'You talk to him, Doc,' Lemmy suggested.

'There's no point, Lemmy,' I said. 'We'd better go up as the – er – Doctor here says.'

'Very well,' said Lemmy, and with that he entered the tiny door and began to climb up the rungs of the ladder.

'Once you get up there and I have closed the door,' the Flying Doctor called after us, 'you can remove your helmets. The atmosphere of the upper cabin is similar to that which you are used to breathing in your own ship – it is kept that way for unconditioned types like yourselves.'

The upstairs cabin was completely bare. There was not a seat nor any kind of control panel to be seen. The walls were perfectly smooth, except for three portholes set at equal distances in the walls. Like the larger cabin downstairs, the upper one also had a flat roof.

As soon as the airtight door had been closed, I unfastened my helmet, lifted its rim slightly and took a deep breath. I suffered no ill effects and decided that the Doctor had been speaking the truth. Lemmy quickly followed my example. It was a relief to get our helmets off after all this time.

'Well,' said Lemmy, moving over to one of the windows, 'at least we can see where we are from up here. That's something. But what's going on, Doc?' His voice was tense and high. 'What are these Martians trying to do to us – send us crackers? And are they Martians? And are we still on Mars? I'm so confused I don't know where I am any more.'

I put my hand on Lemmy's shoulder and pointed towards the pink landscape below. 'Look down there, Lemmy.' I said, trying to calm him. 'Did you ever see anything like that down on Earth? Of course you didn't. Because we're not on Earth.'

'Then do you think this is one of the Martian ships that goes to Earth to pick up victims?'

'Could be, Lemmy,' I told him, 'but it hardly seems big enough for that.'

Very soon we had left the pink desert behind and were flying over greeny-brown country. We travelled in a north-westerly direction, so I assumed that this darker soil must be that of the Mare Erythraeum.

Scattered over its surface were box-like buildings like the one in which we had found Mitch. From the orderliness of the ground and the patches of vegetation we could see, even from the height at which we were flying, I concluded that the earth below was cultivated. 'Hey, look,' said Lemmy suddenly, 'there's another canal directly below us.'

It was much wider than the one in which we had seen the pyramid but seemed to contain the same type of plants. They stood out very clearly against the background of the greeny-brown soil. As soon as we reached the canal the ship followed its course – Lemmy began to speculate as to where it led and what was going to happen to us there.

'They'll never make a farmer out of me, I know that,' he said positively.

'If they conditioned you, Lemmy,' I pointed out, 'you don't know what they might make out of you.'

'Well, they haven't succeeded yet, although they tried hard enough back in that pyramid. Here,' he went on, 'why haven't they ever got at you, Doc?'

'Maybe it's because I'm not a good subject. This conditioning must have something to do with a very deep and profound hypnosis. But whilst I was at medical college even the director of the department of hypnotic medicine failed to put me to sleep. I just didn't react.'

Lemmy was surprised. 'Then what would happen if you were back on Earth and had to have an operation?'

'They'd have to use anaesthetics, I'm afraid.'

'I've heard of people like that, Doc,' said Lemmy, 'but I didn't realise you were one.'

'Yes, I am. That's probably why I'm the only one of us who's not been affected by sleep-inducing sounds.'

'Then from now on,' said Lemmy with resolution, 'I stick close to you, and then if I start hearing that weird noise, you can help me overcome it.'

Approximately an hour and a half later Lemmy pointed out a change in the appearance of the landscape ahead. We were approaching a spot where a number of canals met.

The area had been almost completely cleared of the plants which grew so profusely in the canals. In the place, some five miles in diameter, was a Martian city, consisting of a number of pyramids very similar to that we had seen in the first canal but much smaller in size. They were no more than a quarter of a mile square at the base and I doubt whether their height amounted to much more than five or six hundred feet. The layout of the pyramids was perfectly symmetrical and streets appeared to run between the walls at the base of each edifice.

'What is this place?' asked Lemmy.

'The Lacus Solis,' I told him, 'the lake of the sun.'

'But it isn't a lake, Doc.'

'No, Lemmy. That's just a name given to it by the astronomers down on Earth.'

'Hey, look, Doc,' said Lemmy suddenly, 'down there in the streets.' We were descending to the flat roof of one of the pyramids and, as we neared ground level, I could see that the streets were alive with traffic – peculiar vehicles which from above, due principally to the bright colours in which they were painted, looked rather like ladybirds.

'Well, even the Martians have a traffic problem then,' said Lemmy. 'But why so many colours?'

'Maybe a means of identification,' I suggested, 'instead of registration numbers.'

'Could be, I suppose,' he agreed. Then he looked at me apprehensively. 'Well, Doc, it looks as though we've arrived,' he said, 'but now that we're here, what happens to us? And what about Jet, stuck back there near that farmhouse with only a Whitakered McLean for company?'

'I don't know, Lemmy,' I answered, trying to keep my voice steady. 'We can only wait and see.'

Chapter 18

A gentle bump told us that the ship had landed. It touched down on the roof of the largest pyramid the city boasted. Almost immediately there came the high whine of the mechanism which opened the door to the upper cabin in which we were standing. A few moments later the Flying Doctor appeared, climbing out of the hollow pillar.

'Very well, gentlemen,' he said; 'put on your helmets and let's go.'

'Do you mind telling us exactly what is happening?' I asked.

'Sorry, gentlemen,' replied the Flying Doctor, 'I wish I could. I'm merely carrying out my orders to condition you and bring you here.'

'But we're not conditioned,' protested Lemmy. 'Not Doc and me.'

'No. But at least you're here. And it hasn't been a bad haul, really. Mr Mitchell and the one you call McLean.'

'McLean,' I said, surprised, 'but he's back in one of the land trucks with Jet.'

'At the moment, yes. But his orders were to bring Mr Morgan here, and when orders are given they are always obeyed. And, after Mr Morgan, there aren't many of you left, are there?'

'Aren't there?' I replied, rather lamely.

'We know a good deal about you, Dr Matthews. We knew the scheduled time of your arrival here on Mars.'

'Mars?' exclaimed Lemmy. 'Then this *is* Mars. You admit it?'

'To you, of course.'

175

'Why to us?' demanded the Cockney. 'If this is Mars, why do you go around telling everybody else it's Australia?'

'Because, Mr Barnet, there happen to be a lot of Earth men and women living up in the Argyre Desert who believe they are in Australia. And, unlike you and Dr Matthews, they are all very happy with the arrangement.'

'But,' I protested, 'they live under an illusion the whole time.'

'Down on Earth millions of people live under an illusion,' said the Flying Doctor, 'often for the whole of their lives.'

'Well, you haven't illusioned us,' said Lemmy defiantly.

'No, and more's the pity. You might have been a lot happier if we had. Now, let's get downstairs, shall we?'

'One moment,' I said. 'You said just now that you knew our scheduled time of arrival here. How?'

'Full information was passed to us at regular intervals.'

'By Whitaker?'

'That's right. Pity about him – he was very valuable to us.'

'So Whitaker *was* one of you,' I said.

'Yes. Since 1924. Before then he was on Earth, leading the normal, dull, earthly life. But we gave him something to live for – something to achieve.'

'And look how he ended up,' observed Lemmy.

'Yes,' said the Flying Doctor. 'We hadn't allowed for Peterson. With the exception of yourself, Doctor Matthews, and Peterson, there wasn't a man in the Fleet Whitaker could not, given the time, have brought completely under his influence.'

'So that's why we had all those nightmares whenever he was around,' said Lemmy.

'Yes,' replied the Doctor. 'It's easier to get control of a subject once he is asleep. But if they won't sleep…' He broke off, then said abruptly: 'Come on. Let's go downstairs.'

'Just one thing more,' I insisted. 'Where did you come from?'

He turned to face me. 'From Earth.'

'How long ago?'

'Twenty-five years. Until then I was what I now pretend to be – a Flying Doctor in the Australian bush.'

'But the way you talk you might be a Martian,' said Lemmy.

'I decided a long time ago that there is no point in fighting the inevitable. So I threw in my lot with them. As a doctor I have a way with people. It may be a bit rough and ready but it serves. I'm a go-between; between them and the people who've been brought here. I see to it that their illusion is not shattered.'

'Them? Who are "them"?' I asked.

'The Martians, of course; for whom and by whom the rest of us up here exist.'

'But who are they?' persisted Lemmy. 'What do they look like?'

'I wouldn't know,' replied the Doctor flatly. 'I've never seen them.'

'Never seen them!' For a moment I was speechless. 'Supposing,' I asked at length, 'you had the chance to go back to Earth. Would you?'

'If I were on Earth now I would be twenty-five years older, and I was no chicken when I came here. What prospect would be there for me if I returned?'

'But how much longer,' I argued, 'can you expect to remain as active as you are now?'

'I don't know. But I do know that in the city of Orphir are people who came here from Earth during the opposition of 1879. It is, of course, during the oppositions that our ships leave to pick up new personnel – that is, approximately every fifteen years.

It was all perfectly clear to me now. Whitaker had been picked up in 1924. That's why his memory of Earth and all his associations with it were allied to that date, like the Exhibition at Wembley and the song 'When it's Night-time in Italy'. The sheep farmer and his wife must have come up at some other opposition and I had no doubt that could we have searched the planet and visited every city, we would have found people who had been brought up during the oppositions of 1896, 1909 and 1956.

I must have unwittingly spoken the last date out loud because the Flying Doctor added: 'And 1971.'

'But we, the clever lot,' said Lemmy bitterly, 'had to bring ourselves.'

'Yes – you were the first,' said the Flying Doctor. 'The others came by the usual method – as I did. In my day,' he went on, 'there were many reports of flying saucers being seen, particularly in America.'

'That's right,' I said, 'I remember. When I was a kid a fellow in California wrote a book about it.'

'Yes,' said the Doctor, 'a lot of eye-wash – or so I thought at the time. And then I saw one for myself. Actually on the ground in the Simpson Desert west of Bundooma. Naturally I was curious and approached close enough to photograph it. Then the door opened and a man came out. He spoke good English and invited me in to look around. Five minutes later the sphere took off with me inside. And now I'm here, I make the best of it. And, if you take my advice, you'll do as I've done and do as you're told. There's no escape. Neither you nor your Fleet will ever get back to Earth. Now, is there anything else?'

'I think that's enough to be going on with, thanks,' said Lemmy miserably.

Once down in the lower cabin we were ordered to leave the ship by the door which was standing open and, stepping out, we found ourselves on the uppermost terrace of the giant pyramid. Lemmy and I walked over to the wall to get a better view of what lay below. But, almost at once, the Flying Doctor came over to us.

'Now gentlemen,' he said, 'if you wouldn't mind stepping this way I'll take you down to the Intake Section where you will be categorised for the work most suited to you.'

'Work?' said Lemmy, clearly both surprised and appalled at the prospect.

'Of course. You don't think this is a free hotel, do you? Once you're here you have to work for your keep.'

'But what at?' I asked.

'That is something I don't decide. But you are more fortunate than most. You are all skilled in your own particular professions and should be very useful to us. In fact, your long stay here could be extremely pleasant.'

'Who are you kidding?' asked Lemmy.

'Look down there at the city,' said the Doctor. 'What do you think goes on down there in all those buildings?'

'How should we know?'

'Well, I'll tell you. Each pyramid is a little city within itself. It has its own citizens, a couple of hundred in each; with their own domestic and medical staffs, and directors of culture, leisure and sport. Our aim is to see that every worker is happy, well fed and highly efficient.'

'Sounds marvellous,' said the Cockney; 'just like a colony of ants.'

'But what are they working *for*?' I asked.

'To go back to Earth – eventually.'

'Eh?' interjected Lemmy incredulously.

'For nearly a hundred years,' went on the Doctor, 'they have worked to the end. And, when they return, they will carry the true Martians with them – in the largest space fleet the universe has ever seen.'

'You mean they're building ships down there – to invade the Earth?' asked Lemmy, his eyes widening.

The Flying Doctor didn't answer the question directly. But he said: 'Mars is a dying planet. If its inhabitants are to live they must move elsewhere. And the nearest and best place for them is the Earth.'

'But what about the people who already live on the Earth?' asked the Cockney in alarm.

'And when will this "invasion" take place?' I asked.

'The next close opposition, 1986, should see the beginning.'

'Good grief!' It was all I could say.

'So you see how important it is that none of your expedition gets back.'

'It's all too horribly clear,' agreed Lemmy.

'If people on Earth knew what was in store for them,' went on the Doctor calmly, 'they might make preparations to resist and…' The Flying Doctor broke off and followed our gaze as Lemmy and I turned our eyes skywards.

While we had been talking the distinctive sound of a flying machine had been gradually filling the air. It approached very rapidly, and we had hardly heard the noise and looked up when Freighter Number One passed directly overhead, went shattering by and quickly disappeared.

'Blimey,' said Lemmy excitedly, 'it's Frank's ship!'

The Flying Doctor took hold of his arm. 'I've got to get you down to the Intake Section at once,' he said firmly.

'What's the hurry, mate?' asked Lemmy, pushing the Doctor away. 'Are you afraid Frank might see us?'

'Come on,' said the Doctor, 'do as you're told. Head down those steps to the next terrace.'

'We're not Whitakered yet, you know,' said Lemmy, aggressively. 'Lay a finger on me and I'll give you a right-hander.'

The Doctor ignored the threat and moved forward to take the Cockney by the shoulder.

Then Lemmy's fist flew out and hit him full in the face. He gave a cry, fell backwards against the low wall of the terrace and disappeared over it. Lemmy and I ran to the wall and looked below.

'Oh blimey, Doc,' said the Cockney, 'he went over, straight down onto the next terrace.'

'It was a lucky blow,' I told him.

'Lucky?' repeated Lemmy anxiously. 'But I might have killed him. Look – he just lies there and doesn't move.'

'Come on,' I urged, pulling him. 'We've got to get away before anybody else comes up here.'

At this point Mitch came out of the sphere and walked towards us. 'Hey,' he said as he approached, 'What's going on out here? Where's the Doctor?'

'He's – er – gone down to the next terrace,' said Lemmy. 'Says we're to wait in the sphere until he gets back.'

'And what was that that flew over just now? It was pretty low, wasn't it?'

'Not as low as we would have liked,' said the Cockney.

'It sounds like it's coming back again,' went on the Australian.

I looked up to see the freighter approaching rapidly. It was considerably lower than before and skimmed over our heads no more than a couple of hundred feet above the top of the pyramid on which we were standing.

Mitch, too, looked up at the craft and, as he did so, I heard him say above the roar of the motor, 'Number One – Freighter Number One.'

'Mitch,' I asked urgently, 'do you recognise that ship? Does it mean anything to you?'

' I don't know,' Mitch replied, 'I never saw a plane of such a size and yet it seems familiar. Has its picture been in the papers or something?'

'It certainly has,' I said, 'But not on this planet.'

'On this planet?' asked Mitch vaguely.

'Mitch,' I said, 'go back to the sphere.'

Mitch meekly turned on his heel and went. 'I'm all mixed up,' I heard him say. 'What place is this? It's not Adelaide, is it?'

'Now come on, Lemmy,' I went on, turning to the radio operator, 'this is our chance to escape.'

We had hardly started walking towards the sphere when the familiar voice of Frank Rogers was heard in my ear.

'Hullo, Jet,' it said. 'Number One calling.'

Lemmy and I stopped dead in our tracks.

'Hey, listen, Doc,' said Lemmy excitedly, 'that's Frank calling Jet up on the radio. And we can hear him. Hullo, hullo – hullo, Frank.'

'Hold it, Jet, will you?' I heard Frank say. 'I could have sworn I head Lemmy's voice then. And pretty strong, too. Hullo, Lemmy – come in, please.'

But before Lemmy had a chance to reply to Frank, I was talking to him. 'Hullo, Frank – that *was* Lemmy you heard, and this is Doc. We can hear you, but not Jet. Can you hook us up to him?'

'Yes, Doc,' came Frank's voice, 'you bet I will. Where are you?'

'On the roof of the highest pyramid in the city you just flew over.'

Almost immediately Jet's voice came on. 'Hullo, Doc, I can hear you now. What pyramid?'

'In the Lacus Solis, Jet,' I told him. 'A whole city of them. And Lemmy, Mitch, Dobson, Harding and I – and the sphere we came in – are up here on the roof. Lemmy has laid out the Flying Doctor, and…'

'Yes, mate,' interrupted Lemmy. 'And we've got to get out of here and back home pretty quick. The Martians are planning to invade the Earth.'

'What!'

'It's true, Jet,' I said. 'Watch McLean – he's been instructed to bring you here.'

'But he does everything I tell him, Doc. He hasn't disobeyed any of my orders up to now.'

'Watch him just the same,' I urged. 'The Martians aim to get us – to prevent our warning Earth of their intentions.'

'Doc,' said Jet slowly, 'are you sure you haven't been conditioned?'

'You must believe us, Jet,' I said. 'Let me tell Frank the whole story and have him replay it to the rest of the Fleet so *they* can tell the Earth.'

'Very well, Doc,' said Jet after a pause, 'go ahead. Frank, did you hear that?'

'Yes, sir.'

'Then hook Doc up.'

While Frank was switching over to his main transmitter to contact the freighters still flying in free orbit a thousand miles or more above the Martian surface, I called Jet again. 'Where are you now?' I asked him.

'Still crossing the Argyre Desert – heading in your direction.'

'Well, don't,' I told him. 'Stay where you are. If Frank has enough juice he can drop down, pick you up and take you back to Polar Base.'

'But what about you and Lemmy and Mitch?' asked Jet.

'With luck we might make it, but we have to hurry.'

'I'll say we have,' said Lemmy suddenly. 'Look – there's four men coming up the steps from the next terrace.'

'Into the sphere – quick,' I ordered.

Together we ran across the terrace and through the open door.

Once inside the cabin Lemmy and I paused near the circular opening. 'Well, how do we close the perishing thing?' asked Lemmy. 'We haven't a clue how this ship works.'

'We haven't,' I told him, 'but Dobson and Harding have.'

Dobson and Harding were, in fact, still seated at the control panels. Like McLean, they wouldn't do anything without being ordered. I now tried my hand with the two conditioned members of our crew.

'Dobson,' I said, 'close the door.'

Dobson's hand moved to a control on the little panel before him; there was a high-pitched whine and the sphere's door slowly closed.

Lemmy gave an audible sigh of relief. 'Well, now what do we do?' he said.

'We get them to take off,' I told him.

At this point Mitch came running over. 'Hey,' he cried, 'where's the doctor? Why have you shut him out?'

'Sit down, Mitch,' I commanded, 'and keep quiet.'

'Not before you tell me what's going on.'

'Sit *down*.'

To my relief, Mitch, obviously bewildered, sat down.

At that moment I heard Frank calling Jet. 'We're all hooked up now, skipper,' he was saying. 'Doc can go ahead just as soon as he likes.'

'Did you hear that, Doc?' asked Jet.

'Yes,' I cut in quickly. 'Frank, relay this story back to Control –' Then, suddenly as though right inside my head, I heard the weird sound that we had heard so often since landing on Mars.

Lemmy gave an exclamation of dismay. 'Oh no,' he said, 'listen! Like we ain't got enough trouble.'

I realised what was happening. The conditioning noise – the 'music' or whatever it was – that had induced sleep in Lemmy, Jet and Mitch, had been turned on again, to prevent our takeoff.

'They're trying to put us to sleep,' cried Lemmy.

'You must fight it,' I urged him. 'Use every ounce of your determination and tell yourself *you will not go to sleep*.'

'Yes, Doc,' said Lemmy obediently. Desperately he began to repeat: 'Whatever happens I must not go to sleep, whatever happens *I must not go to sleep*.'

I heard Jet's voice again. 'Go on, Doc,' he said anxiously, 'Frank is waiting. What's happened?'

'Hullo, Frank,' I called. 'Just a minute –'

I looked over towards Mitch, saw him yawn and then collapse. Immediately I realised that if the noise could still affect him, it could affect Dobson and Harding. I gave the order: 'Dobson, Harding – take the ship off immediately. Take off and return to the Argyre Desert, do you hear?'

Dobson at once operated the controls on his panel. A whine and gentle vibrations filled the ship and, slowly at first, then very rapidly, we left the top of the pyramid, climbed into the air and moved off in a straight line back in the direction we had come.

'So far so good,' said Lemmy with relief, and added: 'Whatever happens I must not go to sleep.' He gave a deep yawn. Harassed, I turned again to Frank: 'Hullo, Frank. Hullo,' I called. There was no answer.

'Blimey,' came Lemmy's voice. 'Mitch is out. Asleep on the floor.'

'Hullo, Frank,' I said again.

Frank replied this time, in a very sleepy voice: 'Hullo – hullo, Doc – Jet –'

'What is it, Frank?' I heard Jet say, alarm in his voice. 'What's wrong?'

'I don't know,' was the reply. 'There's that peculiar noise and I feel – so – sleepy.'

'Frank,' I yelled, 'you must fight it, *you must stay awake.*'

'I'm trying, Doc, but the ship, she…'

'What about the ship?'

'She doesn't seem to respond. I can't control her.'

'Oh no,' said Lemmy, much more alert now. 'Not that again.'

'Frank, you've *got* to listen! Take hold of yourself,' I commanded. 'Will yourself not to go to sleep.'

'Do as Doc says,' I heard Jet call, 'you *must* stay awake.'

I glanced aside to notice that Dobson and Harding had now also slumped to the floor and, as we were rising all the time, I told Lemmy to go over to the control panels and see if he could handle the ship. 'Me?' he said. 'What a hope!'

'Go on, Lemmy,' I told him impatiently. 'Have a try. We can't keep climbing for ever.'

'No, mate,' he said as he took his place at the control table.

'It's no good,' came Frank's voice suddenly. 'We're losing height, Doc. I can't – control – her…'

'You must, Frank,' I cried.

'We're almost on the deck now. And – here we go…'

I heard Jet's urgent call: 'Frank!'
There was no reply.
'Frank,' he called again, 'answer me!'
There was still no reply.
'Hullo, Number One,' I said. 'Hullo…'
'What's happened now, Doc?' Lemmy demanded.
'Frank,' I said, 'he must have crashed.'

Chapter 19

Several futile attempts to raise Jet confirmed my fear that Freighter Number One had crashed for, of course, it was only via Frank's transmitter that my tiny personal radio had been able to reach Jet.

Lemmy and I were now on our own – in a strange craft of which we knew nothing.

Lemmy's preliminary experiments to control the ship resulted in little more that the sphere's travelling haphazardly through the atmosphere in all directions. This greatly alarmed him, particularly when, without intent, he turned very rapidly or took the ship into a vertical climb. We had just learned how to keep it either stationary or in level flight when Dobson began to stir.

Lemmy and I watched in silence as he got slowly to his feet and looked around the cabin vaguely.

'Dobson, can you hear me talking to you?' I asked.

He hardly looked at me as he replied, almost mechanically: 'What are your orders?'

'He doesn't seem any different from when he went to sleep,' observed Lemmy.

'My orders are,' I said to Dobson, 'that you return to your control panel.'

Dobson did not hesitate; he went back to his seat.

'Keep your eye on him, Lemmy,' I said, 'See that he touches no control until we tell him to.'

'Right, Doc,' said Lemmy, moving over to the conditioned Earthman.

By this time Harding was also recovering and, on my orders, he, too, took his place at his control table.

'Gives you a funny feeling, seeing them do exactly as you tell them, Doc,' said Lemmy. 'Well, what do we do now?'

'Try to find Frank, of course.'

'But what about Jet?' protested Lemmy. 'He must be going up the wall wondering what's happed to us. Here,' he went on, 'you don't think, after what we told him, that he's still heading this way, do you?'

'Knowing Jet,' I said, 'he probably is.'

'But he mustn't,' said Lemmy anxiously. 'We must get out there and stop him.'

'We will, at first opportunity, but we must find Number One first. Harding, Dobson,' I went on, 'here are your orders. The ship will proceed at a moderate speed in a south-easterly direction.'

Dobson pressed two of the buttons in front of him and pulled one of the levers. We immediately felt the ship change direction.

'He's doing it,' said Lemmy, with satisfaction.

'Then watch him closely and see if you can find out *how* he does it.'

'Yes, Doc.'

I moved over to the observation window and looked below. We were just passing over the city at the height of some five thousand feet. I could see no sign of Freighter Number One. Within a few minutes the city had been left behind and we were passing over the cultivated area again. There was no sign of a ship there either.

We made a complete circuit of the area surrounding the Lacus Solis but without result. Finally, after we had been searching for an hour or more, I directed Dobson to take the sphere back to the city again for, in our short flight across it, we had not, of course seen every part of it.

This time we approached it from the north and almost immediately saw the wreck of Frank's ship lying at the base of one of the huge pyramids which comprised the city.

I at once ordered Dobson to stop the ship. We remained hovering directly above where the freighter lay and I called Lemmy over to the window to look at the scene below. The wreck was surrounded by dozens of the little 'ladybird' cars. There were dozens of men, too. Ordinary men, just like ourselves. Some were just standing around, some were clambering over the wreckage while others were moving in and out of the cargo hatch which, even from this height, we could see was open.

'Are we going down there, Doc?' asked Lemmy quietly.

'If we did,' I told him, 'we'd be delivering ourselves right into the enemy's hands.'

'But we can't just leave Frank there,' Lemmy protested.

'We have no choice,' I said. 'What we must do now is to pick up Jet – if we can ever find him.'

Feeling rather sick, I walked back to the centre of the cabin and gave Dobson and Harding orders to make for the Argyre Desert with all speed. We felt the ship change course, accelerate again and, in a matter of minutes, the city had been left behind.

Meanwhile, as I learned later, Jet was, as I had suspected, still heading towards the Lacus Solis in one of the land trucks with McLean, apparently completely under his control, driving the other.

Failing to contact either Frank or Lemmy and me, he finally called up Polar Base and asked them to keep a listening watch on Number One's frequency in the hope that they would hear from at least one of us. But Polar Base informed Jet that they had been keeping a constant watch, and so had the freighters still in free orbit round the planet, but with no result. The operator appealed to Jet to make for the comparative safety of Polar Base while he was still able. But Jet declared that he had no intention of returning to the ice cap until he was absolutely sure that all hope of recovering Lemmy, Mitch and myself, or even Dobson and Harding for the matter, had gone.

'Well, take care of yourself, sir,' said Polar Base. 'We'd hate to lose you as well.'

'Thank you,' Jet replied. 'I'll do my best to see that you don't.'

And then Jet heard a different voice in his earpiece: 'Hullo, Land Fleet. Are you receiving me?'

'Yes, who are you?' demanded Jet.

'You are in great danger, Mr Morgan.'

'Who are you?' persisted Jet. 'Come to the point.'

'There's no need to raise your voice. I want to help you.'

'Oh, I'm sorry. But how can you help me?'

'Unless somebody does, you haven't a hope of getting back to Earth, not even to your Polar Base.'

'That hardly answers my question,' said Jet angrily. 'How can you help me?'

'I cannot tell you now, in case I should be overheard. I've already brought my transmitter down to its lowest possible power, so that it will reach you and no farther. But every word *you* say is listened to.'

'Then, if they can't hear you, they – whoever they are – must think I'm talking to myself.'

'It won't take them long to realise what's happening, and then they'll come flying out here. Not only to pick you up but to get me as well. And that wouldn't be difficult. I'm only a hundred yards or so away from you.'

'Oh? Where?' Jet glanced keenly around but saw nobody.

'Out of sight at the moment. I didn't want to scare you by suddenly appearing from nowhere.'

'How do I know this isn't another of their tricks? A ruse to get me away from the truck?'

'You must believe me, Mr Morgan. My aim is to help you. And for you to help me in return. If you do get away, take me with you.'

'Back to Earth?'

'Why not? That's where I came from. I have a right to get back if I can, haven't I? We all have, but there wouldn't be room for us all.'

Jet now realised that he was talking to an Earthman and it struck him that, for a conditioned type, he seemed very normal.

'Do you know anything about Doc or Lemmy or Frank?' he asked.

'I picked up their calls to you just before the freighter crashed. If they're not dead, then they'll be prisoners in the city and if you think you can storm that place alone, you'd better think again. Now, how about it? Is it a deal?'

'How do I know I can trust you?' asked Jet.

'You don't. You have to take the chance. You must believe me,' said the voice emphatically. 'At least let me show myself to you so we can talk face to face.'

'Very well,' said Jet.

A few moments later a transport very like one of the 'ladybirds' we had seen in the city emerged from behind a sand dune, drove up to Jet's truck and halted. At the controls was a middle-aged man. There was nothing very striking about him. He was of medium build and had lost most of his hair. The thing that struck Jet most forcibly about the stranger was the pathetically dismal look on his face. He looked as though he had never laughed in his life.

'Well, I'm here,' the man said at last.

'So I can see,' replied Jet cautiously.

'Now do you believe I'm from Earth?'

'All the people we meet on this planet seem to be.'

'But I know where I am and what I'm doing – most of the others don't. They still think they are back on Earth in the year they left it.'

'What year is it on Earth?' asked Jet.

'1971. You see, they failed to condition me. I was the wrong type.'

'Then why did they bother to pick you up at all?'

191

'They have no way of telling good subjects from bad until they have got them. But it makes little difference once we're here. They put us to work just the same.'

'But if you're not conditioned,' said Jet, 'how do you breathe?'

'In the same way as you. I carry an oxygen supply.'

'A space suit?'

'No. A space suit is quite unnecessary if you have the right kind of equipment. Mine is so ingeniously designed that the conditioned people never even suspect – any more than they suspect they're on Mars.'

'Are there any more of you who know the truth?'

'Dozens – scattered all over the planet. Some, like me, with roving commissions, others working in the factories.'

'What at?'

'All manner of things. But the main objective is the completion of the invasion fleet.'

'Then Doc was right,' said Jet. 'They do intend to invade the Earth.'

'Yes, they do.'

'I must get a message back home. Give me full details of how and when the invasion will be made and I'll pass them on to Polar Base.'

'You'd never do it,' said the man. 'The moment you began to give your base any information of that kind your transmission would be jammed.'

'Oh.'

'Your only hope is to get up to the Fleet and tell Earth yourself.'

'And what hope is there of that?'

'A fifty-fifty chance – provided you do all I tell you, without question.'

'That very phrase makes me suspicious.'

'Very well, if you doubt my sincerity I'll get on my way.'

The stranger was already backing his truck when Jet called to him: 'No, wait. What do you want me to do?'

'Come with me – now. It's fairly certain that your side of the conversation has been heard anyway, so we haven't much time.'

'Very well. You lead the way, I'll follow.'

'That's no good,' said the stranger. 'You'll have to come into this truck. Your own is too slow.'

'But what about McLean in the other?' asked Jet.

'What state is he in?'

'He seems to be in a state of deep hypnosis. Does everything I tell him.'

'Does he indulge in any kind of conversation?'

'No.'

'Then leave him. He's too far gone.'

'How do you mean?'

'Of all people brought here his type is the most unfortunate. They have no recollection of anything previous to the time they were hypnotised. They do nothing unless told and have no control over their actions.'

'But they could be revived,' suggested Jet, 'couldn't they? Once we got them away from here.'

'No. They may appear to revive but they don't. Not even when they are sent back to Earth.'

'What? You mean they are sent back?'

'Of course. Some are there now, to all appearance normal people except for an odd way of speaking and a few eccentricities that nobody on Earth would regard with any seriousness. Whitaker was one of those. Didn't you find him a little odd?'

'We certainly did.'

'There are plenty of others like him, already down on Earth. The Martian fifth column, as you might say.'

Jet said nothing.

'Well,' continued the stranger, 'time's running out. Do you join me or do you propose to fight it out alone?'

'What chance have I with Doc, Lemmy and Mitch missing; half the Fleet's crew already in the hands of the – Martians?' said Jet dejectedly.

'Alone,' said the man, 'none at all. But if you come with me there is just a chance of your getting Mitch, Doc and Lemmy back. Even Frank, maybe.'

'And what if you are one of them?' asked Jet. 'Like the Flying Doctor?'

'That's for you to decide.'

'Very well, I'll take the chance.'

Jet then called the other land truck. 'McLean,' he said, 'can you hear me?'

The dull, flat voice of McLean came back almost at once. 'Yes,' he said, 'I can hear you.'

'You are to leave that truck and enter the vehicle in front of this one.'

'Orders were,' replied McLean, 'to proceed to the Lacus Solis.'

'I have changed those orders,' said Jet firmly.

'The orders were not yours to change. And orders must be obeyed without question at all times.'

'Now do you believe me?' asked the stranger.

'McLean,' Jet persisted, 'I order you to leave that truck and come over here.'

There was no reply. And, to Jet's great surprise, the truck in which McLean was began to move off. 'McLean,' demanded Jet angrily, 'what are you doing?'

'He's pulling out,' said the stranger.

'But where's he going?'

'Only he knows that.'

Jet immediately switched on the motor of his own truck and, swinging it round, began to pursue McLean.

The stranger called after him. 'There's nothing you can do, Mr Morgan, believe me.'

'But I can't leave him,' protested Jet.

'You're not leaving him. He is leaving you. Follow him and your chance of getting back to the Fleet is gone completely.'

Jet reluctantly switched off his motor. A few minutes later he was sitting alongside the stranger who immediately started up his machine and set off, at an incredibly fast rate, in an easterly direction.

They travelled steadily for about two hours and, according to the stranger, had about another three hours to go before they reached their destination.

In the next hour Jet learned quite a lot about his companion whose name was Webster. Apparently he was a Sussex man who has been picked up from England fifteen years before, and his one desire was to get back to Earth as soon as he could. He was, of course, very miserable on Mars, doing what the Martians told him. But not to do so, he said, would mean being condemned to one of the underground factories, to live away from the light and work at the dull, monotonous task of building the space fleet. Being a farmer he had been offered agricultural work and had had the good sense to take it. At least he saw the sunlight, and the stars at night.

Quite suddenly Webster interrupted the conversation to say: 'Well, there she is. If we can make that, our chances are good.'

Jet followed the direction in which Webster pointed and saw, on the horizon, what appeared to be a great glass dome.

'But the men working beneath it,' said Webster, 'are like you and me. They need a good supply of oxygen to breathe. And... oh.'

'What's the matter?' demanded Jet.

Webster didn't reply but brought the truck to a standstill and switched off the motor.

'What are we stopping for?'

'They're here,' said Webster.

'What? Who – who's here?'

'Look up there,' said Webster, pointing to the sky. 'Hovering above us – a sphere. They've found us. It's all over. I'm afraid we'll never make it now.'

Unaware of Jet's encounter with Mr Webster, Lemmy, Mitch and I were, of course, still crossing the Argyre Desert in the Martian sphere, hoping to locate Jet in the land truck.

We had been going for about half an hour when Mitch, who was lying on the floor, showed signs of waking up. He opened his eyes and looked into my face as I bent over him.

'Doc,' he complained, 'what's happened to the heating system in this ship?'

'So far as I know,' I said, taken aback, 'it doesn't carry one.'

'What are you talking about? All the ships carry heating systems. We'd better get one of the engineers over to look at it. And quick, before we all freeze to death.'

It dawned on me then that Mitch thought he was back in the *Discovery* and that we were still coasting towards Mars.

'There's nothing wrong with the heating system, Mitch,' I told him. 'It's you that's cold.'

'Cold,' he said, shivering, 'that's putting it mildly. My inside feels like it's frozen solid.'

'Mitch,' I asked, 'do you know who I am?'

'Why shouldn't I?' he said. 'What's the matter? What are you wearing your suit for, Doc?'

'Lemmy and I have to, Mitch,' I replied evasively.

He looked at me strangely and began to climb to his feet. Obviously the effort it cost him was considerable. He breathed very heavily and moved incredibly slowly.

'Now don't attempt to walk,' I protested. 'Lie down again.'

'I'll get up if I want to,' said Mitch defiantly. 'How do I come to be lying on the floor, anyway? And what's happened to the bunks and the cabin? It looks all different. Where am I? What...' He began to breathe very heavily now.

'Doc – my chest,' he cried. 'It feels all tight. I can't breathe.'

'Lemmy,' I called urgently, 'come over here – quick, Mitch is returning to normal but he can't breathe the atmosphere in here.'

'Oh blimey,' said Lemmy, as he came over to my side, 'and we've got no suit for him.'

'That oxygenised cabin upstairs. Harding?' I yelled, 'Open the door to the upper cabin.'

Almost immediately the door in the pillar swung open and, between us, Lemmy and I managed to get Mitch upstairs and lay him on the floor. It wasn't long before the Australian began to breathe more easily and normally, but, before we could get him to the upper cabin he had virtually lost consciousness.

However, I felt that the immediate danger was past which was just as well, for Lemmy, who had gone back downstairs while I examined Mitch, called to me to say he had seen one of the land trucks just below us on the desert.

'Only one?' I asked him.

'That's all I can see.'

'Halt the ship then, Lemmy. I'll be right down.'

'Yes, mate.'

We were both extremely puzzled by the disappearance of the second land caravan and all attempts to raise the occupant of the vehicle over which we were hovering failed. I decided that the only way to find out whether it was Jet or McLean on the desert below was to go down and see.

The moment we landed, Lemmy and I, clad in our space suits, went outside. First we walked round to the front of the land truck and looked into the driving cabin but there was nobody in it.

'Whoever's in that truck,' said Lemmy, 'must be in the living quarters.'

'Then we'd better let ourselves in,' I decided.

A few minutes later we were in the airlock.

But, to our amazement, the cabin when we entered it was empty. There was no sign of anybody. There was nothing for it but to go back to the sphere and continue in the direction in which we had been travelling in the hope of overtaking the other truck which, we could now only conclude, must contain both Jet and McLean.

But, just as we were about to embark, I noticed the tracks of another machine leading from the front of the land truck in which we had expected to see Jet. Lemmy and I walked over and examined them carefully. The marks in the ground had been made by little spheres some foot or more in diameter.

'Come on,' I said. 'Let's get back. We'll fly just a few hundred feet above the ground and follow those trails.'

Before long I noticed down below a strange vehicle, not unlike those we had seen in the city of Lacus Solis. And, apparently, it must have seen us, too, for, as we approached it and hovered above, the thing came to a standstill.

Lemmy was not too happy about dropping down to investigate but I persuaded him that no more than two people could possibly be in the vehicle and, if one of them should turn out to be Jet, we would have, at most, only one Martian or conditioned Earthman to contend with.

But, as it turned out, we had hardly set foot on the ground when I heard the joyful voice of Jet in my radio earpiece. A few minutes later he and his companion had joined us inside the sphere.

After we had been introduced to Webster and all that had happened since we had lost contact with each other had been explained, I told Jet of Mitch's partial recovery. Webster at once asked to see the engineer so I took him upstairs. After questioning Mitch for several minutes, Webster and I returned to the lower cabin.

'Well?' I asked as soon as we had gone downstairs.

'This isn't a bad case. Nothing like as bad as those two fellows at the control panels there. He's almost back to normal. Have you any recollection of his being influenced a second time?'

'By that noise, you mean?' I asked.

'Yes.'

'Yes, I have. When we took this sphere from Lacus Solis that noise came on and Mitch, Dobson and Harding all fell asleep.'

'Then that was it. Had he been handled properly then he could have been completely normal by now.'

'I don't understand.'

'While he is in that sleeping state, it is possible to penetrate deep down into a subject's mind. Tell him he's in Africa and when he wakes up he'll believe it. That, Doctor Matthews, is the Martian method. On the other hand, put him to sleep now, tell him all that has happened to him since the time his memory failed him and, when he wakes up, he'll remember everything.'

'Are you sure?'

'Try it, Doctor, and see.'

'Very well. I'll have to hypnotise him first, of course.'

'Yes.'

Mitch was so drowsy when I did get to work on him that I found him a very easy subject. I told him of everything that had happened to him, and us, since we had landed on Mars and rescued him from the Flying Doctor. I then let him sleep. When he woke up he was perfectly normal but, of course, it was impossible for me to take him downstairs for he had no space suit.

So, telling him not to worry, I left him there and went below to tell Jet the good news.

'Very well,' said Jet, 'he'll just have to stay where he is until we can find some means of getting him some kind of breathing apparatus.'

'Breathing apparatus?' I queried.

'Yes, Doc. Apparently there are such things – used by the inhabitants of that dome we see on the horizon. And Webster told me that if we proceeded as far as there we would find out what has happened to Frank Rogers and the rest of the crew who are missing.'

'That is so, Captain Morgan,' said Webster, 'but the principal reason for going there was to pick up a sphere. Now we have one we can go straight to your Polar Base.'

'But what about Frank – and the rest of the boys?' asked Jet. 'If we don't go to the dome, how do we know what's happened to them?'

'I tell you, Captain,' said Webster, 'it's a hundred to one that they are captives of the Martians. You will never get them back now. And if you want to get back to Earth to warn them of the proposed invasion, you have no time to lose.'

'Look,' said Jet firmly, 'back there on the desert we made a deal. I would take you back to Earth provided you helped me to find out the things I wanted.'

'Very well,' said Webster reluctantly. 'I'll do what I can. Make for the dome – but don't blame me if you end up as the crew of Number One almost certainly have already.'

'That's our lookout,' said Jet. 'OK, Lemmy – take off.'

'And if you must go there,' continued Webster, 'keep at low level. There's less chance of our being detected.'

'Dobson, Harding,' called Lemmy, 'take the ship up. Maximum height twenty feet, course due east.'

I felt the almost silent motors of the ship spring to life and slowly we rose to just above ground and began to head towards the strange domed building on the horizon.

Chapter 20

WhEN we reached it we landed near what appeared to be its entrance. The dome was about half a mile in diameter and perhaps some two hundred feet tall at its highest point. It was made of some kind of thick, transparent substance.

'Well, now, Captain Morgan,' said Webster, 'if you wait here, I'll go and see what I can find out about Frank Rogers and the rest of his crew and, at the same time, I'll try and bring back breathing apparatus for Mitchell.'

'You're going alone?' asked Jet suspiciously.

'You'd look rather conspicuous in that space suit.'

Jet thought for a moment. 'I think it will be best if we come, too,' he said guardedly. 'But first, you go into that dome and bring four sets of breathing apparatus back with you. Is that clear?'

'Yes.'

'How long will it take you to get them?'

'About ten minutes.'

'Right. If you're not back in that time we shall take off.'

'What? And leave me here?' Webster was almost beside himself. 'But you promised you would take me back to Earth with you.'

'Be back in ten minutes, then. Alone.'

Webster left the sphere and the moment he had passed through the door, Jet gave Harding the order to close it.

'What's the idea, Jet?' asked Lemmy.

'I'm taking no chances,' replied our captain. 'We can't afford to.'

'But how do we find out about Frank and the rest of the crew,' I asked, 'if we don't go with him? Or even if he's speaking the truth about them when he does get back?'

'Two of us *will* go with him,' said Jet, 'but we'll put a time limit on our return. And, if we're not back within that time, you, Lemmy, with Mitch, will take this sphere back to Polar Base, board the *Discovery* and head for home.'

Webster was back well within the limited time and, as he had promised, brought four sets of breathing apparatus with him. They were so compact that at first I couldn't believe they would be of any use. But a quick test proved that they were efficient enough. We wore the apparatus round our waists like a belt. From there a tiny, thin tube, no more than an eighth of an itch in diameter, was carried up into our mouths and fixed to our teeth. Through this came the necessary oxygen supply. They were rather uncomfortable to wear at first but we soon got used to them. We took one of the appliances up to Mitch who put it on and then came downstairs.

'All right, Lemmy,' said Jet. 'If we're not back in an hour, you know what to do.'

'Yes, mate,' said Lemmy. 'And good luck.'

'Take care of yourself,' said Mitch, now apparently his normal self again.

We left the sphere and walked towards the airlock.

'What happens if this apparatus gives out on us, Webster?' I asked.

'It shouldn't,' he replied. 'It should last for forty-eight hours of continuous use but, in any case, you need wear it for only a few minutes.'

He was right. We soon reached the large airlock which was entered by a circular door some six feet in diameter. Once inside, the door closed, we passed through another and then Webster told us that we could take off our masks. I did so and found the atmosphere perfectly breathable.

I now expected Webster to open the far door so that we could step into the enclosed area we had glimpsed from outside. But, instead, we turned to a door in the right of the wall, opened it and found ourselves in a long, well-lit tunnel which sloped gently downwards. It was from here that the air, which contained a strong smell of ozone, was coming.

'Where are we now?' Jet asked.

'Inside the wall on which the dome rests. Deep down underground is the factory. Its workers are all conditioned types but it's run by unconditioned men like myself. I'll lead the way.'

We followed Webster for about a quarter of a mile before we came to another door. Passing through it we found ourselves in a long gallery. One side was walled, the other was open. Down below was a huge shop full of machines and men tending them.

'What's this place?' I asked.

'It's one of the assembly shops,' explained Webster. 'We have to pass through it to get to the main control room.'

He led us farther along the gallery and down a flight of steps. As we passed between the lines of men, working at their machines, hardly any of them turned to look at us.

'Don't talk to anybody if you can help it,' Webster cautioned us.

We walked the whole length of the factory and paused before a massive door.

'Where does this lead to?' whispered Jet.

'This is the main control room,' said Webster. 'It is in constant touch with Lacus Solis and, if there's any news to be had about Rogers and his crew, we'll get it here.'

'I see.'

'Now remember, both you and Doctor Matthews are new personnel who landed here only a couple of days ago. You are condition-resisting types and I'm showing you over the place. Is that clear?'

'Perfectly,' agreed Jet.

'Then let's go in.'

We entered the room to find a man seated at a large table. Before him was a televiewer screen on which the whole factory could be seen. He was manipulating the controls and, as we entered, various close-ups of different workers passed before his eyes.

The Controller, for that's all that I could think he was, turned in his swivel seat to greet us as we came in. 'Oh, hullo, there, Bill,' he said to Webster. 'Thought you were out on the Mare.'

'I was, but I was called over to HQ and told to bring these gentlemen over here and show them a few things. They're newly up from Earth and haven't quite got used to the idea yet.'

'Welcome to the fold, gentlemen,' said the Controller cordially. 'You have my deepest condolences. Where did they pick you up?'

'From London,' Jet told him.

'London? It's not the habit of spheres to drop down on populated districts.'

'Well, not London exactly,' said Jet, 'Hampstead Heath.'

'I would have thought even that would have been a little too crowded.'

'Well, it was late at night and it was foggy,' I put in.

'They weren't the only ones,' said Webster.

'I know,' replied the Controller. 'Four more arrived in Lacus Solis this morning. I was talking to a couple of them a few minutes ago.'

'Talking to them?' asked Jet. 'Were their names Rogers and Grimshaw?'

'That's right,' went on the Controller, quite unconcerned, 'two of the types capable of being put into the deepest sleep. Would you care to see them?'

Before we could reply the Controller turned a switch below the televiewer screen and, quite suddenly, we saw the images of Frank Rogers and Grimshaw. They were seated in chairs.

'There they are,' said Controller. 'Undergoing their initial training. Learning to obey orders by remote control.'

Jet could only gasp.

'In a few days,' went on the Controller, 'they'll be coming to work here. By then they'll be used to my voice and to doing exactly as I tell them. Rogers,' he said sharply, 'stand up.'

I looked at the screen in fascinated horror as Frank left his chair and stood to attention.

'Can you hear me, Rogers?' asked the Controller.

'I can hear you,' said Rogers in a flat voice, remarkably like that of Whitaker's.

'Are you prepared to take my orders and act on them?'

'Orders must be obeyed without question at all times,' replied Frank without hesitation.

'Very good,' said the Controller. 'Sit down, Rogers. Now, Grimshaw.'

Grimshaw stood up. 'I can hear you,' he said.

'Turn it off,' demanded Jet.

'What are your orders?' repeated Grimshaw mechanically.

'Turn it off,' said Jet angrily, turning to the Controller. 'Do you hear?'

He approached the man as though about to attack him, but I and Webster quickly grasped his arm and dragged him back.

'What are you getting so excited about?' asked the Controller.

'Where is Frank?' I demanded. 'How far away from here is he?'

'Too far for you to get at, Doctor Matthews. You can give up all hope of trying to rescue him.'

It came as a great shock to find that the Controller knew my name but I hope I didn't betray the fact as I said, as calmly as I could: 'What makes you think I want to?'

'You can't fool me – either of you. I know that neither Rogers nor any of the men with him came to this planet in a Martian sphere.'

'What?' said Webster flabbergasted. 'How do you know?'

'Not fifteen minutes before you came in here a warning that men from Earth had landed on the planet was put out over the intercommunication system. Apparently two of them took a sphere from Lacus Solis. The other is still out in Argyre Desert somewhere and a search for him has already begun. It seems they know about the proposed invasion of Earth. Don't you gentlemen?' said the Controller, deliberately. There was no mistaking his meaning.

The cat was out of the bag now and there was no denying it. Webster appealed to his superior. 'Now, Sam,' he said, 'what you say is true. But you are an Earthman yourself and so am I.'

'I was once.'

'You still are,' said Webster, 'in spite of the time you've been up here.'

'I am a Martian,' said the Controller flatly. 'It is my duty to report the fact that two of the Earthmen are here.'

'You mean nobody knows we are here but you?' asked Jet.

'That is so.'

'Look, Sam,' went on Webster, 'you'd like to go back to Earth, wouldn't you?'

'What would be the point? I came here in 1896. When I left Earth seventy-five years ago I was thirty-five years old – and you know what would happen to me the moment I left this planet. I have no wish to die yet. Now take these men to the living quarters. I'll report their presence here to Lacus Solis immediately.'

'No, Sam,' pleaded Webster. 'Wait. They've promised to take me back to Earth with them – if I help them to escape.'

The Controller laughed. 'You?' he said scornfully. 'What would you want with Earth – you who came here in 1910?

'I didn't,' protested Webster. 'It was 1956 and I wasn't old. Look at me – am I old?' He turned to Jet and me. 'I could still spend a few more years on Earth, couldn't I?' he pleaded. 'Couldn't I?' His last two words were shouted.

'Don't make me laugh,' said the Controller. 'You'd fade to nothing the moment you put your foot on the place. You're not conditioned for Earth, you know. You're not a Whitaker.'

'You've got to believe me, Mr Morgan,' said Webster, appealing to Jet. 'I did come here in 1956.'

'Oh, shut up and get out,' said the Controller. 'And take these Earthmen with you. I have a report to make.'

I saw Jet looking at me hard. 'All right, Doc,' he said resolutely, 'let's go.' And before I had time to realise what he had in mind, he had taken a quick step towards the Controller, brought up his fist and landed it on the point of the man's jaw. Taken completely by surprise, the Controller toppled backwards and lay still.

'What have you done?' cried Webster.

Jet ignored him. 'Come on, Doc,' he said. 'Let's wreck all this intercommunication stuff.'

We wrecked it all right. We picked up the chair on which the Controller had been seated and put it through both televiewer screens. I wrenched the microphone from its position on the table and threw it to the other side of the room.

Suddenly I was aware that Jet was struggling with the Controller who had somehow managed to stagger to his feet again.

Webster was beside himself. 'There'll be the dickens to pay,' he shouted.

'Never mind that,' Jet gasped. 'If you want to get back to Earth, help us get out of here.' That did it. Webster at once went over to where Jet and the Controller were struggling. 'You carry on, Doc,' he said. 'Wreck the lot!' So I did.

When I was through, Jet and Webster were standing, breathing heavily, over the motionless form of the Controller.

'Well,' I said, 'if anybody could get that gear to work now, he'd be a genius.'

'Nice work, Doc. Now let's get back to the sphere, as quickly as we can.'

The thick, soundproof door of the Control Room had prevented the noise of the commotion reaching the factory and, to our relief, we found the workmen were still busy, obviously unaware that anything unusual had happened.

We passed through the workshop, along the gallery and were well on our way up the tunnel before we heard the shouts of pursuers behind us. We hastened our steps and called to Webster to do the same. But, instead, he began to reel like a drunken man and finally he fell to the ground.

'He's fainted or something, Doc,' said Jet, who reached him first.

'Hold on,' I replied, 'I'm coming.' A few seconds later I was bending over the man. 'What happened to you?' I asked.

'I got hurt back there in the fight,' he gasped.

'Then why didn't you say so?'

'I didn't want to hold you up. Leave me – and go on.'

Jet ignored his plea. 'Put his arm round your shoulder, Doc,' he said. 'We haven't far to go now.'

'Right.'

And so, half dragging, half carrying Webster, we came to the airlock.

We had hardly stepped into it when we heard a voice behind us shouting: 'There they are. Hey – stop! Stop!'

But, of course, we didn't. As the door slowly closed we heard the same voice cry: 'Hey, wait – stay where you are.'

And then another voice added: 'Please wait, Mr Morgan. You must listen…' But his words were cut off as the door shut tight.

Two minutes later we were out in the Argyre Desert. Between us we carried the now unconscious form of Webster towards the sphere.

'OK, Lemmy,' I said on reaching the ship, 'give me a hand to get Webster in, will you? And take it easy.'

Somehow we got him into the sphere and laid him on the floor.

'Mitch,' said Jet who was already in the ship, 'we've got to get out of here. And quick. They've already got a search party out after us.'

'But what about Frank and Grimshaw?' asked Mitch anxiously.

'I'm afraid there's nothing we can do about them now.'

'Oh.' Mitch asked no more questions.

'Take a look at Webster, Doc. See what you can do for him,' went on Jet. 'Meanwhile I'll get the ship under way.'

'Come on, Lemmy,' urged Mitch. 'What are you hanging around by the door for? We want to lose it.'

'Those blokes who were following Jet and Doc – they're just coming through the airlock now.'

Even as he spoke he could hear the men calling for us to wait.

Jet ordered Harding to take the ship up to twelve feet above the ground and hold it there. Then he walked over to the door to talk to the men who had now come to a standstill below us.

The moment he saw Jet appear in the open doorway one of the men raised his arms and appealed to him. 'Take us with you, Captain Morgan,' he begged. 'Take us back to Earth!'

'How many of you?' asked Jet.

'Just the four of us, that's all.'

'How long have you been on this planet?'

'Fifteen years. Since 1956.'

'You as well? Isn't there anybody in this part of Mars who came here any other year?'

'You must believe us,' said the man. 'We are young, all of us. And we want to go home.'

'Don't do it, Jet,' I heard Mitch say. 'It's a trick to get us to return to ground level.'

But Jet ignored him. 'All right,' he said, 'I'll take you. But one at a time. Three of you stand back a hundred yards – you will climb aboard in order, as I tell you.'

'Now think what you're doing, mate,' begged Lemmy. 'Four of them could be too much for us.'

'I can't leave them, Lemmy,' said Jet. He turned towards Harding and was about to order him to take the ship down when I intervened.

'No, Jet – wait,' I called. 'Come over here. Look at Webster.'

Jet bent down and gazed at the still form lying on the floor. He gave a cry of surprise.

'Yes, Jet,' I said, 'He's dead. He must have received a hard knock during the fight.'

'But he's old, Doc,' said Jet. 'So very old.'

Mitch and Lemmy joined us. 'From looking at him,' said Mitch, 'I'd say at least a hundred years.'

'But he swore he was young,' said Jet, puzzled. 'Said he'd been up here only since 1956.'

'He wanted to get back to Earth so desperately he lied,' I said.

'But he knew that his age would catch up on him.'

'Maybe he thought he'd have just one glimpse of Earth before he died,' I suggested.

We stood looking at the man in silence for a few moments and then Mitch said quietly: 'Well, Jet, how about those men out there? Are they the same?'

Jet stood up, paused only a moment and then said: 'Harding, close the door. Then head for Polar Base – at maximum speed.'

We hated leaving those men behind but what could we do? Our one thought now was to get back to Polar Base, the springboard for our long journey back to Earth.

The distance was covered in less than two hours and it was with a sigh of relief that we sighted the *Discovery*, still standing on the ice ready for takeoff.

Half an hour later we had left the sphere, were in the flagship and almost ready to fire the motors – and, up to now at any rate – there was no sign of any machine in pursuit of us.

We lay strapped to our couches ready for takeoff.

'Now listen carefully,' said Jet. 'I have ordered Dobson and Harding to take the sphere into free orbit and join the Fleet. I will then have Davis take over two suits from Number Four and tell Dobson and Harding to transfer to Number Five.'

'You intend to take them back to Earth, then?' asked Mitch.

'Why not? The firing of the freighter motors is automatically controlled from this ship. Once they are under way, they will have no choice but to come along with us. Now let's get off. You all right down there, Howell?'

Howell was one of the men who had been in charge of Polar Base while we had been away. 'Yes, sir,' he said. 'Quite comfortable, thank you.'

There were only four couches in the ship and we had had to improvise a bed for Howell. I hoped it would prove as efficient as a couch in protecting him against the effects of the pressure during takeoff.

'All right,' said Jet as the sphere rose into the air and disappeared rapidly into the void, 'that's Dobson and Harding under way. Standing by for firing.'

My heart was pounding as Jet counted off the seconds. Then the motor exploded and we rose steadily from the Martian surface to meet the remaining freighters, still encircling the globe.

Once in free orbit it didn't take us long to manoeuvre the *Discovery* into correct position alongside the freighters. Having lost so many men on the surface of the Red Planet we had only enough now to handle three of the freighters – and Dobson and Harding would be travelling in one of those.

We had started out with twenty men in nine ships. We were returning with twelve, including Dobson and Harding.

'Our trip can hardly be called a success,' I observed, a little bitterly.

Jet took no notice of my remark; he had called up Davis and was asking him to get two suits ready to take across to the sphere.

211

But he had hardly begun to give the order when a cry from Lemmy, who had been watching on the televiewer, startled us all. 'Jet, for Pete's sake, look,' he said. 'Martian spheres – a whole fleet of them!'

'Where, Lemmy?' asked Jet.

'Almost directly below us.'

We all gazed at the televiewer. Looking rather like a flock of birds, the spheres, although very minute at the moment, were clearly ascending rapidly. At the same time, growing gradually louder, we could hear the same noise that we had heard so often in the past few weeks – the strange, hypnotic music that was intended to put us all to sleep.

'They aim to stop us, Jet,' said Mitch in alarm. 'They're trying to hypnotise us before we can get away.'

'How far and how fast can those spheres travel?' said Jet, turning to me.

'According to the Flying Doctor, not very far.'

'Then we'll have to outpace them. Lemmy, let me know as soon as Howell has entered his own ship.' Howell, of course, had had to leave our ship and transfer to his own.

'He's just reached the airlock now,' announced Lemmy.

'Then call up the other ships, Mitch,' said Jet. 'Have them stand by for takeoff.'

'Right.' Mitch set to work.

'So it will be only three ships after all,' I said, half to myself. There was no longer any question of sparing the time necessary to transfer Dobson and Harding to the fourth freighter.

'Hullo, Space Fleet,' Mitch was saying. '*Discovery* calling. Stand by for takeoff. Repeat, stand by for takeoff.'

'Number Three to Flagship – standing by.'

'Number Four to Flagship – standing by.'

The strange noise was increasing in volume now.

'They're giving out with a vengeance this time,' remarked Lemmy.

'Whatever you do,' I yelled, 'don't any of you go to sleep. Fight it!'

'Motor, Mitch?' demanded Jet.

'OK.'

'Then stand by. Position?'

'Three degrees,' said Lemmy. 'Two degrees…'

'Firing imminent.'

'One degree.'

'Contact!'

We felt the great ship vibrate as the motors fired. Glancing to the televiewer I could see the motors of the freighters firing, too.

'Well, that's it,' said Jet. 'All motors fired simultaneously.'

'Good for them,' said Mitch.

'But Dobson and Harding's sphere hasn't moved,' I pointed out.

'I didn't expect it to, Doc,' said Jet. 'By now they are obeying other orders than ours.'

'And the spheres are making no attempt to pursue us,' said Lemmy gleefully. 'We're going to make it.' He began to laugh, a little hysterically. 'We're going home,' he said. And then, again: 'We're going home!'

Epilogue

W̲e established contact with Control a week after takeoff and, as we suffered no interference or jamming from Mars, were able to tell the whole story of our landing, and of the loss of most of our ships and half our men.

The main object of our trip, the exploration of Mars, was virtually unaccomplished; but our escape to warn the Earth of the proposed Martian invasion during the next close opposition was a very definite achievement.

At first Control did not believe our story but, as we passed more and more details of our adventures back to Earth, the truth slowly began to sink in.

'Hullo, Space Fleet,' said the voice from home one day, 'Control calling. Come in, please.'

'Hullo, Control,' said Lemmy. 'Barnet here.'

'It is requested that full details of the construction of the Martian spheres be passed to us, together with methods of operating the same, as soon as possible.'

'Blimey, mate,' protested Lemmy, 'we only flew in those things – we didn't take them apart.'

'Sorry, Lemmy,' said the radio operator down on Earth. 'You don't know the commotion your news has caused down here. A Martian invasion of the Earth was never dreamed of. The last thing anybody expected.'

'I don't see why,' said Lemmy. 'We invaded their planet, didn't we?'

'Yes,' agreed Control, 'but that's different,'

'The Martians didn't seem to think so. Anyway, mate, I'll pass the signal on to Jet. I expect he'll be calling you.'

'OK, Lemmy.'

And so our departed Fleet, consisting of the only Flagship and a freighter on either side, limped home as best it might on its long journey to overtake the Earth which we hoped to do some six months after leaving the hostile planet.

We were constantly at the radio, telling Control everything we could remember; of the people we had met who had originally come from Earth, of the pyramid in the canal, of the great pyramid city in the Lacus Solis. Nothing was left out; most of it was told over and over again.

At last, after six months and two weeks of journeying through space, the ships were turned over and we prepared to make the Moon landing.

Man's first trip to Mars was over. But it marked only the beginning of his dealings with the fiery planet. The invasion of Earth did indeed begin two years later, thirteen years before it was intended. No doubt, now their plans were known, the Martians thought it best to strike immediately. The advance ships of the Martian invasion fleet landed on the world on September 23rd, 1973.

But that is another story…

fantom
publishing

Charles Chilton
JOURNEY INTO SPACE

Between 1953 and 1958, millions of people tuned in to the radio adventures of Jet Morgan and his crew as they left Earth to investigate the universe. Chilton went on to write three best-selling novels based on the groundbreaking radio series.

OPERATION LUNA   ISBN: 978-1-78196-024-0

Destination – the Moon! No adventurers had ever faced greater hazards than the crew of rocket ship *Luna* when she hurtled into space. Jet Morgan, ace pilot, was her captain. With him were her Australian designer, Mitch; Lemmy, the Cockney radio operator; and Doc, whose diary astonished everyone.

THE RED PLANET   ISBN: 978-1-78196-025-7

Blast Off! to new heights of adventure and excitement with Jet Morgan and the crewmen of the spaceship *Discovery* as they lead the first fleet of rocketships to reach across space to the 'Red Planet', Mars. But right from the beginning the expedition seems ill-omened. Uncanny happenings test their courage to breaking point, both on the long space flight and on the hostile planet itself.

THE WORLD IN PERIL   ISBN: 978-1-78196-026-4

An alien civilisation prepares to conquer Earth – and only four men can save her… Jet Morgan and the crew of the *Discovery* return to Mars on the most dangerous and vital mission ever undertaken by man – to obtain the Martian plan for the conquest of Earth. Too late, they find themselves part of the invasion fleet.

Available in paperback from
www.fantomfilms.co.uk

Also available from

fantom
publishing

AUNTIE'S CHARLIE

AN AUTOBIOGRAPHY BY
Charles Chilton

Described by the *Sunday Telegraph* as 'the one genius the BBC ever had on its staff', Charles Chilton MBE joined the Corporation at fifteen as a messenger boy and went on to carve out a 46-year career as a presenter, writer and producer.

Auntie's Charlie tells of his life from growing up on the streets of 1920s St Pancras, via early years at the BBC working for the Gramophone Library, to writing the infamous production *Oh What a Lovely War* for Joan Littlewood's Theatre Workshop.

While with the BBC Charles was sent to the United States to research, write and produce a number of series based on American western history. One of these, *Riders of the Range*, lasted for five years until 1953. However, major international recognition came with his science fiction trilogy *Journey into Space* which he wrote and produced between 1953 and 1958.

Here, for the first time, is Charles Chilton's story in his own words – an autobiography that is frank, vivid, wry and engaging.

Limited edition hardback ISBN 978-1-906263-72-0
Standard edition paperback ISBN 978-1-906263-76-8

Available from
www.fantomfilms.co.uk